ADVANCE PRAISE FOR
THE REVEALED

"Ripe with political intrigue, forbidden romance, and a mysterious group of outsiders who threaten to turn Lily Atwood's world upside down, *The Revealed* is a riveting story about love and courage. It's also a captivating look at a future society where overcoming the odds means finding the power within yourself to become truly extraordinary. Jessica Hickam has written a story that will entrance readers."

—Emily Kiebel, author of *Serenade*

"*The Revealed* will have you hooked from the beginning. Jessica Hickam has written a thrilling story about love, sacrifice, and fighting for what's right. This book will surely lead the pack in the next wave of popular young-adult novels."

—Lauren Joskowitz, entertainment manager, SheKnows.com

"*The Revealed* weaves an adventurous tale of true love, deception, and bravery. Along the way, Jessica Hickam captures the beauty—and heartache—of finding your first true love. And, most importantly, finding yourself."

—Leesa Coble, *BOP* and *Tiger Beat*

"Filled with heart-pounding action and suspense, *The Revealed* is a vivid exploration of one girl's fight against the seemingly impossible—and the forbidden love that helps her survive. The adventure will keep readers wanting more. Jessica Hickam is truly a young author to watch!"

—Neville Page, concept designer, *Avatar*

"There's much to admire in this debut novel."

—*Kirkus Reviews*

THE REVEALED

Jessica Hickam

SparkPress, a BookSparks imprint
A division of SparkPoint Studio, LLC

Published by SparkPress, a BookSparks imprint,
A division of SparkPoint Studio, LLC
Tempe, Arizona, USA, 85281
www.sparkpointstudio.com

Printed in the United States of America.

ISBN: 978-1-940716-00-8 (pbk.)
ISBN: 978-1-940716-01-5 (ebk.)

Cover design © Julie Metz, Ltd at metzdesign.com
Photo illustration © Monica Gurevich
Cover photo © Arcangel Images at arcangel.com
Author photo © Benny Tecson
Formatting by Polgarus Studio

Dedicated to my sisters, Megan and Sarah.
Big adventures are waiting for us.

"Reach for the stars, and if you miss, aim for the heavens."
—Unknown

CHAPTER ONE

If I'm going to be taken, I plan on having at least a little fun first.

Sleek and silver with the latest technology, including dent-resistant metal, my father's Aston Martin is made to drive. The doors recognize DNA and I'm half him, so it's easy to break inside. I just press my hand against the door. The car needs a moment to analyze, then lifts the door, allowing me to slide into the driver's seat. I toss the still-sealed letter onto the passenger seat.

There's no need to open it. I know what it is.

The car's ignition can either be started with fingerprint recognition or overridden by the key. I took the keys from the shelf by the front door while my mother wasn't home earlier this morning.

I shift gears and press my ballet flats on the gas, not wasting any time.

The odometer climbs higher as the car smoothly accelerates.

The sensor in the car's front mirror triggers our gate, and it opens just in time for me to speed through. *Let security try to track me down now.*

Pulling out onto the main road, I press my foot to the floor, going well over the speed limit.

I glance in my rearview mirror.

Security doesn't stand a chance!

My eyes return to the road.

Strategically placed, black SUVs block my path to the freeway. My lungs constrict, forcing the air from my chest. Somehow they're already one step ahead of me.

I grip the wheel.

I'm driving too fast.

My foot hits the brake.

Tires sear the road.

Adrenaline spins through me as I brace the wheel, keeping the car straight.

My knuckles tighten. I feel the road beneath me slipping under my feet.

The Aston slams to a stop, throwing me up against the wheel. The first SUV is only inches in front of me. Relief fills me but is quickly erased by mounting frustration.

I rip off my seatbelt, stomping out of the car.

Jeremy, head of my father's security, stands at the front of the line. There are half a dozen other members of security lounging against the cars as they wait for me to arrive. They straighten to a standing position once I storm toward Jeremy.

Jeremy's lips are carved into a thin line. He looks like he's expecting me to barrel into him and continue running down the road. "Did that scare you enough to get these insane ideas out of your system?"

"You could have made me crash!" I advance on him.

"Good thing you were paying attention then," Jeremy says, opening the backdoor of the SUV. I hand over the Aston's keys and slump inside. The smell of the black leather reminds me of past trips to speeches and conventions. My father used to let me pick the music on the touch screen positioned in the side-door panel, anything I wanted, while my mother would chastise me for turning it up too loud. But my father would just laugh and tell her to let me be a kid. I feel like a kid now more than ever, and it's a hard reminder that I don't get to make significant decisions. Especially when it comes to my life. It has already been laid out for me.

Jeremy tosses the Aston's keys to one of the security guards standing behind him. He'll drive it back into the garage. "You're gonna get yourself killed if you keep pulling these stunts," he continues his lecture.

"Either I do it or The Revealed does," I say as he slams the door, trapping me securely in the back.

Two hundred fifty-two days until I'm nineteen. If I make it until then.

Jeremy is about ten years older than I am, a war vet who came to my family's rescue a few years ago and quickly advanced to the head of our security. He keeps his dark hair short and holds himself stiffly, marching around doing his job. Most of the time he's assigned to watch after me. It used to be kind of a joke. I would see the challenge in his eyes, daring me to find a way to outsmart him. Now he just looks bored, tired of my escapades.

My parents are rarely home these days. They apparently don't have time to supervise their eighteen-year-old only child.

Jeremy opens the door and sits behind the wheel. "How did you know I left?" I ask.

"The cameras caught you taking the keys this morning," he says. He pinches the bridge of his nose and then runs his fingers over his eyebrows. This is all business to him, and it's been a long day on the job.

"Right," I sigh and cross my arms over my chest.

From the front seat, Jeremy turns to glare at me before he starts the car. "You know, you could try listening to your parents for once. They're trying to save your life."

"No one has ever been saved once The Revealed choose a target."

"No one targeted has ever been the presidential nominee's daughter before."

I roll my eyes and look out the window so I don't have to argue anymore. Not that there's much of a view, just trees and grass. Capitol City once had giant cherry trees—thousands of them, all with light-pink flowers in place of leaves at certain times of the year. My father used to take me to the park when we took our regular trips to Washington. I would decorate my hair with the petals. People cut the trees down when the war first started. It was a message of isolationist action, my father always said, since the trees were originally gifts from abroad. Not a very effective message. Now, there's only a monotonous green.

The drive home is short; I'd made it less than a mile. I watch sullenly as Jeremy punches in the gate code, and the tall wrought iron gate splits. The bars may be twisted into a pretty pattern, but the metal doesn't fool anyone. It's at least twice my height and equipped with a security camera and alarm. Once that gate is closed, no one is getting past. I'm not sure if it's to keep The Revealed out or keep me in.

Jeremy waves to the guards on duty at the entrance station as the car passes through.

Our house is laid out on thirty acres. The gate continues all around the property. Cameras are positioned at every entrance and more dot the landscape like decor. There is always someone in the control room watching the footage.

This house is more like a castle than a home. It was built specifically for my father after the war, with over twenty rooms, two kitchens, fifteen and a half bathrooms, a ballroom, two pools, and a guest house around the side of the property. Jeremy lives in the guest house—one of the perks to being head of my father's security team.

This isn't home to me. My home was back in our small three-bedroom house in Oro Valley, Arizona where I was born. I loved that house. Living there was the last time I felt at home. We moved shortly after my father was elected to the Senate when I was eight into a house that was more *suitable* for someone of his stature.

I know it's selfish of me to be ungrateful for this mansion. Selfish of me considering the vast majority of the population now works in the factories and lives in studio apartments—struggling day to day, barely able to make ends meet. I know nothing of working twelve-hour days. I look at my ballet flats and picture them covered in tar. Even the thought of the thick, burnt scent makes me turn up my nose. My house was built on the opposite end of town from the factories on purpose.

I should be grateful, but this house is too big and spread out for the three people who occupy it. My mother hired an interior decorator, of course, and most of the rooms are kept impersonal and bland with ruffles and silk to hide the fact that no one ever uses them.

Jeremy escorts me through the door, catching my arm as I trip over one of the new chair deliveries. I walk inside and ignore my mother fuming in the entry, tapping her foot on the Italian tiles.

Her eyes burn but her face is smooth. She wouldn't want to cause any brow lines.

Men move around me, bringing towering flower arrangements through the door behind me. "Just put them over there," she says, waving at the ballroom entrance. I duck past, hoping the deliveries will distract her.

I hear the click of her heels as she marches after me. "Just what do you think you were doing taking your father's car like that?" She's holding a shuffle of papers but has decided my escape attempt warrants an interruption from her party planning.

I respond by handing over the unopened black letter I'm holding. "This is what I was thinking." With that, I continue up the stairs. My mother follows me, but I don't turn around, not stopping until I reach the back of my bedroom. The entire wall is glass, including the doors. Outside is my balcony. The piece of tape still hangs on the pane where I found the note. It was fixed so you couldn't miss it.

It isn't the first note I've received. In fact, I'm starting to build quite a collection of them.

I turn around and see my mother staring down at the note. Her face is pale.

On the back of the envelope, just under the seal, is a small, silver symbol. It's an open circle that continues around and up with one swift line to create a lick of flame at the top. The circle is dashed through with two lines, slicing it into four pieces.

Soon

THE REVEALED

One word written in bold silver letters in the middle of the note. No name. A name isn't necessary. We both know who sent the letter.

My mother is beautiful—tall and slender with fair skin, bright-blue eyes and deep chestnut hair that matches my own. She has this observant look behind her gaze. She never misses a beat—though I really wished she would, at least occasionally. She scans the letter, and I can see fear transform her face.

"Keeping me locked in this house won't keep me safe," I tell her, leaving the room to escape her terse gaze.

My mother, still staring at the note, turns and leaves the room, presumably to show the latest threatening evidence to Jeremy.

The letter is from The Revealed. Their notes started arriving four months ago on my eighteenth birthday. They're taunting me with their warnings. It's a game to them, and posting these letters is the way they prove they've already won.

It doesn't matter that my parents live on thirty gated acres, with security patrolling twenty-four hours a day. Forget the security system that sends an alert every time a window is so much as tapped or a door nudged. The cameras around the premises shouldn't even be wasting electricity, because they never catch anything on video that's useful. And they've vetted everyone who works for us so many times it's become a monthly routine.

No, The Revealed slip through every time, and yet I'm still ordered to stay locked inside this house for "my safety."

No one can keep me safe.

The kidnappings started less than a year after the war ended and have continued for the past five years. There are over four hundred missing now. All of them eighteen when they were taken, and none of them ever seen again. They're called the Taken Eighteen. No one knows why The Revealed are kidnapping teens, only that once the teens are gone, they don't come back. There's something weird about The Revealed, too. They have this ability—this way of making things happen that no one can explain. They're able to make trees fall and lights flicker out. That's why they call themselves The Revealed. Because they have some understanding of how the world works that no one else does. They're able to tap into this somehow and abuse it to ruin the harmony our new nation is struggling for.

A lot of people think the Taken Eighteen are dead. It's a good possibility. What would an organization of any kind be doing with four hundred teenagers? Parents say having one is hard enough.

I think there's more to it than just a killing spree. The Revealed are too smart. There's some higher aim here than slaughtering innocent people. They just have yet to clue the rest of us in on their motives.

But what do I know?

Not much, it seems, because everyone around me insists on telling me how to run my life. Since turning eighteen, I haven't really been allowed to leave the house. My parents hired tutors who come to keep me occupied throughout the day. My schedule is strict. My parents are one of the "lucky" couples that are rich enough to justify locking their daughter indoors for a year. Between our mansion-sized house and my father's reputation, it's expected. Most parents with eighteen-year-olds view them as a prime labor force and send them to the factories out of sheer desperation.

My father wants to see this changed. I mean, so does the rest of the world, but he seems to be the only one with a vision and the right amount of charisma to carry the idea. It's why he's a good politician. He's been vital during the reconstruction process following the war. His military background makes him the perfect candidate to step up to the plate in the country's time of crisis. He's big on reorganizing the states and allowing them to keep their democratic rights. People like hearing that in a time where everything they own—including their liberty—is at stake.

We've been reduced to the trembling sliver of colonies that was our nation's beginning. The wastelands start just east of the border between Louisiana and Texas. The boundary line extends north, slicing between Tennessee and Arkansas, snaking up through the middle of Kentucky and Ohio, and ending in the center of New York. Everything west of the line is uninhabited. Sure, there are rumors that some drifters float past the line, never to be seen again. But the attacks came from the west, and pushed farther and farther inland until the East Coast was all that was left of the once-great nation.

Again, I was lucky. When the attacks began, my father was on congressional business in DC. My mother and I were with him like usual. If we'd been at our home in Arizona, we wouldn't have survived the first attack.

Now my father is running for president, asking these newly reformed little areas along the East Coast to vote for him in the first election since the war.

It's hard to believe that six years have already passed since that day when the ground came alive and the sky fell. Today, the clear, blue skies mingled with wispy clouds are a sight I thought I'd never see again. For months after the war, the sky was a pitiful shade of gray. It was like being trapped in limbo. Either humanity would crumble, or we would find a way to pick up the pieces. That gray sky hung over our heads, pushing down on us, taunting us with the helplessness we all felt.

During the war, no place was safe. My parents had considered sending me to Barcelona or Stockholm, since they had trusted friends in both places. Good thing they didn't. There wasn't a country on this planet that was left unscathed. The District of Columbia was considered a prime target for violence, but my father refused to leave. He said he had a duty to protect his country. He wouldn't abandon it in its time of need. And he didn't. Put that on the posters.

When the war ended, Americans were scattered. People became nomads. There were always hopeful rumors that certain areas were free from the bombings. People would evacuate on foot with dreams of finding a safe paradise. That wandering existence went on for years. But slowly, as it became clear the destruction was over, people began to set down roots again. Cities attracted people, and DC is now the most-populated of them all. So much so that the previous infrastructure couldn't support the masses. Apartments were raised, stacked like LEGOs on top of one another until they towered in the sky. At least most everyone has a bed.

No one—least of all my father—knows what to expect with this election. All he has is hope and a handful of dreams on his side. His opponent, a man named Roderick Westerfield, has radical beliefs—he's an isolationist and pro-military, spouting radical ideals about the importance of protecting our state at any cost via law and order. Only votes will tell which one the public prefers.

I walk onto the veranda and breathe fresh air, ignoring the men draped across the overhang installing chandelier lights. Immediately two security guards close in, their eyes trained on every move I make.

"Don't worry guys," I say, "I'm not going to leave the house. I just need some air."

I'm under house arrest until my birthday next year, unless The Revealed take me first. I'm betting on The Revealed. With all the inky black notes I've been receiving, my odds of making it to nineteen don't look good. But I've accepted it—come to terms with the prospect, unlike most of my peers. It isn't like I'm really doing much living here anyway.

I lean over the railing and take a deep breath.

"Lilith?" my mother calls.

I hate when anyone calls me that, but especially my mother. It's Lily to everyone else. Always Lily. I clench my teeth, "Yes?"

"Mr. Shieh is here for your history lesson," she says, her voice rising to my room from downstairs.

By history, she means politics. By lesson, she means brainwashing session. Mr. Shieh doubles as an advisor to my father's campaign. His instruction leans heavily to one side. It's the side my parents want me to adhere to. Little gems of information like states should make their own decisions. Our Founding Fathers wanted the central government to have less control, and the people to have more say. The government should provide healthcare and education to all and use taxes to further these causes.

The lesson today is lost on me, though. It isn't exactly a typical day, not that I usually have trouble drowning out Mr. Shieh's declarations of democracy. But the house is buzzing with life. There are people everywhere. It's why I chose today to try and leave. I thought maybe the cameras would miss me slipping out in the midst of the commotion.

Only two days from now, my family is hosting a celebration at our estate to honor the anniversary of the war's end and recognize and appreciate our progress as a nation since that moment. At least, that's how the invitation reads. While August 6 is the sixth anniversary of the war's ending, it also means there are only about three months before the election. It's a win-win situation. My father hosts the party, and gains support and positive press all in one night.

Electrical crews hustle in and out, hanging lights. Delivery personnel bring in flower arrangements. Chairs and tables are ushered in.

My father is out of the city on the campaign trail until the night of the celebration. I haven't seen him in two weeks. The election keeps him busy, and the only reason to be excited for this event is because it means he's coming home. This house always feels better when my dad's here. He asks my opinion about his campaign. He wants me to edit his speeches. He cares about what I think. He's the only one who seems to care about my opinions. My mother just wants me to keep my mouth shut and look like a lady. She's always worried I'll embarrass her.

After my lessons, I glance down over the railing to see my mother marshaling the press around her, arms gesturing in graceful, fluid motions, like a conductor. She's allowing them to cover all the setup activity to give audiences just a taste of what attendees at this spectacular event can expect.

"Press will be stationed here in the foyer, so you can get interviews with the guests as they arrive."

She leads them into the ballroom, which is on the west side of the house. It's a breathtaking room with gold fixtures and rustic Italian tiles. It's two stories tall. The second floor is open so guests can look down on the dance floor and orchestra. Large Grecian-style pillars support the second-floor balcony and decorate the room, providing a gazebo-like setting indoors.

"And over here is where the orchestra will play." She sweeps a hand toward the corner. "It's the local symphony and they are absolutely marvelous. An open bar will be located near the kitchen, over here. We all know how politicians get when champagne is offered," my mother says, laughing lightly and bringing her hand daintily to her chest. "I'm kidding of course."

The reporters chuckle along with her, passing each other looks like, *Isn't she just the greatest?*

One reporter extends her phone, which she's using as a recorder. "Can you tell us what the campaign's been like for your family? Has it been trying?"

My mother's smile doesn't quite reach her eyes. She's annoyed at the reporter's too-eager stance. Must be someone new.

"Of course it has its moments," she says and smiles, "but what job doesn't? My husband and I have devoted our lives to serving our country. It's all we know how to do, and we wouldn't want anything else." She goes in for the kill. "We know the nation feels the same."

The journalists all nod in agreement. They are an elite group of nationally syndicated reporters chosen for this tour. They'll all repay the favor by talking graciously about my family. Not that they don't normally anyway. My father led the efforts to make television media possible again. These reporters all owe him their jobs. Jobs like theirs are considered rare—a real luxury in our current world. They won't soon forget his work on their behalf.

My mother takes them outside and even leads them around the gardens. She shows them the rows of plush chairs being stationed where the fireworks show will close out the evening. She then shepherds them to the parking lot—that's right, my house has a *parking lot,* and says goodbye.

She walks back into the house and her mousy event planner, Charlotte, flits around her, checking the RSVP list. My mother holds out a hand. Charlotte purses her lips and scrambles, handing my mother a stack of formal, sealed envelopes. They look like fancy wedding invitations. My mother sighs and paces across the floor. Charlotte follows closely behind holding the invite list. The soft click of my mother's heels echo through the foyer.

"Rogers?"

Charlotte scans the list. "He has confirmed."

"Hayes?"

"She is also confirmed."

"Jacobson?"

Pause.

"He's not on the list." Charlotte waits behind my mother.

My mother's eyes narrow in thought for a moment before she concludes, "Don't follow up." She shrugs. "If he doesn't attend, it won't hurt the campaign. No one will miss him. But make sure Marg Lancing is on that list. She will bring a lot of support if she backs Mark. I want to ensure her endorsement." The hint of a confident smile lifts the corners of my mother's mouth.

"Yes ma'am." Charlotte makes a note on her list and then scurries from the room with her task at hand.

My mother is still perturbed about the incident this morning, I can hear it in her voice as she calls upstairs to me in a strained but ladylike whisper, "Lily, would you mind going to the kitchen to see if they are on track with the menu?"

"Sure." I don't even try to hide the excitement in my voice at the assignment. I move down the stairs, walk through the foyer and down the hall, and turn left.

The main kitchen isn't your average kitchen. It's restaurant-style, bigger than most people's houses. It's complete with a walk-in freezer, a cooking line, a head chef, and full staff on duty seven days a week. There's not just one refrigerator, but a wall of them. Stoves, large enough to cook for thousands, and every other appliance known to man fill the cavernous room. It sits adjacent to the ballroom, with the backup facilities on the other side of the house in a smaller kitchen setup, typically used for staff meals or for big events.

I spend a lot of time in the kitchens. It's a good way to stay busy—learning professional cooking techniques while I'm forced to stay inside. The head chef's name is Ilan Levy. He studied with the best in France for years before coming back to the states. Chefs of his caliber are hard to find after the war, and my mother quickly hired him to take advantage of his talent.

I walk through the kitchen doors and almost collide with a tray of hors d'oeuvres.

"Lily!" Rory's face lights up. She's an intern in the kitchen. She swings the tray down and turns to me. "Here to get your hands dirty?" She always keeps her long blonde hair fastened back in a ponytail. The lush curls fall across her shoulder. Rory is a tomboy to the core, so I've always found her perfect curls to be deceiving. Her sharp brown eyes confirm the fire she holds just under the surface.

"My mother sent me to check on the status of the preparations for the party."

"Well, wash your hands. We have some plates you can help me decorate."

"Really? Okay." I smile, moving to the sink.

"Please," Rory says, moving plates off the tray, "you're a better decorator than I am, babe. Well, almost," she smirks.

Rory is my age. She turned eighteen about six months before I did, but she has to work and doesn't have the means to even try to protect herself against The Revealed. She lost both her parents in the war. She's one of the lucky ones, though. She found a way to pursue her cooking passion, avoiding factory work. It isn't easy living, but my father is planning on making a lot of changes during his term. He wants to return the nation to what it once was—a land of promise.

Rory and I have grown close in the few months she's worked here. I count her as one of my best friends—actually, she's one of my only friends. When you aren't allowed out of your house, it's hard to maintain friendships with others. My classmates have moved on. The rich ones are planning for college while stuck in their own homes during their eighteenth year, like me. The others are hunting for jobs. I'm the only one waiting to become a Taken Eighteen. No one else I know has received black letters.

My parents made sure I kept up with my schooling even during the war. They said it was vital I get an education. In fact, rebuilding the nation's educational system is one of my father's key campaign messages. After the war, when schools started forming again, I was sent to an elite preparatory school with rich kids and other politicians' children.

I miss school. My parents let me finish out my semester in December with the rest of my classmates. But because my birthday was that April, they began homeschooling me in January. I've been at home ever since.

Rory hands me a decorating bag filled with a lemon-pepper mousse, which I begin swirling over the salmon and dill bruschetta. Rory has a bag of her own and works on the other side of the table on a duck rillettet.

"So anything exciting happen lately?" she asks.

"Well, I stole my father's car this morning and tried to make it to the highway."

"What?" Rory's hand tightens, and the cherry-port compote she is plating smooshes across the plate, ruining the dish. She sets down the bag, "Lily, you did not." She bites her bottom lip and squeals. "Why didn't you tell me? You've failed so many times, you at least have to let me try to help you next time."

"Not with your job on the line," I shake my head.

"I could meet you somewhere. We can do all those things you want to do—go out to a club, go shopping at a real mall." She pauses. "Well, I mean, you can shop, I'll just tag along and pretend I have money to burn."

"Yeah right, like my parents give me money," I say.

"But you know where they hide it," she replies, swirling a spoon in the compote, tasting it.

That's true. But I don't know if I'd ever have the guts to take it. My parents gave me the safe code for emergencies only. Still, the idea is tempting.

"Ooh," Rory says suddenly, an idea lighting across her chestnut eyes, "We could go to the college. You would love it. So many boys, and all of them are rich and sexy."

"You wouldn't go after a guy just because he's rich," I frown at her.

Actually, I long for the colleges like in the movies, where campuses were filled with diversity and self-exploration. If my father could recreate the system like that, he'd get my vote. As it stands, I'm not sure I want to place a ballot at all.

She shrugs. "Not all of us can have the future president for a father. We have to hope we marry the future president."

"You have no idea what you're asking."

"So where were you planning on running without me?" she asks, pouting.

I shrug. "Maybe the fields? I'm just tired of it all," I sigh. "I got another note. It was taped to my bedroom window. I saw it and just lost it. Staying inside isn't keeping me safe. If anything, it's like a red flag letting The Revealed know exactly where I am. It's not like I wouldn't have come back," I shrug. "I just wanted to get out for a little bit. I think I at least deserve to see some of the world before The Revealed take me."

"Stop it," she says, and reaches across the table to lightly smack my shoulder, "don't say that."

But it's true.

I'm ready to change topics. "So how about you?" I ask. "How's it going with Coltan?"

"Ugh," she scrunches her face. "Over it. We started talking about the election. He's voting for Westerfield!" she says aghast. "Anyone who isn't voting for your dad is crazy."

I laugh to lighten the fact that her statement is spoken like someone who believes all the propaganda. Sure, my father means well and really wants all the things he talks about for the country, it's just not going to be that easy. Not by a long shot.

"Anyway, I met this new guy last week at this restaurant I went to," she says, "and he asked for my number, so maybe that'll turn into something. He was cute. But there was also this other guy on Friday. I went to that new club Frost, which is great for meeting guys, I discovered." She considers that for a moment. "Eh," she continues, shrugging, "I've got options."

"I'm jealous," I admit. A boy named Tristan Olivier once kissed me on a dare when I was thirteen. That's the extent of my love life. Having a father running for president is deterrent enough. Being locked in my own home seals the deal.

"You've only got eight more months of this staying-inside crap and then I'll take you out!" Rory promises, a wild child at heart. "The second you turn nineteen!"

"Done." I say, though it feels like a lie when my mind floats back to the note on my window.

"What are you two doing?" Ilan says, balancing a large tray on his belly and shuffling around to the refrigerator. "Rory, are you getting Lily into trouble again?"

"Always!" she sings, adding another dollop of cherry compote to the top of the rillettetes.

Ilan drops the tray and comes to inspect our work. He rolls up his sleeves, displaying arms covered in tattoos. He places his hands on his hips, red face peering at our plates. "Lily, I should hire you on as part of the staff." Ilan admires my appetizer through keen brown eyes. The bright-yellow lemon-pepper sauce dots the tray in an intricate pattern. "At least while you're stuck in here."

"Why, so my parents can pay me, chef?"

"Well, someone should." He grabs one of the metal pans off the rack. "Although with you two talking so much in here, your speed is lacking. We only have today to prep the amuse bouche. I've barely started on the entrées. Rory, as soon as you're done with those rillettetes, make sure they're back in the cooler."

"Of course, chef," she says and nods.

My mother walks through the door. "Lilith." She looks at me expectantly and adds, "What's going on? I thought you were going to come back and tell me how things were going."

"They're great!" I hold up the decorating bag.

"Yes, well, come on," she says, motioning for me. "We don't have time for that. You have your final dress fitting."

My lips curl into a frown.

Rory laughs. "I'll go if you want."

"Wish I could trade you," I say, but follow my mother.

CHAPTER TWO

To me, being targeted by The Revealed seems like having terminal cancer. At first, you're devastated. You want to fight, claw at every possible escape. There's anger and frustration at not having any control. You try anything to get out. But at the end of the day, the cancer keeps growing. Just as the black notes keep coming. Eventually, you realize it's a losing battle. You want to fight, but it isn't a war you can win. Whether it's terminal cancer or The Revealed, they've already won. There's nothing left to do but enjoy the time you have. I've accepted it. My parents have not. They're clinging to every scrap of hope they've got. Even though the outcome is so obvious.

Most kids don't face this fight. I'm the only one I know who's ever received letters from The Revealed. For most rich eighteen-year-olds, the year inside has become a rite of passage, a step into adulthood. They succumb to their house as a prison because they know there will be years of life on the other side. Sure, no parent wants to see their kid go through this, and no kid wants to turn eighteen. But for most kids, the odds of actually being taken are slim. The Revealed have become as much a cautionary tale as a reality. Most eighteen-year-olds don't really have to face their fear of dying. They most likely won't be taken and the time spent indoors is fleeting, so it's endurable.

I know my eighteenth year is also fleeting. But not because I will soon turn nineteen. Because The Revealed will come for me. And that will be the end of life as I know it, whether they kill me or not.

It makes the pomp my parents insist on all the more ridiculous.

My mother sits in her favorite plush chair while I stand on a raised platform in my ball gown for tomorrow night. Gold and plush, the dress corsets my body, pulling everything into tight, womanly lines. When it reaches my hips the dress explodes in silk and ruffles, the fabric draping like a curtain to the floor. The seamstress floats around me, tacking on little flowery details as she goes, completing the effect of the dress.

I'm a cupcake.

I glance over at my mother to gauge her reaction, but she's got a newspaper covering her face. On the front page is a boy with dark hair hanging in his eyes, framing his sharp face. Bright green-and-gold eyes peek up at the camera, bemused, as he wades through the press. He's in a crowd with his friends, smirking against the camera flashes. He's holding a girl's hand. Two more boys stand around him. One of them has an arm extended to keep the paparazzi at bay, bulging biceps warning against any attempt to get too close.

I know them all. We went to school together. They were a year ahead of me. Most kids just pretended like I didn't exist. But Roderick Westerfield's son Kai, the dark-haired boy in the photo, was the worst.

My mind flits back to preparatory school, the day the presidential candidates were announced almost a year and a half ago. I already knew and so did most of my classmates, but the official word from Congress sealed my fate.

I was in the auditorium, sitting on the indoor wooden bleachers that were raised at least ten stacks deep. My classmates surrounded me in that awkward shuffle of cliques that haunted teens even after the war.

Kai Westerfield and his friends sat in one corner, talking and laughing. He was so carefree. He wore his uniform without the required tie and kept a few buttons of his shirt undone. It was just the right amount of practiced dishevelment. The girls in the group had hemmed their skirts well above their knees so they had to sit with both their legs to one side to keep from showing the world what was underneath. As if giving people a sneak peek wasn't the point.

I wasn't the only one stealing glances at the group. Kai Westerfield was considered the North American Sector's most-eligible bachelor, and he wasn't even of legal age. All the girls in the auditorium were glancing at him, hoping to catch his attention.

He, on the other hand, kept his arm draped around a busty blonde who was splayed across his lap. I don't even remember her name now. Just his arm candy of the week. She kept nibbling at his ear. He allowed it without giving her so much as a glance. This made her pouty. When she curled her bottom lip and had the nerve to speak to him, he pushed her from his lap. She smacked onto the wooden bleachers and huffed, open-mouthed at Kai, but didn't have the nerve to call him out.

Kai didn't even glance in the girl's direction.

Another girl, this one auburn-haired, reached out an arm and placed it just above Kai's knee. She stared hungrily at him. He gave her a fleeting look before ignoring her, too.

I glanced at him only for curiosity's sake. Didn't he feel the same pressure I always did to uphold his family's reputation? The auburn-haired girl ran her hand farther up Kai's leg.

He and I had the power to ruin our parent's careers if we chose. How did he keep that worry from his expression? I felt like it always weighed mine down—like my eyes would shine brighter if only I didn't fret so much about the opinions of others.

Jeremy silently waited for me at the auditorium door. My parents had authorized clearance for him to attend all of my classes. He spent every weekday watching over me, standing outside the doors of my classrooms.

There was a reason people kept their distance from me.

My professor played the news for the school and we watched. Well, I tried to watch as lead anchor Riley Fisher made the announcement standing outside the Capitol Building. He kept the suspense for as long as possible before revealing the contenders.

Mark Atwood and Roderick Westerfield would vie against one another in the first presidential election since the war.

No one was surprised. But this was the official announcement. Before, it could be waved off as friendly speculation. Now the election and my father's involvement were strikingly real.

My eyes immediately returned to Kai, who was receiving high fives and pats on the back from his friends. They were whooping and laughing, causing quite a ruckus. One boy, Kai's best friend Micah, even held up Kai's hand and shouted, "Future First Son!"

I sank down on the bleachers, trying not to look at the other students who were staring at me.

Kai could have the title, for all I cared.

One girl in my class, a little blonde named Keira who had always been friendly enough, put a hand on my shoulder. "It won't be so bad," she grinned encouragingly. Her father was a neurosurgeon, some kind of scientist at the Pentagon or someplace. She had no idea.

I peeked over my shoulder, and my gaze caught Kai's. For just a moment we looked at each other. Was he remembering those days in California, too? Our families used to meet at a beach house in Malibu every summer. I was seven, Kai just eight. We were friends, in the sense that we ran around outside together, making sand castles and collecting seashells.

My throat caught as I thought about our family dinners beside the fireplace. My mother would be chopping leaves for a salad, Kai's mother making strawberry shortcake for dessert. And my father and Roderick Westerfield would be throwing hamburgers and hotdogs on the grill. Kai and I would occupy ourselves at the table. I would set the plates down neatly, and he would follow behind me, rearranging them until I got angry.

It was simple then. Things made sense. Sure, our fathers had different political opinions, but they were friends. They still found enough common ground to appreciate one another.

Then Kai's mom died during the war. And Roderick Westerfield became a different man. A vengeful man. Harsh and hard. There were rumors that during the war, he had killed men with his bare hands when he and Kai needed food. Not that those rumors were rare. People became desperate when they hadn't eaten in weeks. But with Roderick Westerfield, it was different somehow. Darker. Not born out of desperation but desire. As if he had to prove to the world that he was top of the food chain, most powerful of them all. It wouldn't surprise me if the rumors about

Westerfield were true. You just knew with a glance at him that he wasn't a man you wanted to make angry.

Part of me pitied Kai, but he was growing up to be just like his father. It was difficult to feel sorry for someone once they were capable of making their own decisions. I watched the auburn-haired girl's hand creep even higher until it made me blush to keep watching. It was more difficult by the day to sympathize with him.

By the time Kai and I found our way to prep school, we hadn't talked to one another for years. We were strangers. He had his jock friends, and I had parents who were grooming me for an election.

He loved being the center of attention. He had a different girl on his arm every week, model types who fawned after him. He was the son of a powerful man, and that attracted a certain desperate type of girl. He played into it though, and played them, going through almost every girl in our school.

I avoided him, not interested in his games or the show he put on for attention. I hid from the spotlight while he reveled in it, squeezing out all he could.

Our mutual gaze in that auditorium ended quickly. But the memories of that beach and our families still made my heart twist. Not with longing, but with sadness for things lost.

As the bell rang, I piled my books under my arms and bolted from the room, slipping past Jeremy and not giving him time to follow. I hid under the bleachers outside and cried.

I thought the spot I'd found was safe, but quickly learned otherwise as voices drew near.

My cries dried in my throat. I sank deeper into the shadows, huddled amongst the dust and spider webs. Feet clanked against the stair treads. Two voices carried from above.

"I mean, it's pathetic really," one boy said. It sounded like Micah.

And then Kai spoke, and I knew I'd heard right. "She just thinks she's too good for all of this. Did you see how she ran from the auditorium?"

There was a snipping sound as they fired a light. Then I smelled the smoke from the cigarettes as it wafted through the crevices in the bleachers. They were smoking between classes, which was not allowed but a lot of the students did it anyway.

"I mean, everyone knows she's the biggest snob at the school. And in a school full of snobs, that's saying something. Look at you, your dad's running for president too and you still have friends."

"She clearly just can't handle it. It's her parents' fault. You should see them outside of TV. Her mom is like this pathological liar. The woman will say anything if she thinks it'll help her family in the polls. Her dad's spent so much time and energy creating his career, he can't see past that to anything else. Of course Lily's fucked-up."

The boys jumped over the railing and onto the dirt. If they looked over their shoulders, they would see me.

The boys put out their cigarettes, grinding their feet into the dirt.

"Whatever, man, I want nothing to do with that girl. She's weird," Micah went on, raking a hand through his hair and spitting in the dirt.

Kai agreed. "Weird and a snob. Not that she has a reason to be a snob. All you have to do is look at her face to see that."

The boys snorted laughter and their voices grew faint, but I stayed hunched in the corner. I sat in the shadows for a long time. I was too humiliated to leave before I was positive everyone else had gone home for the day.

Kai's comments surprised me, though I knew they shouldn't. Everyone whispered things like that behind my back. I was the biggest snob, the girl who wanted nothing to do with people she thought were beneath her, which meant everyone, according to my peers.

But ugly? I mean, I'd never thought I was some drop-dead gorgeous stunner or anything, but ugly? And he'd said it without any hesitancy, with such conviction that it made it feel like well-known truth.

I know Kai and I didn't speak. But I thought he of all people would know what I was going through. It would make sense to him, if to no one else.

Clearly, I'd been wrong. Really, stupidly wrong.

I pulled my hair from its ponytail and ran my fingers through the front pieces so they didn't tuck behind my ears and fell firmly into my face. With my books clutched in front of me, shielding as much of my face as possible, my eyes panned to the path at my feet, I found Jeremy, and went home.

Kai's words echoed in my head. *Not that she has a reason to be a snob. All you have to do is look at her face to see that.*

And as any girl would do, I looked to my mother for affirmation that I didn't deserve those words. That I was worth more than that, that my exterior appearance didn't define me.

"Lily, what happened to you?" my mother paraded toward me as I entered her wing of the house. Her fingers danced across her ear as she secured the back of her earring. Then she began running her fingers through my hair and pulled it back into its slick ponytail. "Your face is a mess. Have you been crying?" she sighed. "Maybe we should leave it down then. I can have Meredith come up to give you a hand with the styling."

More tears stung my eyes. But I strangled them back.

"Don't purse your lips like that," she tapped them. "You'll get premature wrinkles. You need to clean up. We don't have that much time. You know it's a big day for your father. He's talking to Jet and his PR team now to go over the plan for tonight. Did they show the announcement at school?"

I nodded stiffly.

"Good," and now she added a hint of glee in her eyes. "It's all going so well. We just have the dinner tonight. You just have to get through the Congressional dinner. Put your dress on and a smile. You don't have to do anything else. You're father and I will handle the press. Maybe say hello to Kai. He'll be joining Roderick this evening. It would look nice for the campaign if you two were friendly."

I couldn't speak without letting free the flood of tears.

My mother paused only then to look at my face. She didn't need to voice the disappointment I saw there. "What am I going to do with you?"

It was then I realized no one was going to comfort me. There weren't going to be warm embraces and soothing words anywhere in my future. Only hard interiors and forced smiles. So I conformed. Became the statue everyone expected. Faked grins and donned pretty dresses.

After that day, I wore my hair down and my head low. I waited out the days until Kai turned eighteen, which was only a few weeks after I overheard him talking. Then he was pulled from school and kept indoors.

He survived his eighteenth year without being taken and joined the military on his nineteenth birthday. I'm sure it was his father's idea. It would look great for his father's campaign to have two military heroes in the family. And Kai was destined to be a military hero, with all his charisma and charm.

My mother pulls the newspaper from her face. She insists on having paper copies hand-delivered each morning, even though everything is available online now.

Her face is placid and she nods, "That will do." She waves the seamstress away with one hand. My garment is complete.

"I see Kai's home from the military," I tip my chin at the front page.

My mother glances down at it like she hadn't even noticed his picture. "Yes, well, apparently he's on leave for a while to help his father with the campaign. Not sure what help that boy will be able to provide, though. All trouble if you ask me."

My mother stands and unzips my dress. She holds it carefully while I step out.

"Watch the hem," she warns. I do and step down onto the plush carpet, pulling my sundress back over my head.

My mother hangs the ball gown for me. The maids will deliver it to my closet later. Wouldn't want to risk the dress by placing it in my hands for longer than necessary. I may ruin it, and this dress cost enough to fund the gala itself.

"Am I done?" I ask, trying to keep my irritation from my words.

"For now," she says, and I run upstairs before she can change her mind.

With headphones in my ears and the Internet to keep me occupied, I drown out all thoughts. Knowing if I allow myself a second to think, it will be of inky black notes and silver symbols that promise my time is almost up.

CHAPTER THREE

Two days later, the house fills with so much activity I barely have time to take it all in. I'm grateful for the chaos because it keeps my mother from having time to further address my latest escape attempt.

My father arrives home just an hour before the party is about to start. My mother is already dressed, and I'm in my room doing my hair, down and curled. I don't even hear him come inside.

"I'm home," he sings, walking through my hallway.

Quickly, I set down the brush and run to the door. He must have gotten ready in the car because his dark hair is slicked back and styled. I see the hint of foundation on his cheeks, which makes me smirk. But Jet, my father's publicist, insists it makes him look better on camera. He must not have had time to shave though, because there is the barest dark shadow playing on his jawbone.

"Dad!" I wrap my arms around him.

Hovering outside my room is a string of advisors and security. Jeremy nods at me from the doorway, his face blank. Behind him is my father's publicist, a sharp-looking guy named Jet Roth. I don't remember the last time I saw my father without Jet by his side. As usual, Jet is talking animatedly on the phone—something about a speech for my father. He's really concerned about the wording when discussing funding for employment and job training programs.

"Hi Lil," my dad says and chuckles. "Sorry I'm late."

"What took you so long?"

"The usual," he sighs. "It takes a lot of time and energy to win an election. What have you been doing?"

"Um, Mark," Jet steps into the room and lowers the phone to speak to my father. "Winston is sending over the draft for the conference on Wednesday. Can you read through it and get back to him by Sunday?"

"Put it on my calendar for tomorrow," my father says, nodding. Then he turns back to me. "Sorry Lil, what were you going to say?"

I wave my hand in the direction of the ballroom. "Just that this event is all Mom's been able to talk about for a month."

"I heard about your little getaway attempt," he says.

"Mom called you, of course."

He nods.

"I won't stay locked up in this house for another eight months," I say, turning back toward my mirror.

"Would you rather become one of the Taken Eighteen?"

"No, but if they want me they'll take me whether I stay inside or not, won't they?" I counter.

Talking so personally despite all of the people around has become normal for my father. This group is sworn to secrecy under all circumstances anyway.

Jeremy walks up to my father. "Sorry to interrupt, sir," he says, "but I just got word that the press is getting restless. Mrs. Atwood is requesting you downstairs as soon as possible."

My father checks his watch, then turns back to me.

"Keeping me in here isn't going to stop them," I add before I lose him to the party. "You want to see all the letters I've gotten? And most of them have been taped to my bedroom window."

My father's shoulders tighten in discomfort. "Unfortunately, right now I need to please your mother. We'll talk more later. Enjoy yourself tonight, okay kiddo?" My father doesn't like discussing the letters. Avoidance seems to be my parents' favorite tactic whenever I bring up The Revealed. They just want me to stay inside and not argue about it. That's what other rich eighteen-year-olds do, after all.

"I'll try," I say grudgingly.

He leaves with his entourage close at his heels, and I turn back to getting ready. I slip off my robe, grab my dress off the hanger, and pull it on. I trace my hand over the shimmery material as I zip up the back. I glance at myself for a long while in the full-length mirror, trying to make the look feel right on me. I turn to the side, then the other side, then face front.

I look like a doll. A pretty doll, but a doll nonetheless.

I pout my lips and lean toward the mirror like it's a camera. I furl my hair and twirl around. Still, I look breakable. I wish I were fierce and powerful. When people saw me they would know I was someone important.

But that isn't real.

I'm a snob, I remind myself. The sting of the words makes my throat constrict. I bite my lip against the memory, but other unpleasant thoughts invade my mind. I'm eighteen years old and stuck inside a house twenty-four hours a day. Not very glamorous.

The media tries to paint my life that way. They will all be here tonight, showering me with questions about where my dress is from and what I plan on doing when I turn nineteen and how I'll feel if my father wins the presidency.

I walk onto the balcony outside my room, watching people stream in through the doors below.

Rows of limos stretch down the road. The valets work quickly to make sure none of these people wait. They are the most-powerful people in the world. They wait for no one.

A red carpet is unrolled down the walkway, and soft light keeps the setting intimate and alluring. Inside, guests are led through the foyer, pausing for the photographers and reporters, and into the ballroom, which is lined with round tables and red-and-gold accents. A live orchestra plays soothing music, and I can hear laughter and the hum of conversation from my balcony.

No doubt my father will make his appearance in a matter of minutes.

I smooth out my dress, not ready to become a spectacle yet. Ever since turning eighteen, I am somewhat of a focal point during conversations. It's hardly a secret that I've become a big target for The Revealed. People are even betting on the Internet, guessing the date I'll be taken.

Two hundred and fifty days until I'm nineteen.

"Lily?"

I jump. Rory stands in the doorway.

"Sorry, I didn't hear you come in." I smile sheepishly at her.

"I'm supposed to be working but had to see your dress." She runs toward me and grazes her hands over the material. "Oh my God, you look like something out of *Vogue*! Too bad it isn't still around or they would have died over your dress. They would have wanted you on the front cover." Rory is always too complimentary of me. It's embarrassing and only makes me turn crimson. Not a flattering color against the gold.

I shake my head, "It looks ridiculous. I look ridiculous."

"Shut up, babe." She rolls her eyes. "You're perfect. And get downstairs. You're missing the biggest party of the year."

"So are you," I remind her.

"Yeah, but no one cares about me." She shoos me out the door with a light smack on my rear to get me going. I squeal and head into the hallway. She scampers past me with a wink, and starts off for the back stairs that lead to the kitchen and servants' quarters.

As I make my way down the hall to the main stairway, I can hear the ballroom music, and a muffled undertone of voices and movement.

There are a lot of people here.

I remind myself to take deep breaths and move slowly as I walk down the sweeping staircase into the grand foyer.

As if on cue, all the cameras turn in my direction.

"Lily!" they yell, "Lily, look here!"

I keep a smile plastered to my face. Even the guests' heads turn. I'm the center of attention. It's a rare opportunity for people to look at me since I never leave the property. I glance toward the doors, wondering if I can make a break for it if need be.

"Lily, have you received any more messages from The Revealed?"

"Lily, do you think your father will be able to save you?"

"Lily, how much time do you think you have left?"

Jeremy comes up beside me and takes my arm. He steadily leads me through the line of press, recorders, and television cameras shoved in my face. I don't answer any of their questions. My goal is to simply make it through the night gracefully. But the media are like bloodhounds on the trail. They follow me, while Jeremy attempts to block their path. "Give her some space folks," he says, holding out a protective hand. "Back behind the media line, please."

One good thing about staying inside is it keeps me away from the cameras. They can't get inside the fence surrounding the house, though a few certainly try. To them, I'm just another sideshow to boost ratings. Not a real person with feelings.

"Thanks Jeremy," I mumble.

My mother floats over and kisses my cheek and then goes about tucking my hair behind my ears. "There," she says with this warm, motherly smile I only see when we're in front of the cameras. She holds out my hand, being sure to tilt our faces toward the lenses. She loves the attention. A few flashes of light, then she shifts her attention to Marg Lancing, a congresswoman from Pennsylvania. She and Marg have been friends for years; they're both social climbers, obsessed with their appearance and social standing.

I move through the crowd toward an empty table.

"Watch out!" Rory shuffles by in her pressed black trousers and white blouse, holding a plate of hors d'oeuvres. I see the neatly arranged salmon with lemon-pepper mousse dotted on top. If only I could be helping Ilan now instead of standing in this ballroom.

"Rory," I say, standing to talk to her, "need some help?"

I wouldn't mind sneaking back to the kitchen.

She keeps walking. "Of course not!" She flaps the end of her dishtowel to keep me away. "You're supposed to be having fun. But I gotta go serve these! See ya later." She grins, and I lose her in the swarm.

I sit back down at the table and stare at the guests around me.

Fun. Right.

Really, my presence here is just for show. This is how the Atwood family proves to the outside world we love each other. We make appearances together and support my father's campaigning efforts on his political bulldozer to the presidency.

"You look like you could use a dance."

I turn around in my chair. Instantly, my expression melts into shock, and I feel the danger of the situation creep into my spine. I glance around the room to see if any cameras are pointing my way. "Mr. Westerfield." I stand up, trying to remain pleasant and polite.

The man in front of me looks carved from stone. Everything about his features is sharp, from the cut of his jaw to his dark brow. One eyebrow is raised just slightly, as if he's amused. He is always playing a game. Each conversation is a test to concoct ways to manipulate.

Roderick Westerfield is not a friend. He's the competition. But it isn't polls I'm concerned with. That isn't my problem with this man. Westerfield has always made me uncomfortable. Since his wife's death, Westerfield's sole purpose has been to win the presidency. This man doesn't fool anyone, either. His radical policies aren't a secret. He wants to renegotiate the border lines and isolate the North American Sector from any country that doesn't agree with our trade standards. Doesn't he realize that's what got us in to this mess in the first place? But in a time where people are paranoid about their own neighbor, they seem to want a leader who will fight if need be. The war brought out the fear and violence in a lot of people.

If Westerfield is elected president of the North American Sector, who knows what the new nation will get itself into in the name of security.

Westerfield's gray eyes sparkle, but with cunning, not good spirit.

"Ms. Atwood," he extends his hand, "you look as beautiful as ever."

I don't take it, glancing nervously at the crowd, ready to get out of the situation at the first opportunity.

"What are you doing here?" My eyes narrow.

"I was invited, naturally." He's playing with me.

Westerfield seems to be enjoying my discomfort. For appearance's sake, I can't be bluntly rude, but all I want to do is run. Westerfield still holds out his hand. He's taunting me, but I don't know what the game is yet. There must be something he's playing at.

"I'm sorry." I take a step back.

He laughs, loudly enough that it catches the attention of those around us. "I insist."

What does he want? A dance? He must be drunk. I stare at the thick golden drink in his hand.

"I said no. If you are trying to cause a press scandal, I'm not buying," I say in a low voice. "Save it for my father. Your competition is with him."

"Who says I'm competing tonight?" he responds, louder than I'm comfortable with, putting a hand on my shoulder.

I cringe from his touch. His skin is just as slimy as his words. How this man can deceive the public into thinking he is a level choice for president is beyond me. I'm seriously considering making a run for it. The exit doors aren't far. I pull up my dress so that he can't touch me again, but by now people are beginning to look at us. Presidential candidates are never in the shadows at functions like this, especially when they are talking to the opposition's daughter.

"I heard a rumor from a journalist friend that you were recently spotted out for an afternoon on the town, making quite the scene." Westerfield leans comfortably on the back of a chair.

The color drains from my face as I remember stealing my father's car.

"Your father's Aston Martin, huh?" He smirks, knowing he's got me pinned under his thumb. "Good choice."

There's his punch line.

"I don't know what you're talking about," I tell him tensely. "I don't think you have your facts straight."

He continues with his devious grin, "No? But I *do* have pictures."

This is a new low. My heartbeat quickens at the thought of my picture—probably standing by the door of the car and staring defiantly at Jeremy—splashed across the home page of every major Internet site. My father will be horrified and my mother ... oh God, my mother will kill me!

I have to get away from him. "Are you trying to blackmail me? I'm sorry. Excuse me."

I turn from Westerfield, but he grabs my upper arm. "Do not underestimate what I am capable of Ms. Atwood." His words slither across my cheek. "I am intent on winning this election." A camera flashes. "And I think that you are the catalyst to get me there." He drops his hand and holds up his drink. The ice clanks against the glass. "Cheers, to Daddy's Little Girl."

I am frozen, watching as Westerfield slurps down his drink with such smug satisfaction. I raise my hand, wanting to knock the glass from his mouth. I want to tear that smug expression from his face, prove to him that he can't hurt me.

"That's enough." A hand wraps firmly around my arm and leads me to the middle of the dance floor. I yank my arms away from whatever security has been sent to collect me. Clearly, Jeremy's decided it's time to intervene.

"Take my hand."

Another camera flash snaps me back to reality.

I look at the person I'm now dancing with for the first time. He's wearing a military outfit, decorated with a splendor of pins and medals, some to show his rank, others recognize his achievements and awards. He doesn't even pause as he begins gliding across the floor with me. It's the sharp cut of his features that takes me off guard. The childish lines have faded, replaced by striking cheekbones and a firm jaw. But his dark hair falls across his forehead in that way it has since we were children, and that mischievous look in his green-gold eyes still spells trouble.

"Kai!" I try to pull away, but he holds my hand tighter, keeping our steps perfectly in time. "Why are you doing this?" I keep my voice low through clenched teeth, even though I want to scream at him.

Another flash.

We're in the middle of the dance floor. There is no way I can hide my face from photographers.

Kai holds my hand tightly. "Relax."

"Relax? You and your father are trying to ruin everything!"

Kai Westerfield is trouble. The kind of trouble I've always tried to avoid. I haven't said a word to him since we were children. The last time I was near him, it was the day I was hiding under the bleachers, and he was telling his best friend what an ugly snob I was. I'm not the least bit interested in the way he goes through women or his affinity for partying. I know it, even if the rest of the country wants to paint him as the military hero. He's just like his father.

"Lily," he snaps, "if I wanted to ruin you, I would have left you with my father."

"Oh, like this is any better!"

"The press is much more interested in you and me dancing than in my father having a five-second discussion with you. If I've learned anything, it's that paparazzi aren't hard to please. Better pictures of you and me on the cover than you and my father."

"What about the other pictures your father has?"

"I'll take care of it," he says.

"You'll take care of it?" my voice rises skeptically.

He purses his lips, amused, like he's watching a two-year-old throw a tantrum and knows that intervening is not worth the energy. "Yes. And your father should be able to as well. He's the one who reinstated all these journalists, right?"

My stomach sinks to my feet. Though my father is the last person I want to share those photos with, I don't have a choice. I haven't even been at this party for fifteen minutes and already I've ruined the night and possibly the election. Imagine the headlines, "Atwood can't even control daughter, how will he handle the country?" Then a nice shot of me handing over the keys.

"If you had simply left," Kai continues, pausing for a moment to spin me in a circle, then pulling me close again, "the media would have immediately picked up that something was wrong. But now it looks like we're friends. Now the press can write about how great the Westerfield and Atwood families get along. It might even be wise for your father to slip in a couple words about how he and my father go way back. We both look good."

Slowly, I nod my head. His words are beginning to make sense. It still doesn't change the fact that his father is now out to make my life a living hell. Leave it to Kai to know how to manipulate the press.

"Aren't you supposed to be on some military mission or something?" I demand.

"I'm on leave right now."

"So you decided to come crash our party?"

"Actually," Kai twirls me around again and this time when he pulls me back I worry for a moment that our heads will collide. But he's in control, stopping me just before we hit. Enough to both shock me and make me realize how close we're dancing. "I was invited." His eyes don't waver from mine, and I suddenly feel like we're the only two people left in this ballroom. "Despite what you think, our fathers are actually more alike than different. They are both masters of PR."

The song ends, and there is light applause as I realize that most of the guests are watching us on the dance floor. My cheeks are deep red by now, I'm sure.

I catch sight of my mother in the crowd; she looks like she's waiting for the perfect moment to give me a good lecture. Thankfully, the guests begin to mumble and the crowd begins to shift.

Rory comes up to my side, and I'm glad for her company. She's holding a plate. It's filled with the rillettes amuse-bouche she was plating yesterday. "Lily, your mother—"

Kai raises an eyebrow. "Rory?"

Rory lowers the tray while she takes him in. Recognition filters through her eyes. "Kai? I can't believe they invited you and your father here!"

"You two know each other?" I can't help but sharply add my two cents. This night is getting weirder by the second.

"We met last weekend," Kai says smoothly.

"At that new club that I was telling you about," Rory says, "called Frost." She turns back to Kai. "I didn't think you'd remember me."

"Of course. How could anyone forget that argument?" Kai laughs.

"Argument? You got into an argument?" I'm glancing between the two of them. "Why didn't you tell me about this? About him?" I sound more accusatory than I should.

"Well, I wanted to, but your mom dragged you out of the kitchen before I had the chance," Rory explains. "Anyways," she says, turning to Kai, "Thanks again for covering that tab. I kept trying to explain to that guy that I had cash out in my car but he just wouldn't let me leave to get it." Rory turns back to me. "I even told him he could walk out there with me, but because I hadn't paid my bill they wouldn't let me out the door. They said I should call someone or something. I don't know what I would have done if Kai hadn't covered for me." She glances back at Kai and adds, "By the way, I owe you nine dollars."

"No," Kai says, waving her off, "no, you don't. I told you that already the other day."

She shrugs. "Well, I really appreciate it. Kai Westerfield of all people, coming to my rescue. Who would have thought?"

I know my face is twisted into a mix of shock and disapproval. Not a flattering expression, but I can't wipe it away. Kai and Rory? And Rory is actually acting like she likes this dude. No way. No way! Sure Kai Westerfield is charming, but I can't believe that Rory of all people is buying it. Everyone knows he's a playboy. And Rory knows the history between Kai and me.

Soft string music plays in the background as some people dance and other groups of people around the room talk, keeping the noise level even.

I find my father in the crowd. A glass of champagne in his hand, and he's laughing. A grin spread wide across his face as he talks to Roderick Westerfield. And it isn't his politician grin. It's his real one. The one that makes him look like a dad. My dad. During the days of backyard barbecues and summer nights. Sure,

Westerfield is my father's competition and rival, but I sometimes forget there was a time when they were good friends. It dawns on me that the nostalgia must mean something to my father. There must be some part of Roderick Westerfield that my father still feels he understands. Well, I'm not clouded in my judgment of Westerfield. I don't trust him, and I *don't* like him.

No one else is unsettled. They have all gone back to their business.

Just like Kai said. We dance. The media gets their pictures. We all go home happy.

Except I'm not happy right now. Is this—my eyes drift up and down Kai's frame—what Rory meant when she said she met someone new last weekend? The idea makes me angry. She shouldn't be going after someone like ... him. I've told her all about Kai. I told her what he said about me. She's my best friend. Shouldn't she be on my side?

Kai catches me watching him, and I curtly turn my gaze to Rory.

Kai's always flaunting around, making these big spectacles at events, smiling and acting like such the confident hero. Cocky, if you ask me. Girls swoon over him, and he eats it up. Did she say he came to her rescue? She should know better. It wasn't to defend her honor or whatever bullshit he spews. It was for the attention. So he could play the hero and, at the end of the night, everyone would just love him even more.

I glance back over at him through my eyelashes. Clearly, not as subtly as I thought. He's still staring at me and our eyes meet again.

He's not even listening to Rory. But then, I guess, neither am I.

I turn my attention to her words just in time to catch the end of her last sentence, "Your mom wants you. She's up near the media line with your father. I think they're going to take more pictures or something." She shrugs and adds, "I have to get back to serving. Ilan's having a fit in the kitchen. There are so many people. It was good seeing you again, Kai." She whisks away, tray in hand.

My eyes return to the crowd. At least Jeremy isn't hovering nearby. But that probably just means he's reported back to my mother about my "scene," which is exactly why she wants to see me.

"I have to go," I blurt to Kai. I want to get lost in this party for just a little bit longer before my mother drags me back to reality.

"Wait," he says and grabs my hand, forcing me to turn and face him.

"Look, I appreciate what you did," I say, "the dance and all but…."

"But what?"

A grin pulls at the edges of his lips, and he tilts his head in playful amusement. I can't tell what the expression means. It's almost a replica of his father's. Only, it's also the opposite of the expression Westerfield wears. Kai's is laced with sincerity and an authenticity I don't understand. It nevertheless fills me with suspicion.

"It was really good to see you again, Lily," he says before I can finish my sentence. "It's been a long time."

My face melts before I can harden my gaze. It's then I realize my hair has fallen over my shoulder, my cheeks are bare all the way to my ears, lending myself like a book to his gaze. I've never felt so exposed in my life. And I want to pull my hands up, shy away from his look before his eyes can take in the sight of my face. I don't want to watch his expression as he analyzes my appearance. I don't want him to see me and find the disappointments.

His eyes narrow and then his expression drops, yanking my chest and my lungs down with it.

But his face doesn't mock.

Eyes widen. Jaw slackens. He doesn't meet my gaze.

What?

Before I can verbalize the question, he's grabbing my wrist.

"Get down!" he yells, yanking me roughly to the floor.

I catch sight of Marg Lancing, who shrieks. The room seems to take a collective shudder. My body vibrates with surprise. Everything suddenly comes into focus. People are dropping all around us. Glasses are tossed aside as something piercing and crashing pulses through the room.

On the floor, Kai wraps his arms around me. My heart jumps into my throat. An attack? Are we being attacked? I peek through Kai's arms at the commotion. The back windows of the ballroom are completely shattered, leaving piles of broken shards.

The music stops, replaced by an orchestra of frantic screams as people recognize the danger, causing chaos.

The doors slam shut on their own and something translucent creeps along the hinges, cracking as it climbs up the sides of the door. *Ice.* Ice is forming along the doors!

My feet want to move. I scramble up, but Kai pulls me back to the floor. "Stay down," he commands. A few people grab the door handles and try to open the doors, but they don't budge.

All of the glass in the ballroom explodes—champagne flutes, light fixtures, serving platters. Everything. A sharp wind whips through the room like a bomb. Blackness sweeps over us with only the dim moonlight left to illuminate the room.

"Keep your head down!" Kai orders, and I tuck my face between my arms. Some of the flying shards hit my skin and I cringe at the sting, yelping as the pieces rake my flesh.

When the glass stops raining again, I dare to glance up.

My breathing is sharp and inconsistent. My limbs shudder uncomfortably, my muscles tensing repeatedly. I've felt this enough to know it's caused by adrenaline. I just need to stay calm, take deep breathes.

We're under attack.

And who knows what kind of attack. But it's all-too familiar, this ducking under objects to protect ourselves from shrapnel.

Kai helps me to stand. He snaps into some sort of soldier mode and has this look in his eyes that says he knows exactly what to do. I cling to that look, praying it's real. He takes my hand and pulls me back along the wall, hiding us behind the crowds that are running away from the broken windows. Everyone has cleared the dance floor. The musicians have abandoned their instruments, which lay strewn about the hall.

Kai grabs a napkin from a table and takes my wrist, blotting the tiny beads of blood on my arms. His jacket protected him. I wasn't so fortunate. As he dabs the cuts, the pain settles in over my skin. I flinch at the sting, and my eyes water. Normally, I would snatch the napkin from him and tell him to shove off, but right now I'm too stunned. My eyes are shifting to everything around me. My vision adjusts to the darkness. The shadows dance along the walls as people scatter in frantic attempts to get away. If Kai wasn't holding my arms, I probably would do the same.

"I'm fine," I mumble. We just need to get out of here. My eyes scan for a way out. There has to be a way out. This is my house. If anyone can get out of this room, it's me.

There's movement just outside in the grass. Shadows shift as someone or something approaches the now-empty window frames. The hall falls silent and still as the uninvited visitors walk inside the room. As they step inside, a wind picks up and circles around the room as though it is alive. It whips through the crowd. My skin prickles with fear.

As my eyes adjust to the moonlight, I glance over the outfits the new visitors are wearing—black pants and black tanks tops. Something shiny is embroidered over their hearts. It's the silver symbol.

These people are The Revealed.

I'm not the only person that seems to have noticed.

Stunned gasps fill the room.

My father stands at the front of the crowd. Always the brave leader. "What do you want?" he shouts.

Is this it? Are they going to take me right now? In front of everyone?

A striking woman stands at the front of the group, and I can tell she isn't someone you want to mess with. She holds herself high, not the least bit afraid of anyone in the room—including security with their guns drawn, only waiting for the command. Her eyes scan the crowd.

"Stay where you are or we'll shoot," Jeremy warns.

The woman stops and gives him a stern, disapproving gaze. She flings out her hand and the gun is torn from Jeremy's grip and slides across the floor. There is the sharp succession of cracks as weapons fire, but not one of the people in black fall to the ground. Instead, there is a light *ping, ping* as the bullets fall to the floor like rain, stopped mid-flight.

I feel my limbs begin to shake all over again. Everyone's heard stories about The Revealed's abilities. But to see them used like this—as though they are simply an extension of their own bodies—is as stunning as it is terrifying.

A hand reaches out to my face in the dark. "Look at me." My eyes connect with Kai's green-gold gaze. "Breathe."

Shakily, I nod and begin taking quick, shallow breaths.

A man tries to make a run for it, sprinting through the broken glass. One of The Revealed reacts. He flicks out his wrist and a plant from outside comes twisting in through the broken pane. It wraps around the man's waist and pulls him to the floor.

Someone screams.

They are controlling the plants, making them grow and move.

"How—"

Kai places a hand over my mouth, silencing me. He positions himself so that his body is in front of me, shielding me from view as much as possible. Sure he's taller and broader, but I'm like a beacon in this dress.

The woman's attention snaps, and her gaze connects with mine. She tilts her head, staring at me. Suddenly I'm frozen.

This is it. I've waited for this moment. Since the notes started arriving, I knew this time would come. I wish I could stand and be brave. But I can hardly remember how to breathe, let alone be valiant.

But then her gaze moves past me to the rest of the crowd, scanning over everyone.

"We're only here for one," she says. She doesn't seem even the least bit fazed by the security. Their weapons are gone or out of bullets. They're just as defenseless as the rest of us.

Two of The Revealed break off, turning to the sides of the room and scanning the guests. They move quickly through the crowd, sweeping the room before returning to the others' sides.

My muscles tense until they ache. Kai, still standing in front of me, is gently pushing me back against the wall. The Revealed whip past us without stopping, and I know that despite Kai's efforts, they see me.

If it isn't me, then who are they after?

"I have to find Rory," I say in Kai's ear. His arm doesn't give. "She's eighteen, too."

I push against him but his grip is firm.

"Kai." My voice is foreign and cracked.

"Gone," one of The Revealed says to the woman at the front.

"It appears so," she says, and nods. "This isn't the last time you'll see us," the blonde leader warns. "Let's go," she says to the rest of her group and they retreat out the windows again, quickly disappearing into the night.

As they leave, the ice on the doors recedes. People yank them open and begin sprinting madly from the house. Security tries to follow The Revealed out into the night but can't find their trail. Patrols are immediately dispatched to search the area, but I know they too will come up empty-handed. The Revealed never leave evidence.

"Someone call the police," my father orders.

The media begin snapping pictures of the destruction. Jeremy finds me and grabs my shoulders. "Are you okay?"

I look around the room. "This is not okay." I try to keep my thoughts straight. "Rory. I need to find Rory."

"She's fine," Jeremy promises. "I just saw her in the kitchen. Ilan's a mess though," Jeremy's ill-timed attempt at humor falls flat. He clears his throat and straightens out his shoulders. "Here," he says, shrugging out of his jacket and wrapping it around my shoulders.

I glance back at Kai. My eye contact is the only thanks I can muster before Jeremy takes me from the room.

The night is clearly over.

CHAPTER FOUR

There are tabloid stories: at least a dozen of them the next day. Each one a front-page headline screaming different sensational tales.

Lily Escapes Being Taken!

———

**Atwood House Destroyed in Revealed Blast
Intended to Be Lily's Demise!**

———

**It's Only a Matter of Time Before
The Revealed Try Again!**

———

**Will the North American Sector Finally
Declare War Against The Revealed?**

I willingly stay inside, not wishing to be hounded by the press. Jeremy's security team has managed to keep them off the estate so far.

I didn't think tightening security was possible, but my mother has found a way. She's doubled the number of personnel assigned to the house and has detectives in and out for the next week, investigating every inch of the property. Not that they'll find anything.

No fingerprints. The Revealed didn't touch anything, though they somehow managed to lock the doors, melt the barrels of heavy metal weapons, and shatter every piece of glass in the room. No footprints. There isn't a single mark in the dirt outside the window. The cameras around the house went out during their entrance, so no footage of their break-in was collected. Their abilities make them ghosts.

I switch off the news report on the television in my room. It's almost over, and after the news ends the programming goes static until the next run of reports. I sink down onto my bed, shut my eyes, and slump back onto the pillows. My fingers trace along the tiny scabs all over my arms. They weren't bad enough to warrant stitches, but they are a stark reminder of yesterday.

Why didn't The Revealed take me?

I was right there. The blonde woman definitely saw me. The ones searching the crowd definitely saw me.

The answers aren't in my room so I head down the hall. My father's home office is in the east wing. He stayed home today to manage the investigation. There is a high risk the destruction caused at the gala will cost him a few points in the polls, and my father is doing everything in his power to ensure that doesn't happen. With the investigation pouring through every nook and cranny, any shred of evidence will help, but we don't know much.

His office is decorated with mahogany bookshelves. My father loves books. He has quite the collection of rare novels. During the war, saving books was the last thing on most peoples' minds. Novels that were once available everywhere are now prized possessions. My father spent a small fortune on a few of the works in his collection. The dusty, sharp smell of paper hangs in the air.

My father sits in his leather chair behind his hand-carved desk, concentrating on something on his computer. It's one of those rare times when he's alone, which means he's working on something important. His eyes are narrowed on the screen and every few minutes he types something out rapidly. He doesn't even look up from his computer, though I know he must have caught my movement.

I know better than to interrupt him when he has that look in his eyes. His eyes are so light, the document on the computer screen reflects in them. I almost think that if I got close enough, I could read the words in his eyes.

"Is it *suppose to* or *supposed to*?" he asks without looking up.

"Supposed to," I tell him leaning against the doorframe. "With a *D*."

"Right." He nods, types, and then clicks before looking up at me. "What can I do for you, Lil?"

"Just wondering if you've had any leads?"

He sighs, and I know he's a bit perturbed at the interruption though he's holding back from admitting it. "None."

"What are you working on?"

"Going over the notes Jeremy sent from the investigation. It seems like The Revealed exited the property to the south. We found evidence of tire tracks from some kind of Jeep or Range Rover that didn't match the guest vehicles. The trail goes cold once they reach the main road. We took plaster casts of the treads and some dirt samples, hoping we might be able to pinpoint the car based on its tread or at least track where it has been. It's a shot in the dark."

"What about the woman? The one at the front of the group? Who is she?" I ask.

He shakes his head and says with a wave of his hand, "No one knows. It isn't the first time we've seen her though. She appears to be some kind of leader. If we had records like we used to, we would have found these bastards by now." My father never swears in public, and I always feel like I'm seeing this secret, real side of him when he slips around me. "As it is, everything is outdated since the war. We've depended on people to come forward to reregister of their own volition. She could be someone that was declared dead long ago. If I find anything, you'll be the first to know."

I know my father too well to believe that's true. I'm always the last to know anything important. But this isn't just about the gala or The Revealed. It's about me. The Revealed had a clear shot at taking me last night so why leave all those inky black notes and then pass up an opportunity like that? It surely would have drawn attention, and The Revealed have made it clear they love attention. The theatrics make me sick.

"Do you still think they want to take me?" I ask my dad hesitantly.

His eyes sharply flit to mine, then back to the computer, and finally rest on me again. He sighs. "I'm not taking any chances."

"But they could have taken me last night if they wanted, right? Maybe it's a mistake and those notes weren't serious or something."

My father's dark eyebrows pull together. "That sounds like a stretch, Lil."

He types something on the computer and then looks back at me expectantly. Conversation over. I turn from my father's office but am surprised when I hear his voice calling me back. "Lily." He's even taken his hands entirely off the keyboard this time.

I move back toward him until I'm standing in the center of the room.

"They can't have you," he says and stares at me hard.

Looking in my father's eyes has always been a bit like looking in a mirror. We have eyes that can't seem to settle on a color. Officially it's hazel, but there are blues and grays with the greens, golds, and browns, too. The colors can't seem to make up their minds, unlike my father, who is resolute.

"They can't take you." He says each word in a cold, clipped voice.

I don't know what to say, how to comfort him when I'm just as afraid. "I'll always be your daughter," I say.

He nods once, then is back to business on his keyboard. The moment has passed.

I walk back down the hall, but instead of going back to my room I head down the stairs and out the side door. I tromp onto the grass and make my way down to the guesthouse below the main quarters.

I knock on the back door. "Jeremy?" I continue knocking. "Jeremy, it's Lily."

After a few more knocks, the door opens.

He's wearing jeans and a simple white T-shirt, not his usual crisp white button-down shirt and dark-suit uniform. "What do you know?" I ask him.

"I've been at home all morning, Lily. I don't know anything."

"I don't believe you." I step around him and walk inside.

Jeremy adjusts his shoulders so he's standing squarely. I've bothered him, I know, but I'm too curious about the investigation to care. I need information.

"Maybe you're working from home," I say pointedly. "I just talked to my father and he's going over *your* notes."

The familiarity of his house always strikes me. My mother gave him all of our old furniture and decorations from the house in Arizona. It's a southwestern style, with rustic leather couches and pictures of cacti and sunsets on the wall.

"I don't know what to tell you." He turns. "Want some tea?" His words are curt, as rigid as his stance.

"You're going to tell me the head of my father's security really has no idea what's going on with the investigation into last night's attack?"

I head into the living room. Jeremy has his laptop lying out on the coffee table and papers arranged all around in neat little stacks. It's just the organized mess I was hoping to find. I pick up one of the papers. It's a police report from last night.

I hold up the report and raise my eyebrow. "Off duty, huh?"

"Lily," he says, grabbing the paper, "you know that's classified information."

"Come on Jeremy." I clench my fists at my side. "Last night affected me probably more than anyone. There's a very good chance I was the reason they were there in the first place."

"We don't have evidence to know that for sure."

"I've got plenty. Want to see the collection of little black notes I've received? Why are they sending them if they aren't planning on following through? Is it just a game? Do you even know what they want?"

Jeremy sighs, clearly without the answers I so desperately seek. "We have nothing. They're ghosts." He picks up some of the papers, scans them, and then throws them down. "Nothing."

I plop down on his couch.

He remains standing stiffly by the door.

"There has to be something we're missing." I have long since grown impatient with The Revealed and the lack of answers. "What about the plants from last night? Did you know they could do that? They used them like weapons."

"There was a similar incident in Florida last month."

"What kind of incident?" It's like pulling teeth to get anything out of him. If he'd just tell me what he knew, I'd leave him alone.

"With a man. He'd been tied up with vines."

"The Revealed did that?"

"So he claimed. He said he was attacked without motive."

"And the glass?" I press on. "How did they shatter all the glass like that?"

"The Revealed's powers come in their ability to manipulate things around them. We've compiled records of incidents regarding their abilities. Anything elemental is under their control. They can create fire, wind, water," he gestures like he's pulling something out of the air.

"Anything elemental?" I consider this. "So everything?"

"We don't know their limits yet. But there are limits. Some are stronger than others. Once we find their weaknesses and limitations, we think we can fight them."

"That's it?"

"That's all," Jeremy sighs. "You'll be the first to know if I find that missing link."

"Jeremy," I groan, "you can't just brush me off so easily. I want to know about the other incidents. And, if they control the elements, how did they make security drop all their guns? How did they shatter the glass?"

"It's classified," he stresses again. "All of it."

"I somehow doubt that," I grumble under my breath. That's a classic line just to get me to leave things alone, but this time his tone made it clear the conversation was over.

Jeremy gives me a surly look as he watches me leave.

I walk back outside and march through the grass feeling frustrated. I hate the unknown. I've never liked surprises. Clear paths are always best. Plans. I need plans. And keeping me locked up in this house is definitely not a solid plan. I don't know how much more proof The Revealed need to give my parents.

The property seems to close in on me and I wander along the lines of the fence, tracing my fingers along the rails.

I think of the gala and the way The Revealed marched in as if they were on the VIP list.

Though I would never admit it out loud, thoughts of the gala make my mind stray to Kai, and I lose sight of my mission for information. Just the thought of him makes my pulse spike and my jaw clench in frustration. He is so arrogant! And the way he smiles, like he knows everything. He's just used to getting his way because he's good-looking and charming. And what was he thinking, helping me like that at the gala? He always has to be the hero. Why does he have to try so hard? Does he always have to make sure he impresses every single person?

As I approach the entrance gate, I notice a parked black car, hidden around the corner and out of view of the house. I crouch down and hide myself behind the trunk of a tree. Security drives Escalades. I have no idea who else would have reason to be parked outside my house.

Paparazzi? Or something more sinister?

I peer around the corner of the tree trunk. The car is idling. I reach in my pocket for my cell phone. Jeremy's number is on speed dial. It's better if he's perturbed I interrupt him again than if someone breaks onto the property.

A hand covers my mouth.

CHAPTER FIVE

I shriek and drop my phone. Instinct kicks in, and I move to fight. I throw my arm back, but a hand catches my wrist and pins it against the tree.

"What are you doing out here?" a familiar voice whispers in my ear, so close I can feel the warmth of his breath.

"Kai!" I spin around and the hand drops from my mouth. "What are *you* doing out here!"

"Trying to figure out a way to get your attention without alerting your mob of security."

"You probably already have!" I say, pointing at the camera in the corner of the entrance gate, which pans back and forth over the property.

He raises an eyebrow, and a small grin dimples his cheek. "A camera?" he nearly laughs. "Please, I disabled that thing as soon as I got here. It's on a continual fifteen-second loop now until I press here," he points to a button on his cell phone.

I just stare at him with my mouth gaping a bit, unsure if he's joking with me.

"Technology's kind of my thing," he explains with a shrug. "Why do you think the military keeps me around?"

He's not kidding. I look back at the cameras, wondering if he can teach me that trick.

"You disabled my camera?" I stammer. "Why would you do that? Why are you even here?"

"Because I found *these*," he says, holding out a folder, "in my father's office. I figured you'd like to hang on to them. Or destroy them."

I open the envelope he hands me and a series of images fall out into my hand. Images from my joyride the day before the gala. Westerfield wasn't lying when he said he had evidence of my escapade.

"Do you have a lighter?" I ask, flipping through the images.

"Don't smoke," he shakes his head.

"That's new," I blurt out before I can stop myself.

"What?"

I wish I could take it back. "You used to. Smoke."

"A few times in high school, I guess. How did you know that?"

I shrug quickly, tearing into the photos, until they're shreds around my feet. I grind the shards into dirt. The moisture from the soil bleeds into the edges, further ruining the images.

"You sure didn't waste time making sure they disappear."

"No," I breathe feeling relief swell in my core. "I didn't want to have to explain. Those are the last things I want my parents to find."

"It's done." I can tell his answer is also a promise to me that he will keep this secret.

"Well. Thanks again." I turn toward the house. I have to get back inside before the security patrols notice me. Kai being here won't go over well. He's the son of the rival candidate, after all.

"Don't," Kai says and stops me before I can take a step.

I glanced back at him with a questioning gaze.

"Don't go back inside."

"What?"

His eyes say he already has a plan. "You don't want to."

"What?" My gaze narrows.

"Come out with me. We can go anywhere you want. I'll have you home by dark."

"Oh you're funny." I roll my eyes.

He doesn't smile, just watches me.

I snort, "Go outside with you? I wouldn't even get past the—" I gesture down the road before glancing back at the cameras. "My parents would ki—"

He raises an eyebrow. "That's the point, isn't it? To do something unexpected?"

He has me there. My voice hitches.

There are a million options in this moment. The right one is to tell Kai to leave. I could insist he go, or call Jeremy. I could say thanks, but no thanks. This is a bad idea.

It is a bad idea. Kai Westerfield is a bad idea.

But going back inside that house—staying locked away for my life because I'm scared of the outside world—is an even-worse idea. The Revealed had their chance to take me. I'm not just going to wait around for them to try again.

Instead, I walk right up to Kai until my face is only inches away from his, studying those deep green-and-gold eyes until I'm sure he isn't playing around. His expression is unflinching.

"So what do you say?" he asks.

I keep waiting for him to laugh, but it doesn't happen.

"Anywhere I want?"

"Anywhere."

"Before six?"

He nods. "I'll have you home before six."

It's almost like he's challenging me. But there's something more behind his gaze. It's adventurous and encouraging.

I don't want to say no.

Two hundred and forty-nine days until I'm nineteen. Unknown days until The Revealed come for me. What if today is my last?

"Fine," I walk to the driver's side door and hold out my palm, "but I get to drive."

He grins in an earnest way that crinkles his cheeks and tosses the keys over the car. I get in, and he pushes the button on his phone, reprogramming the cameras back to normal. I can't help the gawk that surely covers my face. "How do you—" I gesture to the phone.

"There's an app for that," he says and shrugs, chuckling. "I like programming, so I just modified an existing software. You know how you can use devices to sync with your lights and music?" He waits until I nod before he continues, "Same idea, just with a camera. I hacked into your property's security system and then applied the setting to the specific camera."

My face is blank with confusion. If I didn't know what Kai looked like, I'd say the boy talking right now would be wearing suspenders, a white button-down shirt, and a pocket protector, all while pushing his round-rimmed glasses up his nose as he spoke. But I can see the sinewy muscles out of the corner of my eye and watch as he smoothly flicks that trademark dark hair from his face.

"Who are you?" I ask.

He laughs. "Your worst enemy."

I don't laugh, because according to the press and the rest of the nation, that's kind of an accurate statement. Our fathers are now the biggest rivals in the country, if not the world.

He seems to catch on to my train of thought but breezes past it. "Being good at technology definitely comes in handy. So where are we going?" he asks, staring out at the road around me.

"Hold on." This time I do allow a smirk and press the pedal to the ground. The car revs to life. I breeze past a billboard featuring my father's face, huge and centered. It reads, "For a better tomorrow. Mark Atwood for president." It makes me feel like I'm being followed. In fact, I most likely am.

"Security will probably still track us down," I tell Kai, glancing again in the rearview mirror.

"I'm sure they will if they're anything like my father's. You'll have to lose them. If you can."

"Challenge accepted," I say, running a yellow light and turning onto the freeway.

The surprise of freedom lurches through my veins.

It's been over six months since I've been on the road like this, and I was never allowed to be in the driver's seat. It feels so freeing to be in control. If I wanted, I could keep the car in drive for as far as it would take me. It's liberating, though I'm not planning on going to the end of the Earth. Instead, I pull along the road heading down a familiar path until the houses thin and all that remains around us is empty land.

There are large fields on the outskirts of town, run by the state as part of reconstruction. Some of the genetically modified crops—corn, sunflowers, and wheat, among others—are almost as tall as houses. The taller the crop, the more produce they yield and the more mouths the country can feed. The harvest is only a few weeks away.

That is where I drive.

I remember when I was a young girl—twelve or thirteen—going out to these fields with my father after the first planting. As a symbolic reflection of new beginnings, representatives from across the colonies came to help sow the seeds. These crops now sustain the population, making it possible for our new nation to rebuild. My father helped oversee the process. I was even allowed to plant my own seed. Now there are so many fields stretching out across the acres that I can't remember where it was. It doesn't matter. The point is that we all had a part in getting to this place.

I park the car on the grass, and we get out. A few people work around us. I can see small silhouettes for miles on end. They will lose the light soon enough, and their day will be done. They don't pay any attention to us, though. The fields are open for anyone to visit any time. It isn't uncommon to find people here just enjoying the sun.

I run through the blades, hitting the shoots at full sprint. The stalks reach out to me, gently slapping my arms. It's like being a child again, laughing and feeling the world at my fingertips. At the center is a small, circular clearing—a marker to prevent people from getting completely lost. I lie on the ground in the center of the circle, spreading my fingers along the dirt. I close my eyes and breathe in the air, smiling as the sun kisses my face, neck, and legs.

Kai breaks through just behind me, and I can hear him stop.

Silence fills the space between us.

"What?" I ask, not opening my eyes, though I can feel his gaze.

He shakes his head. "Nothing," he says, and sits down beside me. "Out of all the places you could go … ?"

I shrug. "I feel comfortable here."

In fact, lying here in the dirt, I feel better than I have in a long time. I stretch out and know that these fields continue for as far as the eye can see. No fences in sight. The sky above me has no limits. All the stress about The Revealed and the unknown seems to melt away in the middle of this field with Kai.

Really, I shouldn't think like this. I don't know him. I haven't even spoken to him since high school. Even then we didn't hang out. Ever.

If you had told sixteen-year-old me that two years later I would be lying in a field with Kai Westerfield, I would have called you crazy. But I guess if you'd told me that I would be in these fields because he gave me the only way to escape my house, I guess that would have made sense. I was never made to stay in one place. I always had dreams for bigger things, faraway places.

"Someday I'm going to leave this city," I tell him, "and never come back."

"You say that now," he replies lazily, "but you'll miss it."

"Maybe I will, but I won't come back. Isn't that why you joined the military? To get away?" I open my eyes and turn my head to look at him.

He's staring back at me. His eyes are glinting with curiosity. He scans my face and I realize how close we are. My nerves hit me.

"I guess that's part of the reason," he admits, his voice low, "but I also want to be part of the new nation. I want to help it grow, be the best it can be." His cheeks curl as he smiles. "Kind of cheesy though." He looks back up at the sky.

"It isn't," I shake my head.

I have this urge to reach out to him. As if a tangible connection would make him see I understand.

But I keep my hand at my side.

The truth is he scares me. He never had any interest in me before. Not that I tried to get his attention. I didn't want it. I wasn't one of those girls who needed it because I had to feel wanted. And he left me alone, just like the others. Because I'm the spoiled rich girl.

The memory pricks in my throat and tears spring to the corner of my eyes. *Of course Lily's fucked up.*

I stand.

All you have to do is look at her face.

I pull my hair from under my ear, letting it fall across my face, almost into my eyes.

"I have to get home," I say, feeling the need to get out of here as soon as possible. My eyes sting, and I swallow against the tightening in my throat.

"What?" Kai looks up at me as I scramble to get the stray grasses and grains off my back. "We just got here."

"Can you take me home?"

"Why?" Confusion clouds his features while he gets up.

"Because I don't want to be here anymore."

He's taken aback. "Did I say something?"

"Yes," I blurt, then quickly correct myself. "No. I mean, why do you care? Why did you even bother taking me from my house? I'm just a spoiled little rich girl right?" I cover my face in my hands, frustrated that I said that last sentence. Infuriated that I care. I shouldn't care what Kai Westerfield thinks.

He takes a step back, baffled. "What are you talking about?"

It makes me even angrier that he doesn't remember what he'd said. It was bad enough the words came from his mouth. But he'd said them so passively they didn't even matter to him. It wasn't a big deal to him at all to talk badly of someone that way.

"Forget it. It doesn't matter." I begin pushing through the stalks of grain. "I just want to go home."

"Whoa," he says, chasing after me, "Lily, just hold up a second."

He grabs my arm. "I don't think you're a spoiled little rich girl."

"Please," I jerk away from him.

He holds fast. "I don't know where you even got that idea."

"I got it from you!" Now I'm just embarrassed. I never should have brought this up. I should have ended it before it began. Coming out here with him was a mistake.

"Me? I—" he stammers, and realization fills his features. "Shit." He runs a hand through his hair, pushing it back only to have it fall messily around his forehead. "That's how you knew about the smoking. Are you talking about high school? How did you even hear about that?"

"I heard you and Micah talking after the election announcement," I grumble.

"God, Lily." He grips his neck as if he's straining to find a way to justify his words.

"I really don't need you to explain." I step back away from him. "It's not like you were the only one with that opinion. But you'll excuse me if I don't want to be your friend."

"I had no idea what I was talking about," he says, "I'm sorry, Lily, I'm really sorry. It was such a stupid—I just let myself get caught up in that shit in high school—all the gossip and the attention. It was wrong. I was wrong."

"High school wasn't that long ago."

"It was for me," he says. "It feels like a lifetime ago. And you're right to hate that guy, but this one now, in front of you, wants a chance. A real chance."

"No." I can't help the suspicion. I can't just let it go. "You could have any girl you could possibly want. Hell, you've had quite a few. I won't just be the next in line because you're charming."

Okay, that was a rude comment. And it makes him mad. I see the spark ignite in his eyes.

"You're the most-stubborn person I've met!"

"You're the most arrogant!" I fire back. "I see the way people look at you. More importantly, I see the way you look back."

"You have no idea what you're talking about. Who are you to judge how I handle the attention around my family?"

"I think out of anyone on this planet, I'm the most qualified, actually."

"Oh, right, because you handle all of this so well. You hide inside of yourself so afraid of people actually seeing you."

"Seeing me? Not everyone can be as good-looking as you, Kai. Not everyone gets to prance around the streets and be adored. You have no idea what it's like to be—"

I falter, not just because I can't say the word. *Ugly.* But because our faces are so close it's dangerous. The tips of our noses are a breath away. I can see every small fleck of gold within his irises. My breath hitches.

I want to reel back inside myself, unable to believe I lost control like that. I've never lost control of myself around someone besides my parents.

His gaze holds me tighter than any embrace. "You have no idea." He swallows roughly, his jaw stiff and clenched. His words become strained. He's barely keeping his cool like he wishes he could grip my arms and give me a good shake or two. His eyes register every inch of my face. "You have no idea how I see you. Everything I said about you was a lie. I was lying."

I can't move. So much as a twitch and I think our shoulders would collide. I'm not sure what would happen if we touched. My handle on control is so slight as it is.

And he's imploring me with his eyes to let go and break. He's begging me to snap and give in to him.

I don't snap. I don't allow my guard to fall entirely. But I do lower it an inch or two. "One more chance," I breathe.

He nods, and it sends butterflies rattling around in my stomach.

Cars.

I hear cars pulling over the dirt.

"Great," I mutter, snapping out of the trance that is Kai's gaze. I can tell by the sound of the engines that the cars are Escalades.

Kai hears them, too. "Stay next to me, okay?"

He takes my hand and puts himself protectively in front of me. All I can focus on for a moment is his hand on mine. His fingers curl around mine, strong and warm. He doesn't know who is coming through the field, but I do.

"It's okay," I say and walk around him, through the grasses.

There's a line of five SUVs parked next to Kai's car. No surprise there.

Jeremy is standing in front like usual.

"Oh, your parents are just thrilled about this one," he says, and shakes his head sarcastically.

"I'm sure they are."

Kai stands with his arms crossed over his chest. "I can take her home."

"Oh, I think you're well past done," Jeremy says, leading me away.

I get in the backseat of the car without an argument. What's the use?

I glance over my shoulder at Kai once more before Jeremy closes the door. My head sinks against the seat as we begin to drive back to the house. I push my palms against my temples, resisting the urge to smile. What am I getting myself into? Kai was so close to my face that I could feel his breath dancing across my cheek. Heat rises to my face. And all I do is think of him until we arrive back at the house.

Then reality sinks in along with the chill of dusk.

My father is standing at the base of the stairs with his arms crossed tightly over his chest. My mother is next to him. She takes one look at me and makes a dramatic exit up the stairs, looking resigned.

My father lets the silence hang over us for a few more moments. He's waiting for me to speak, but I won't give him the apology he seeks. I don't have anything to apologize for.

"Do you have any idea what you put us through when you run off like this?" he finally says. "And only a day after The Revealed break into our own home? Jeremy said you were with Kai Westerfield? What were you thinking? Not only did you leave the house, leaving yourself completely vulnerable to The Revealed, but you are seeing that troublemaker? How long has this been going on?"

"Nothing's going on." I shrug off his questions. "We're just talking."

"It's one thing to make small talk at events. It's another to fraternize with the competition. You are not to associate with that boy. For your own good. You think I don't see him in the papers? I would have thought Roderick would have raised him better. Clearly, losing his mother has done bad things for that boy. You think you're old, grown up? You think you know so much, but you have so much to learn. If I could make you understand, I would. I know that family better than anyone in the North American Sector. Kai Westerfield is bad news."

"Maybe. Maybe not. But there's a chance you're wrong about him, and I'm willing to take that chance to find out."

"I'm not! And neither is my campaign." My father throws his hands up in exasperation. "I have too much to worry about regarding the election to be concerned about you and that Westerfield boy. You are not only making a fool out of this family, you are risking your life when you leave like that. I forbid you from seeing him."

"Not happening," I snap back.

"It doesn't matter. You don't get a say in this."

"Like hell!"

"You do not want to test me," he warns. My father has never talked to me like this before. Ever.

"I'm not testing you, I'm living my life."

"You don't have the luxury of making mistakes like other girls, Lily. This Kai Westerfield will hurt you. It's only a matter of time."

CHAPTER SIX

It doesn't take long. Less than twenty-four hours, in fact.

My mother slams one of her old-fashioned newspapers down in front of my breakfast plate. I look up at Jeremy, who is standing in the corner. His eyes stare blankly through me. No help at all.

I glance from my mother to Jeremy before looking back down at the tabloid.

I read the headline: *Lily Atwood Plans to Vote for the Other Side,* and practically spew my cereal all over our cherrywood table. I grab the paper and my mouth falls open. On the front page is a picture of Kai and me at the fields. We're in the middle of the stalks, and he's so close to me it almost looks like our lips are touching. Our lips almost *were* touching. My eyes are completely connected with his as though I'm in a trance.

I inhale sharply and quickly begin to sputter when a cornflake gets caught in my throat.

Fear and embarrassment shoot through me. Please let this be a joke. I can't look away from the picture. I cover my mouth with my hand, afraid I'm going to be ill. I feel the urge to run, but there's nowhere to hide. Everyone will see this picture. Something meant to be intimate and personal. I can only imagine this image splashed across every home page in the colony.

Where did this photo come from?

"I hope you know how much trouble you're in young lady," my mother scolds. "First you try to steal your father's car on Friday, and then you just run off without a word yesterday! While your father and I were worried sick about you! What's gotten into you?" Her voice is rising haughtily.

I shake my head, too stunned to verbalize an answer.

"And now this story?" She smacks her hand across the paper, "This is the result of your reckless behavior."

"There has to be an explanation," I stutter unconvincingly. "We didn't do anything."

I read over the column. Whoever wrote this story definitely had some inside information. They know how terrified I am that The Revealed might take me. They know I don't want to be in the spotlight anymore. They wrote about my escape attempt and the resentment I harbor against my parents.

"We just went to the fields!" I say.

My breathing builds as I feel more and more overwhelmed. I shut my eyes tightly and rub my forehead. The absolute worst part of this article is the picture. Kai's strong arms reaching out to me gently. His dark hair falling loosely around his strong jaw as he peers down at me with concerned eyes. Concerned eyes that are meant for me. And me with *that* look on my face. I look shy and surprised at his attention, peering up at him between my eyelashes. I'm inviting his look. We didn't even kiss!

My mother is fuming beside me. "How could this happen?"

All I can say is, "I don't know," over and over again.

Who knew all of this? Unless I leaked this information to the press myself—which I definitely hadn't—then no one could know all these details. No one was there in the fields when this happened. Just me and—

I stand up from the table.

The revelation is like a slap in the face.

I grab the paper and rip it to shreds, throwing the pieces around the breakfast table. Before I realize it, I'm in the entryway.

My mother catches up with me. "And just where do you think you're going?"

"I'm getting some air," I huff, feeling my frustration spiral out of control.

"Lilith," she says through clenched teeth, "you will not walk away! You will explain this and apologize."

"Apologize?" I turn on her. "You want me to apologize?" I am so out of control, so on the edge, and she just stands there with her hands pressed neatly against her hips. Her magenta lips are on the verge of pursing, but she doesn't allow them to completely. God forbid she shows any emotion that could cause wrinkles.

There is nothing I can say to reason with her. She's too selfish to even see me, let alone listen to what I have to say.

I yank my coat from the closet and head outside.

I don't hear footsteps behind me, or the sound of a door opening. Just the guards patrolling, and I know they're watching me keenly. One nods in my direction, but none approach me. They don't try to strike up a conversation, which I appreciate. Silence folds around me. Finally, it feels like I can think. But my thoughts aren't clear. Kai did this to me, and that I can't understand. No matter how many times I see that photo in my mind and tell myself I've been betrayed, it isn't something I can accept or come to terms with. Confusion and betrayal blanket around me.

Is he really that good a liar? He looked me in the eye and told me he wanted to know me. For just that one moment he made me feel like I was something more than Mark Atwood's daughter. I really believed he was interested in me.

And now I feel like an idiot.

I think of those girls back in high school who flitted about him like little birds opening their mouths for attention like sustenance essential for life. He just shoved me off his lap, just like he discarded those girls, and left me on the bleachers without a second thought.

He played me against my family to get Roderick Westerfield votes.

I walk to the gardens on the east side of the house. The smell of gardenia reaches me, and it's calming, almost intoxicating.

I try to rationalize my thoughts, think through my next move. My mother will want me to speak with the press. That's always my mother's answer to any crisis. She thinks the public loves us enough that any explanation will suffice. Hopefully, Jet will veto that idea. It's better if we don't draw more attention than necessary.

How could Kai do this to me? Worse, how could I let him? I hate him. I've never hated anyone more in my life.

CHAPTER SEVEN

I find Rory in the kitchen the next day, working on the filet mignon entrée for my father's luncheon with his campaign staff. I try not to think about my father and the look on his face as I stood in his office and my mother presented him with the article. I disappointed him. He wasn't surprised, though. He just chewed for a moment on the inside of his cheek as he looked at it, then tossed it to the corner of his desk and got back to work at the computer.

"Dad, I—"

He held up a hand to silence me, then looked to my mother. "Call Jet, have him do some damage control. Set up some articles with reporters you trust. Find a way to explain this."

My mother's efforts to explain this are that we are silly children who've known each other for years. Our families used to be good friends, of course. So why shouldn't we see one another? My being out of the house was another cover they had to devise. My mother said that from time to time she allows her daughter to get some fresh air, closely monitored by security, of course. And that's all the picture was. Just an image made worse by gossip.

The reporters printed it.

The explanation ran in the paper this morning. But no one is buying it. No one really cares what my parents' excuses are either. They want to know how deep my relationship with Kai goes now that it's been confirmed.

The events of the last day are grating. Every time I think of Kai my eyes began to sting and my throat squeezes in on itself. It feels like prep school again. Not that I've forgotten what it's like to be alone, but to have the loneliness shoved in my face repeatedly feels even worse.

"Hey," Rory greets me, looking up from the pan where she is sautéing a mix of vegetables.

"How's everything going?" I ask, leaning against the counter.

She shrugs. "Same old. I saw that story yesterday." She cringes. "You and Kai Westerfield, huh?"

My stomach churns, and I try to not focus on the nausea. Plus the fact that I think Rory was developing a thing for Kai. And now that I'm ... *was*, I mean ... for just a second thought he and I were— "It just sort of happened."

I'm beyond frustrated with myself. Even after he sells me out to the papers, I can't stop thinking about him. I keep trying to rationalize his behavior like it was somehow justified. I don't want to think he could really be that coldhearted. But he is, and he always has been. I made the mistake of forgetting that for one moment of freedom I'm now paying for.

To my relief, she rolls her eyes and grins, "I know how that happens, babe."

"Yeah, well, the whole mess is kind of why I'm here. I could really use a break from all this."

"Guess you were right when you said he was bad news. Wanna talk about it?"

"No," I say, a little too quickly. There's a moment of silence as I collect myself. "I don't want to talk about it, but there *is* something I'd like to do."

"What did you have in mind?"

"A night on the town. I want to go out—with you—to that new Frost place."

"Looking for a rebound?" Rory nudges me with her elbow.

"No." I smile at the look on her face.

"Yeah right, you want to get over Kai. And you think booze and boys is the way to it."

"I don't need a boy," I counter.

"Of course you don't. That doesn't mean it isn't fun." Rory shimmies her shoulders suggestively.

"So you'll take me?"

Her shoulders drop. "I wouldn't know the first thing about getting you out of this house."

My mind flashes to Kai and that mischievous smirk as he explained how he'd turned the cameras on repeat. He was the only person I'd ever met in my life who could do anything remotely close to that. The system was otherwise foolproof. My own escape attempt had ended with a roadblock less than a mile from my house.

Despite my determination I admit, "Neither do I."

"And you've had more practice than me."

If only I could fool the cameras like Kai did. I have no idea how. But maybe I can do something else. Suddenly, a plan sparks in my mind.

If we can't trick the cameras, maybe we can trick the eye.

Just like we practiced. I take a deep breath and glance up. She's standing on the balcony, silhouetted against the moonlight. Her hair is coiled into a bun on the top of her head so it's hard to make out any distinguishable characteristics.

The floodlights cast an eerie white glow over the property. I see the shadows in the distance as the security figures patrol the perimeter.

I pull the chef's apron tighter around my waist and flip up the hood of my sweatshirt. My fists tighten at my sides and the keys in my hand press firmly into my palm.

Staff parking is around the corner from the main entrance, and I trek down the grass, sure to keep my head down.

The first patrol guard I pass is Darren, just like Rory and I talked about. Darren always has this patrol shift. He's Jeremy's second-in-command, and a little too eager. This is the best time because Darren's shift is almost over, and he won't be as cautious.

"Goodnight, Darren," I say, keeping my voice low and casual.

"Night." He brushes past me without a second glance. "Have a good weekend."

The car squeaks open with a click of the unlock button on the keys. Rory has an ancient Honda Civic. The red paint is fading away in large patches all over the vehicle. When I open the door it creaks loudly. I glance back over my shoulder. Darren isn't paying any attention. I settle into the driver's seat and wait.

Darren continues his patrol around the perimeter. At the end of the lot, he meets with another man. I can't see his face but assume it's Evan, who will take over the post. I check my watch. It's 10:00 p.m. exactly. Right on time.

But the two begin to talk, chatting on and on about who knows what.

I anxiously watch in the rearview mirror.

Maybe they caught on. Somehow they figured out what Rory and I have been plotting and are waiting, laughing at us until we try to get through the gate. Then the joke will be on us.

They're still talking, quiet shadows at the edge of the parking lot.

And then they shake hands and Darren wanders out to his car, calling it a night.

I skooch over into the passenger seat and sink down, careful to make myself still so Evan won't notice anyone in the car.

Darren's car flashes to life, and he pulls from the lot. His headlights hit my mirror briefly, and I tense. But he passes by and no one starts running toward the car.

Evan circles back to the other side of the lot and begins his patrol. He's swinging the flashlight back and forth, tipping his head from side to side. He turns his back to me to march the other way, and I slink deeper into the passenger seat. My eyes focus on the rearview mirror. Waiting.

What's taking her so long?

Evan turns around at the end of the parking lot and starts walking back to the opposite corner. He's all scrawny limbs, which make his movements jerky.

A bead of sweat begins to trickle across my forehead. Even though the night is chilly, the nerves beat it from my body. I pull the sweater over my head and yank the ties open on the chef's apron, tossing both in the backseat.

Then I focus back on the rearview mirror, but my eyes collide with Evan's. He's staring in my direction.

Shit.

Can he see that it's me in the darkness?

He hesitates, then whips around suddenly.

"Hi, Evan," Rory calls through the darkness. I can see Evan relax.

"Hi, Rory." He grins. It's a grin that all boys give Rory when they're privileged with her attention.

"How's your night so far?" she purrs.

"Well, I just started. It isn't bad." I can see Evan struggle to stand a little straighter and puff out his chest, posing for her.

"That's good." Rory brushes past him. "Goodnight," she says over her shoulder.

But he runs after her. "Let me walk you to your car."

"Don't be silly," she says, waving him off. "I'm a big girl."

"An eighteen-year-old girl," he corrects. Clearly this isn't Evan's first attempt to gain Rory's attention. "Can't be too careful."

"Oh, I'm careful." Rory produces a can of pepper spray from her purse and holds it out for Evan to see.

He snorts, "You think that's gonna stop The Revealed? You were at the gala weren't you?"

"Of course I was there," Rory replies, "but a girl does what she can." With this she gives him a snarky smile. Rory doesn't need a hero.

"What you need is this," he produces his gun, tossing it from hand to hand.

Rory rolls her eyes. "Yeah, 'cause those were *so* useful that night. Look, I have to get home." Rory brushes past him again, this time not giving him a chance to cut her off. "See you tomorrow."

She opens a back door, dropping her stuff in the backseat.

Evan is still watching her, and I'm careful not to twitch a muscle.

Rory plops down in the driver's seat and wordlessly takes the keys from my hand.

I glance in the mirror. Evan is still watching. Then he shakes his head briefly and starts marching again.

I slink down so I'm curled at the bottom of the passenger seat, just under the dashboard.

Rory slowly pulls out of the parking lot, not even so much as glancing in my direction. She rolls down her window and waves to the guard station. I'm so focused on holding still I don't even breathe.

Our plan depends on the fact that whoever is on duty should be more concerned about who's getting in, not out.

The assumption is correct.

I can hear as the metal gates creeks open.

As soon as there's enough space for the car, Rory guns it, flying down the road surrounding my house.

I unfurl from my hiding place and burst out into laughter, feeling lightheaded at the initial breath of air. "I can't believe Evan went so far as to show you his gun!"

She just chuckles. "Wasn't the first time he's tried."

"Gross." I stick a finger in my mouth, mimicking a gag.

I pull my nude wedge heels from the bag I brought and slip them on.

I dressed up, wearing dark denim jeans and a lacy white top beneath the sweater. Once I pull my hair down, it falls in soft waves around my face. I offset my mascara and liner with a streak of gold eye shadow, which makes my hazel eyes pop. I relish the feel of pampering myself, of actually getting ready for an event attended by people under the age of forty.

When Rory said I was looking for a rebound, someone to take my thoughts away from Kai, she was wrong. For some reason, I seem to like the burning ache in my chest when I think of Kai. He's become this dull throb at the back of my mind. Over and over I just want to know why. And through all the pain and rejection, I still shiver thinking of his body so close to mine. I imagine his hands touching my face, circling down to my waist.

It's wrong, so wrong. I hate myself for having thoughts like this. I don't want to be so stereotypical. But no matter how wrong I know my feelings are and how disgusted I am with them, I can't make them go away. But tonight I will force them away. Tonight is about letting go. Just for one night I will have fun instead of always being afraid.

We don't have to wait in the line that snakes around the building. The bouncer at the front doesn't even check our IDs. He takes one look at me and simply unhooks the gate with a polite, albeit surprised, "Ms. Atwood, I thought it would be another eight months before we saw you here."

Rory grins and pushes me inside, saying, "She has the night off," over her shoulder.

I'm suddenly not as comfortable. He recognized me too quickly.

"Maybe we should have him sign something, or ask him not to tell anyone I'm here. I mean, what if he calls the photographers or—"

"Stop," Rory cuts me off with a quick hand. "Don't forget, this is the new hangout for the DC elite, they're used to seeing important faces. They would lose a lot of business if they started asking questions and snitching on people."

She's right, of course, so I relax and take a moment to enjoy where I am.

This is the place everyone wants to be on a Friday night. No matter what happens to a civilization, people still love drinking. Bars and nightclubs always seem to have a place in society.

The entire venue is lit in an icy-blue hue. The booths that line the walls are a striking sapphire color. All of the silverware and plates are made of glass, which reflect the light like crystal. The entire tabletop is coated in a smooth layer of ice that keeps drinks cold and allows for a unique, refracted look.

I stare at the glass on the table and imagine the tabletop exploding into a thousand fragments. I trace my fingers down the small scabs that have formed over the cuts from the glass at the gala. I remember the fear, but I also remember Kai's strong hands around me, telling me everything would be okay.

Two hundred and forty-four days until I'm nineteen.

"Let's do shots!" I yell over the music, grabbing Rory's hand and leading her to the bar.

"Whoa," she laughs, "Slow down, babe. We have the whole night to get there."

"I'm ready to have fun now," I insist.

"Shots?" A bartender overhears. He's probably been trained to read lips what with the music blasting through this place.

"Four," I say, holding up the fingers to be sure. "Make us something fancy. What's your specialty?" I ask, leaning over the bar.

"It's called Ice," he tells me, close to my ear.

Appropriate.

"Great, four of those."

The bartender raises an eyebrow at me. "Are you sure you want four?"

"Are you crazy?" Rory demands. "One of those shots is enough to make a normal person lightheaded. And you never drink!"

The bartender sets the drinks in front of us. It's an electric blue, with sugar rimmed around the glass like cracked ice.

"I'm only taking one," Rory insists.

"Who said any of them were for you?" I dare her with a grin. I pull out the wad of cash I stole from my parents' dresser and hand the bartender a hundred dollar bill. "Keep the change," I tell him.

I pick up one of the shots and hand it to Rory, taking one for myself.

Her eyes go wide. "I can't believe we're doing this."

"You and me both," I say, and now I feel the rush of adrenaline. I see it in Rory's eyes as well. Tonight will be amazing. "Cheers!"

We down the shots without hesitation and quickly take the second after that. The shot is like liquid spearmint, and it burns until I can feel it settle in my stomach. Then it spreads like tendrils through my veins, all cold fire.

I never drink. Occasionally wine with dinner when my parents feel like it's a special occasion. But other than that, I don't go near the stuff. This is the first time, but I've watched enough old movies and heard enough of Rory's stories to know how this works. We drink, we dance, and we forget our problems.

People around us are tinged with blue from the lights. White and black is the preferred color of attire. Only a few hints of color pop throughout the bar. It makes sense. White is cheap but can more easily be made to look expensive, compared to the drab brown-and-tan uniforms of the factory workers. Any vivid shades of cloth are more expensive and rare, unless it's a faded hand-me-down. The vintage look isn't in right now. Vintage just means you scavenged through some abandoned store somewhere down your path to refuge during the war. I'm glad I chose white with my jeans. Rory is in a fitted black cotton dress. We look like we belong.

The fun doesn't stop with the shots. I drag Rory to the dance floor, and in between songs, guys offer to buy us drinks. None of which I refuse. The Revealed could be coming for me tomorrow. I might as well live it up. There's no use wallowing over my pathetic life.

Over it.

And each time I take a swig of alcohol, I'm proving it to myself. I don't need anyone. I can be independent. I can be a normal eighteen-year-old girl. I don't have to be perfect all the time. I don't have to always say the right thing and act a certain way. I can be free. I deserve to be free.

Rory is dancing with some guy that holds her close. He's all arms and blue eyes. I don't blame her for returning the attention. If only for one night. By tomorrow, she won't even remember the guy's name.

I move from the bar and through the crowd.

"Lily Atwood," I hear some of them gasp. "No way!" And then whisper amongst themselves.

Someone catches my shoulder.

"Whoa, slow down there." I don't recognize the boy who blocks my path. He has long hair that hangs in his face in slick tendrils, and his breath smells stale from alcohol.

I try to weave past him, but he's quick and spins in front of me again.

"Can I buy you a drink?"

"I've already had one, thanks." I try to keep my words straight since it's definitely been more than one drink.

"You're Lily Atwood aren't you? I recognize you from your picture in the tabloids the other day."

"Thanks for the reminder," I quip. Apparently I'm not drunk enough because it still stings. I imagine Kai's hand on my shoulder instead of this boy's. Kai wouldn't be grabbing at me like this. He would be confident and strong.

I wave this strange boy off with my thoughts, but he thrusts a drink into my hand.

A picture of Kai flashes through my mind again, almost like I'm seeing him in the crowd. His image burns in my mind; emotion wells up inside. Not numb enough.

I take the drink all in one gulp. It burns on the way down my throat. I sputter a little, but after a moment the warmth makes me feel better. It makes everything numb and meaningless.

"Alright!" The guy's laugh sounds distant. "Someone came to party. What'll it be?"

My mind is fuzzy, which is such a relief. It really is just so nice not to think or feel. It's wonderful to let it all go, to be numb, and not care just for a little while.

"Let's dance," the guy says, and takes my hand.

And before I even know what's happening, we're among the crowd dancing, and the guy's hands are entwined around my waist. He keeps trying to pull me closer.

Swaying with the beat, we dance among throngs of bodies for I don't know how many songs. Everything seems to be moving fast now, time included. I've lost sight of Rory in the crowd, and though I want to find her, I can't seem to make my body follow suit. It's taken on a mind of its own, dancing among the crowd.

People say my name.

"Look, it's Lily Atwood!" someone says.

"Alright, Lily!" they cheer me on.

Others laugh, "Get it girl!"

I'm feeling too liberated to focus on their words.

Time is fast and slow all at once.

My drink is gone, and I toss the plastic cup onto the floor.

I'm living in the moment, but at the same time I'm moving in all directions at once. The music flows with me and through me, and it's all I care about.

Then my stomach lurches.

I stop moving. Well, my feet stopped moving, but my stomach is spinning right along with the room.

"I think I need some air," I say, feeling heat rising to my cheeks.

I break outside, and the crisp air hits me like a cold shower. My hands grip the railing of the wraparound porch. Thick screens enclose the porch so no one can exit or enter this way, but I can still feel the brisk air. I rest my head against one of the wood posts and am grateful for the breeze catching my face.

"What did I drink?" I ask, not really to anyone in particular, as I breathe in and hope the night air will clear the clouds in my mind. My cheeks feel puffy and tingly.

"Well, I gave you a shot of tequila, but I don't think that was all the help you had." I didn't even realize the stale-breath guy had followed me out.

I groan.

The guy—I don't even know his name—is suddenly close to my face. He's too close. I just need air. I shrug him off, wishing he would just let me breathe.

He doesn't.

Instead, he moves closer still.

"You know, for a daddy's girl, you're pretty hot." He reaches out to me, catching the end of my blouse and pulling me against his chest. "You're legal now, right?"

I try to push his hand away, but my fingers fumble awkwardly.

He leans his face into mine and wraps his hands around the back of my arms, pulling me closer. His lips graze against my cheek, and I can feel his stubble against my face. His kisses are sloppy as they reach my mouth.

I try to turn my head, but his grip is tightening.

His tongue leaves a hot trail over my lips.

"No," I tell him, trying to push away, but my arms aren't quite working right.

"Come on." His voice is gruff. "I know you want me. You don't have to pretend to be good."

His hand slips under my shirt.

My stomach heaves and this time it isn't from the alcohol. "Stop."

I push on his face, but he's much stronger than I am. He ducks out of my hold and moves his lips over my neck.

"Don't! I have to find Rory." I shove away from him.

Now I'm scrambling to get out of his grip with all of my might, but every move I make seems ineffectual and weak.

"Stop! No!"

He's too strong and the alcohol has made my struggles even more pathetically worthless.

"Hey!" A voice breaks through the haze.

Before I even know what's happening, the guy is ripped off of me. I hear something that sounds like a body hitting the ground. I grip the railing, sucking in air. Rory steps over the guy groaning on the ground. "I've just spent the last twenty minutes searching this place for you! You can't just walk off like that! Do you know how worried I was? And—apparently—I had good reason to be."

No amount of air can stop everything around me from spinning.

Rory wraps her arm around me, lifting me up. "It's time to go."

I look down at the ground, where the guy is still curled in a ball, whimpering.

"Where'd you come from, Wonder Woman?" I ask.

"He'll be fine. Just a little lesson on how not to treat a lady. Are you okay?"

I shake my head no.

"Yeah," she nods, "you don't look so good."

Rory helps me walk to the front door, though we quickly decide that isn't the best way to leave. There are hordes of people still milling around. And I, especially, know that people means cameras and cameras mean pictures.

"Let's try the back door." Rory quickly steers me in the other direction.

"Perfect!" I throw my hands in the air and nearly lose my balance in the process.

"Come on." Rory rolls her eyes. "I think we can get out through the kitchen in the back. I can't believe I agreed to this," she adds under her breath.

"Can I help you?" A manager stops us before the door.

I shake my head. "We're leaving."

"The exit is the other way," the manager points back at the masses of people.

"Look," Rory tries to reason with him, "we're just trying to get home. I thought I saw an exit back here and there are a lot of people up there and—"

"I'm sorry," the manager says, holding up his hand, "this exit is for employees and emergencies only."

He has no idea who I am, which is a good thing. But also a bad thing because if he makes us go out front, somebody may take advantage of the photo opportunity. Drooping eyes, running mascara, disheveled shirt—I'm not ready for a close-up.

It's better if I just fill him in. "You don't know who I—"

Rory quickly scrambles to cut me off. "Can't you just make an exception?"

I glare at her. If she'd just let me tell him, he'd let us out. After all, he doesn't look like the negotiating type.

My stomach rolls. "I don't feel so good." I turn away from Rory, with the intention of finding the bathroom. I just need to sit down for a minute.

I stumble. Hands grip me, catching me and propping me up.

All I see are green-and-gold eyes. His hair falls into his face as he stares down at me with inquisitive concern. At first I think I'm hallucinating. But alcohol doesn't cause hallucinations. Right?

"Mr. Westerfield," the manager says in surprise, "I didn't realize you would be here tonight or else we would have reserved you a room."

"Vince, how many times do I have to ask you to call me Kai?" He pauses to make sure Vince knows he's sincere. "I was just leaving and these two are with me. I have the car waiting in back."

"Of course, of course. My apologies. I didn't realize." Vince moves aside.

"I am *not* with you," I shove Kai, but end up wobbling myself. He catches my wrist. When I try to wiggle away, he responds by scooping me up into his arms in one fluid motion.

"What does that mean?" he asks Rory over his shoulder as I shove against his chest. He needs to put me down. He's ruining everything.

"She knows you planted that story in the papers," Rory says, grabbing the door.

Kai stops in his tracks, "That I, what?"

My hand stops on his chest and my eyes go wide as I realize I'm touching him. His shirt cuts into a short V and my eyes are level with the smooth lines of his sun-kissed skin.

"Put me down!" I push him again. I just need air. If I can just sit down for a minute, I'll be fine.

"Please," Rory waves a hand, "the one of you two in the fields. I have to say, Kai, I know we just met and everything, but I really thought you were better than that."

We walk back outside where a car is idling, like Kai said.

"Put me down!" I repeat because neither of them seems to be listening to me. "I'm *fine!*"

"You don't smell fine," Kai says pointedly.

"Oh, right," I roll my eyes, "like you're the poster child for good behavior." And for some reason I find that so amusing that I begin to giggle. The giggle turns into a laugh, and I can't stop. I cover my mouth and fall back in Kai's arms, laughing at my little joke.

He takes me out to the car and puts me in the passenger side.

"You're going to sober up," he tells me sternly. "Then we're going to talk."

"I never want to talk to you again," I turn my face from him. "Why are you even here?" I push on Kai's stomach as he leans over me to buckle me in like a child. "I don't want to see you."

"Well, that isn't really an option after your father called mine tonight demanding to know where you were. Apparently, he thought you'd snuck out with me again."

I can't hide my horror. "My father called you! They were supposed to be out all evening!"

"I'm so dead," Rory groans behind me.

"No, you're not," I wave her off with a sigh. "It's fine."

"Lily! Do you have any idea what will happen if they find out I was with you tonight?" Rory's voice goes up an octave.

"Don't worry," Kai tells her, "I'll take the fall for this one. I'll just say I lied when I told my father Lily wasn't with me. I'll make up something about how I didn't want to get her into trouble or some story like that."

All Rory does is swallow roughly and nod. I can see the fear on her face. She knows as well as I do that Kai can practically get away with murder. The only repercussion he might face would be a verbal admonition, if that. Rory on the other hand, wouldn't be so lucky.

I don't want her to be afraid. "See. It's fine."

"Do you have your car here?" Kai asks Rory.

She nods. "It's parked out front."

"Take a cab." He hands her a wad of cash. "We'll worry about the car in the morning. I'll take care of Lily until she sobers up and then have her back at her house before her father can call the CIA to have me assassinated."

"Like hell you will!" I cut in defiantly. "Rory, you can't leave me here with him."

Rory gives me a sidelong glance. She knows what happened between Kai and me. But I also know she still has a soft spot for the guy after their interlude here a few weeks ago.

"I'll take a cab," I tell her. "I can just take a cab with you."

"That sounds even less like a good idea," she tells me.

Rory watches me carefully as I weigh my options.

At this point, it doesn't really seem like I have a choice. Either I stay with Kai or Rory gets fired. I can't allow my best friend to take the fall for this. I hate Kai. That's a given, but I don't think he's a murderer.

"Fine," I grumble.

"Are you sure?" Rory asks.

"I'll call in an hour though," I say. "If I don't, assume it's his fault and feel free to call my father's security."

Rory raises an eyebrow, but agrees to the call.

"There's water," Kai gestures to the unopened bottle between the front seats. I don't look at him. He doesn't push it, and walks Rory to the back door of the club, asking Vince to hail her a cab.

Returning to the car, Kai shuts the passenger door for me and gets behind the wheel. He doesn't start the engine right away. "How did you get here?" he asks, and his cheeks wrinkle with amusement.

I don't answer. I don't want to talk to him. I just want him to take me home and cover for Rory.

"I've got time." Kai throws the keys up on the dashboard and leans back in his seat. So much for getting the hint. "You have some sobering up to do anyways."

I don't make eye contact with him. The silence stretches out between us. It's so quiet that I can hear him breathing next to me.

I rub my eyes and then stuff my hands under my arms and slink down in the seat. My vision is too fuzzy, but when I close my eyes everything starts to spin.

It's too hot. I shove my cheek against the window. Being in this car with him is making my blood boil. I don't want to be here with him. He tricked me. He lied to me. Again, he made me feel more inferior than anyone I've ever met in my life. The fact that he holds such power over my emotions is terrifying.

When he finally speaks, I nearly jump at the sound of his voice. "I didn't leak that story."

I clamp my jaw tightly, and refuse to look at him. But I can feel his expression reaching out to me, demanding that I believe his words. Why does it matter so much to him what I think?

The silence falls over us again. I wrench the water bottle from its place in his middle console and take a long swig. It helps to cool the burning in my stomach.

"Damn it, Lily!" He hits his hand against the steering wheel and I flinch. "I'm not my father!"

I can't take it anymore and get out of the car, slamming the door as I go. I stumble a bit before realizing this isn't the best idea and lean my back against the alley wall, closing my eyes. The spinning returns so I force them open again really wishing I'd brought that water with me.

A few seconds later, I hear the car door open and Kai's footsteps walking toward me. He marches right up to me, and I can hear his hands clap against the wall next to my shoulders as he steps right in front of me.

I stare down at the street.

"Look at me," he says, his voice rough, close to my face.

I shake my head, keeping my eyes on my feet.

"Look at me."

"You're just saying all of these things, and I can't think." I press my hands over my forehead.

"You feel like all of your life people have treated you like something you're not, that you've always been in your father's shadow. Do you think you're alone? I'm *not* him. I'd never do something like plant that story."

Slowly, I allow my eyes to meet his, which are unwavering and so sincere. It's as if he wants me to believe him because it will counteract all those times people have accused him of being just like his father, as though my one opinion will matter that much.

This is too much.

"Can you just take me home?"

His hands slip from the wall and he stands up. His eyes don't leave mine. "Yeah," he finally concedes. "I can take you home."

We walk back to his car and this time he turns on the ignition immediately. He quickly pulls onto the street, driving the familiar route to my house. I call Jeremy on my way home to let him know I'm coming, and he's waiting for me at the gate when we arrive. The only light overhead is the lamp, which bathes everything in a soft, white hue. Around us, it's pitch black and silent; only a light breeze disturbs the complete stillness.

Kai parks in front of the gate and gets out of the car with me. "This was my fault." Kai puts up his hands as though he's surrendering. "Lily and I just lost track of time and—"

"Noble," Jeremy says and sighs. "But I, at least, know better by now, Mr. Westerfield. Lily is her own person. She went out tonight because she wanted to, not because you or anyone else convinced her."

I actually like hearing Jeremy say that.

"I wouldn't," Jeremy says, raising an eyebrow at my reaction, clearly too plain on my face. "Your parents will, no doubt, agree. You aren't in for good times."

That definitely makes my expression fade.

Jeremy opens the gate for me and holds out a hand to usher me inside.

I pause. "Will you give me just a minute, Jer?"

His hands drop. "A very quick one." He emphasizes "very."

I walk back to Kai, still standing at the door of his car. I meet his gaze unsurely. "I want to trust you ... about the story."

"I want you to trust me."

"Good." Maybe it's the alcohol that's making me brave. Maybe it's my desire to believe the best in everyone or the sincerity behind his expression. He did, after all, cover for Rory tonight. I breathe, "One more chance."

He nods and his eyes light up with surprise. "Saturday. Can I see you tomorrow?"

"I'll be lucky if my parents don't want to keep me locked inside until I'm twenty after the stunt I pulled tonight," I sigh.

"Here," he grabs a pen from the center console along with a scrap piece of paper and quickly jots something down. "I'll wait for you. Ten a.m."

He gives me the paper with his phone number scrawled across.

"I don't think—"

"Come on Lily," Jeremy calls.

"I'll be here. I'll wait," he tells me resolutely.

I lower my voice, "I'll try."

But Jeremy isn't quite finished yet. "Mr. Westerfield," he calls to Kai before he can get into his car.

Kai turns back.

"I just want to remind you of the repercussions if you so much as breathe a word of this to *anyone*—"

"It's okay." I put a hand on Jeremy's arm to stop him. "He won't say anything. I trust him." I glance back at Kai and meet his gaze again. This is his chance to prove he deserves it. "Goodnight."

My mother and father are waiting in the entryway.

"Go upstairs. Go to bed. We'll talk in the morning." My mother's eyes are hollow.

My father stays quiet, his expression dark.

"I—"

"Do not," my father says sullenly, "even try to rationalize your behavior this evening. This," he waves his hand at me, "is not the daughter I raised."

His comment takes me off guard like a punch to the stomach. Tears well in my eyes because they don't understand. I can't make them understand what's happening to me.

So I just brush past them both and go to my room.

I collapse onto my bed and scream into my pillow. I've never done it before. It was always something in movies that seemed juvenile. But now I understand. The emotions in me have been bottled up for way too long without anyone hearing them. And I need someone to hear me, to listen.

My parents are not those people.

A sharp ring snaps me from my stupor.

I sigh as I realize it's just my cell phone. The blue light dances next to me as Rory's name pops up on the screen.

I pick up the call. "Hi, Rory," I sigh into the receiver.

"Lily," she sounds exasperated, as though she's been watching the clock for the past hour counting down the minutes until she could call.

"Sorry," I mutter.

"Are you home?"

"Mm-hmm," I say. "Just faced the parents. They want to kill me."

"I might just strangle you too! You didn't call! I was getting worried!"

"I'm sorry," I say, without the strength to make it wholehearted. I just need sleep.

"And Kai was a gentleman?"

"If that's what you want to call him," I murmur. "He didn't plant that article. I mean, I don't think he did. It's confusing."

"Hmm," she muses, "sounds like someone's interested again."

"I wasn't ever interested."

She laughs into the phone.

"It's Kai Westerfield. I *can't* be interested."

"We always want what we can't have."

"No," I whine. She sees through me too easily. "I don't want to talk about it."

"Fine. Not tonight. We'll talk more tomorrow. After tonight, I can only imagine the sleep you need."

"Yup, you too. Goodnight."

I click the phone shut. Lazily, I open my eyes and stare out at the moon. But it's half-blocked by something taped to my window.

What the....

As if this night couldn't get any worse.

It's a small black square.

The hair on the back of my neck stands on end. My stomach rolls over, tossing the alcohol.

I can see the silver crescent symbol in the center sparkling against the moonlight.

My throat tightens as I rip off the sheets, stumble to the window, and tear the back of the envelope open. In my panic, my movements are hurried and clumsy.

April 13

My sleepiness goes right out with the breeze. April 13 is my birthday. The letter seems to make it clear that I won't be reaching my birthday next year.

It's all I can do to reach the bathroom before spilling the contents of my stomach in the toilet. As if tonight wasn't already rough, I spend the remainder of it huddled with my back against the wall on the bathroom floor, the note clutched in my fist.

CHAPTER EIGHT

Daggers.

There are little daggers stabbing their way around the back of my eyes.

I try to blink away the pain but it stays with me. I groan as I reach for my clock. It's still morning. I've never been one to sleep away the day, though today very well could have been the exception.

In my bathroom, I find two Advil and slam them back without a second thought before making my way to the kitchen.

My mother's voice carries through the foyer before I see her and my dad in the dining room. I grip my head as the stabbing returns.

"Marg called this morning," she says. "She's backing Roderick."

My father is still here, which is surprising. He answers, "Even after the gala? Did she say why?"

"No, no she didn't say why," my mother quips. "He probably offered her a cabinet position."

"We offered her a cabinet position."

"Secretary of Transportation. Everyone knows that's the most-useless position, Mark. I told you."

"She isn't exactly qualified for much else."

"She wants State. Her ties with foreign diplomats have strengthened since the war."

"I already promised the position to Timothy."

My mother sighs. "Who offers more support? You need a woman up there as well, Mark."

I can see them talking from where I stand at the base of the stairs. The dining room is to the left while the kitchen is behind me.

"That's why I have you dear," my father kisses my mother lightly.

I try to slink past the stairs and make it to the kitchen for something covered in butter before they both eye me.

"Sit. Down." It's amazing how my father's voice can go from affectionate to cold in only seconds.

I cringe. Judging by the tone, I know he's talking to me. I shuffle into the room and fold myself into the nearest chair, which is three chairs down from my mother, the closest parent. Not a choice I make by accident.

Luckily, the Advil is kicking in and I'm already feeling the stabbing pain dull down, otherwise my father's next words would have sank into my head like a cheese grater rubbing against my temples.

"Do you realize your mother and I have been up most of the night working to make sure all our bases were covered so we wouldn't have another headline about you on our hands?" I'm sure he doesn't want me to explain how I spent my night just about as much as I don't want to hear about his. "We paid off the manager of the club, in case you were wondering, so he would sign a nondisclosure agreement." Shame fills his voice.

"Sorry," I grumble.

"I don't know who you are anymore," my father knocks his fist against the table. "What has gotten into you?"

"I'm growing up," I tell him, gratefully accepting a cup of coffee from one of the serving staff.

I take a long draw of steaming caffeine and accept the soothing warmth all the way down to my toes.

"According to whom? You think last night is a sign you're growing up?"

I shake my head, "I won't be who you want me to be. I won't fit in a little box of what is acceptable to make you proud."

My father purses his lips, "All of that aside, you are putting yourself right in harm's way. When will you understand? Those letters you keep receiving aren't normal, no matter how much you would like to deny it. The Revealed have their eyes on you."

"Exactly. This house isn't going to save me."

"Oh and that Westerfield boy will?"

I'm not sure what my father expects to accomplish by this conversation. I won't revert back to that little doe-eyed daughter. I'm growing up. There is no going back no matter how much he wishes for it.

My father continues his lecture, but I haven't heard a word.

Kai. I promised to meet Kai at 10:00 a.m. I glance at my watch. It's fifteen minutes after.

"I have to go," I fling back my chair and stand. "Homework," I say simply, not caring that it's an obvious lie and ignoring their demands I return.

By the time I climb over the gate around the property, it's 10:25.

But Kai's black Audi is still waiting. I glance at the cameras suddenly wondering if maybe this time it would be best for security to catch me, though I know Kai has switched them on repeat.

I suddenly feel guilty for running out on my parents on bad terms. It seems like lately all we are is on bad terms. Maybe I should go back. I glance over at the house looming behind me and feel the overbearing pressure that comes with everything inside of there.

I look back to Kai, sitting so comfortably in front of my house. He's holding his phone in his hand with that arrogant pride at his technological abilities. I grin in spite of myself.

Kai hops from the car to whisk open the passenger door for me.

He sees my expression and shakes his head, "Today I get to drive."

I stare at the passenger seat. It isn't too late to go back. I stare over my shoulder at the security patrolling the premises. They haven't seen me yet. I timed my exit well. But they will soon.

"You can trust me."

His words take me off guard, and my gaze flickers to meet his. It only confirms his sincerity.

I get into the car. "Where are we going?"

"You'll see," he says, and pulls out onto the road.

Great, just the way to elicit my trust. Convince me to get in the car and then don't tell me anything. There's no use harping on it now, though. I made my decision.

The top is down and I stretch my fingers into the air, enjoying the way the wind dances across my outstretched hands. I close my eyes and lean back against the headrest. A comfortable silence falls over us. It's peaceful, which makes it easier to forget my uncertainty.

I glance over at Kai, keeping my head pressed against the seat. He has one hand casually draped over the wheel, his bicep bulging underneath his long-sleeve shirt, which he has bunched at his elbow. His eyes are trained ahead, gleaming with the thought behind his eyes I can't pinpoint. He's so good-looking it makes my chest ache. I want to take a picture of him, capture that look, and study it for hours.

Do I trust him?

Yes.

I know I shouldn't feel this at ease sitting with him. I should be wary. But I'm not. Not at all, which makes me foolish, I suppose.

Feeling my eyes on him, Kai glances over at me. He quickly glances back at the road, but a smile plays at the corner of his mouth now.

"I don't think I'd mind if we kept driving," I tell him.

"What do you mean?"

"I don't think I would be upset at all if I never went back to that house."

"Someday you won't have to."

"Someday, I'll get into a car, put it in drive, and never look back."

He smirks. "I might do the same."

Maybe we'll go together.

Neither of us says it, though it seems to hang in the air.

"But that won't happen for a while," Kai adds as an afterthought. As though we are talking about reality here instead of the wishful thinking it really is. "I gave my word that I'd give my country another year. My leave of absence is almost over. Plus, one of them will become president whether we're here to see it or not.

Running won't stop the reality of all this. But someday," he adds, "someday."

As if "someday" serves to preserve a hope for our future.

Kai takes me to the middle of the city where smoke billows from the factory smokestacks, turning the sky gray and orange. We're told the society we live in now is comparable to that of the 1920s. The war set us back over a hundred years. Technology is for the wealthy. Cars and computers are rare commodities that I often forget not everyone has. Being in the city is a stark reminder. The transit bus is in full swing. It operates nearly twenty-four hours a day, and is the primary mode of transportation for most people. Those who don't live far from their work usually bike or walk. Only the factory owners are rich enough to own a vehicle.

Amidst the browns and blacks of the city, there are random splashes of color: vivid sapphire and stark crimson. The blue signs support Atwood and the red are for Westerfield. Posters are affixed to the sides of buildings; they feature my father's tall and proud image, his eyes glinting. "For a better tomorrow," the signs proclaim. Westerfield's banners show a man with a harder look. His chin turned slightly to the sky. His signs promise, "Never again."

Seeing the heart of the city splashed with the campaign propaganda is a revelation. Even if The Revealed take me and this is the end of my life, I've lived these eighteen years in vivid color. The other ninety percent of the people in this city live with monochromatic hues. It's dirty and destitute.

Kai notices my expression.

"It won't stay like this if your father becomes president," he says. "Kids will go to college again, really go. Not just the ones who have money. It will be like those old movies where kids our age have fun and play around with life. Your father will find The

Revealed. He'll make it safe again. People will get out of their houses, become innovators, grow. This'll be a place of promise again."

I give a curt laugh. "I wouldn't be too sure."

"We'll have more of a chance than with mine. My father loves the power he holds. He says these people deserve the way they live. Like they've asked for it or something. I've heard him say it before. He doesn't think they're worth saving. He likes the system without a middle class. This country could be great again, you know, if the government would just give people the right resources, they could really make this place something."

It's obvious he's passionate about the country. It's also surprising. I've never seen this side of Kai before. He has a true desire to help. And he's right. The city doesn't have to be this way. Maybe someday it won't be. Maybe Kai will be a part of that change.

It's too bad I won't be around to see it.

Kai pulls into a parking lot.

It's a small place. I didn't even notice the building until we were sitting in front of it. Trees line the median strip between the parking lot and the road, successfully blocking this area off from the rest of the city.

I read the name at the top of the building: Elias Fitness. "A gym?" I ask.

"Come on." He leads me inside, where a bulky man is waiting for us at the counter.

"Perfect timing," he tells Kai and takes us through two glass doors that lead out back. "I'm Elias." He holds his hand out to me, and I shake it. This guy has arms the size of tree trunks, but the features of a child. His face is round and slightly red, topped by light-blond hair, which only makes his complexion look pinker. He's in his mid-thirties, from what I can tell.

"Lily."

"Pleasure." He takes us through a large gym to an empty studio. There are only a few people around and none of them pay us much attention, too focused on the weights in their hands or the boxing dummy in front of them.

"Don't worry," Elias says, winking knowingly as I scan the building. "We added your name to the nondisclosure form I signed for Kai months ago. You'll need these." He hands me a pair of boxing gloves from a rack hanging on the wall.

Kai is already lacing up his pair. Elias helps me with mine.

"We're really doing this?" I ask warily, looking over my shoulder at Kai as Elias secures the gloves around my wrists.

"Self-defense." Kai holds his hands up and shakes his gloved wrists back and forth.

"What?" My jaw nearly drops.

"You were the one who said sitting in a house won't save you. You're right. But this might." He playfully throws out his hand and socks me in the arm.

I flinch.

"It's self-defense."

"Okay?"

"So defend yourself," he laughs, throwing out his hand again.

"I don't know how," I admit, but smile sheepishly nonetheless.

Elias comes around beside me. "Let's start by having you work with the bag instead of Kai," he laughs. "We don't want you hurting that pretty-boy face of his."

"Watch it." Kai drops his arms.

Elias leads me to the center of the studio, which is one large room. Mirrors line the back wall where half a dozen weight sets are assembled. Heavy bags dangle from the ceiling in a line, one after the other. In the middle of the room is a boxing ring made of simple mats with ropes strung around the perimeter.

Elias directs me to a punching bag. "Alright," he says, moving behind me, "hit this."

I look back at him hesitantly before throwing out my fist and connecting with the thick cushion.

"Okay," Elias says, "needs some work. But okay. First things first, you want to reposition your feet so they are staggered." He bends over and lifts my right foot, pushing it back behind my left. "Now loosen up." He grabs my knees. "They should be slightly bent. When you punch, use your whole body, not just your arms. Follow through on your shot and move with it, extending your arm out as part of the natural rhythm. A straight shot. Imagine hitting two inches deep into your target. Don't curve your hand around. Keep your wrist straight, and your thumb tucked on the outside of your fist. Get the power from your hips."

Elias moves out of the way. "Go ahead and try it again."

I swing out. This one is better. I can feel how it is better, though it doesn't really show much strength. I don't see the bag move. But I can feel the movement in my body.

I can't help but drop my mouth in awe of the strength and excitement that pulses through me. I'm suddenly empowered. The rush of emotion comes with the adrenaline, and it feels like I can breathe again for the first time since turning eighteen.

I punch the bag again.

My body understands the movement. Though I know my motions aren't yet coordinated, there's something so fluid and natural in it.

"Better," Elias says and nods, "but you want to keep your other hand up." He moves my left fist up near my face. "If you ever do have to defend yourself, it won't be in front of a bag. There will be another person, and they aren't just going to stand still while you punch them. Keep your hand up as protection."

I do as I'm told and punch again. Then again.

"Much better," Elias says, encouraging me.

He makes little corrections as we go along. He teaches me different ways of striking. He explains it's best to ball my hand in a fist and use a hammer motion to the side. If I don't have gloves on this will keep me from hurting my knuckles.

Once I've gotten the hang of punching, Elias teaches me some other simple self-defense moves. It doesn't take long before my arms begin to feel heavy. No doubt the muscles will hurt in the morning.

But I'm alive. And I'm proud of myself. Taking on this new challenge is invigorating. It makes me feel like I have a chance.

"Alright, come here Kai," Elias motions him over. He positions Kai so he's behind me.

Elias moves around us and says, "Now Kai, I want you to wrap your arms around her and grab her as though you were an attacker coming up behind her."

Kai does as he's told. His arms encircle my arms and waist. The bare skin of his forearms is warm against me, and I feel his breath against my neck. The rest of his body is aligned with mine. I'm tense with the sudden awareness of him touching me, touching him. I try not to get distracted from what Elias is saying, but being this close to Kai does weird things to my mind.

"Your right foot on his," Elias is saying.

My right foot where?

"Lily?" Elias glances over at me.

"Um ... yeah. Right." I blush. "Sorry, could you repeat that?"

Kai chuckles and my cheeks flush.

Elias rolls his eyes good-naturedly. "You're going to start by stepping on his right foot with your right foot, okay?"

"Right," I nod. "Right now?"

"Let me explain the rest of the move," Elias says.

"Right."

"You're going to step on his foot and then push your body out to create some space, throwing your elbow behind you as you do this. Let's try it in slow motion first. We don't want anyone getting hurt today."

"Okay." I do as instructed, pretending to step on Kai's foot and then pushing my elbow back. I can't get my arm out of his grip. He's too strong. I struggle for a moment before Kai starts laughing.

"Well," Elias says, "obviously it doesn't work very well in slow motion because it's your momentum that will carry you through."

"She can try it full force," Kai tells Elias.

"Maybe it would be better if she practices with me. I've been punched before, and I can take a hit. I don't want you getting hurt. Then the whole country would be after my ass."

"Don't worry about it," Kai brushes him off. "I've been training in combat. I'm in the military."

"Kai, are you sure?" I ask hesitantly.

"Of course. Come on." He puts his arms around me again. "You won't hurt me."

"Okay," Elias says skeptically. "One … two … three."

I step on Kai's foot with all my strength, throw my weight forward like Elias showed me, then jab my elbow back. But instead of it connecting with Kai's ribs, he dodges out of the way, wrapping his arm around my elbow and dropping me lightly on the ground, falling next to me on the mats.

I sprawl out on my back and start giggling. "You're such a show off!" I roll over and push his shoulder.

He shrugs. "I told you. It's the military."

"What do they teach you? How to assassinate people?"

"It's top secret," he says and stands to help me up.

"Did I even hurt you a little?" I ask, taking his hand.

"Maybe," he says and grins, keeping hold of my hands.

"Not even a little?" I pout.

"What? You wanted to hurt me?"

"Not badly."

He lightly socks my stomach and I grip his elbows, squirming to push him away, laughing.

"Come here." He tries to reach out to me, and I pull back, preparing to run. Instead, he grabs me around the waist and hoists me up, swinging me over his shoulder.

"Kai!" I'm breathless as he tumbles with me to the ground again, gently tossing me as though I'm weightless. I can't stop the smile that spreads across my face, and we're both laughing euphorically. I can't remember the last time I did anything like this. Not since I was a child, living in Arizona, did I feel so carefree.

"Alright." Elias walks between us, reminding us he's still in the room. "I think that's enough for today. You better get Lily home before her family realizes she's gone."

My attention snaps to him and then to the clock. I need to get home.

Elias extends his hand. "It was nice meeting you. Hopefully we'll be seeing you again soon."

"Yes," I agree. My cheeks are flushed, and I feel light with energy.

Kai drapes his arm around my shoulder, and we walk out to the parking lot comfortably in sync with one another. We get into his car and head back to my house.

"So can I see you again tomorrow?" he asks as we pull up to the gate.

"I have class," I say, falling easily into my skeptical nature.

"On Sunday?"

I look over at him and just as quickly wish I hadn't. I avert my eyes. "I don't think so."

"Alright, what about next Saturday?" he asks but doesn't give me time to answer. "Saturday at five o'clock it is. I'll take you on a real date this time. To dinner. So wear something nice." I can hear the smile in his voice.

I clear my throat. "I said I don't—"

His hand covers mine, and I repeat my mistake. My eyes glance over to his. He holds my stare.

Then he replaces his hand with his lips and for a moment, I'm his. He captures my mouth, wrapping my hair in his fist so he can pull me closer. I shiver in surprise, but sink into his hold. Desire coils in my stomach. It's hard to breathe again, but not in an uncomfortable way. I'll never breathe again if I can be close to him like this always.

Crap.

I pull away.

"This is a bad idea," I say, my voice shaky with the emotions that kiss left behind.

"You only think that because it's what your parents tell you." There's that playful sparkle in his eyes. His thumb grazes across my lips.

But the smile fades from my face. It's a bad idea because I trust Kai, and no matter how much I try to fight it, it's like my body has some internal signal I can't figure out how to turn off. And until I do, it's pushing me to make decisions that aren't safe. I can't trust myself right now.

I move to get out of the car, but Kai's grip on my hand tightens. When I look back his eyes are filled with determination and resolve. His hand moves from mine and cups my face. His rough fingers run down the line of my jaw. I'm so lost in his gaze that I don't even realize how close he is until he speaks, and I feel his breath across my lips.

"Saturday night."

It isn't a question. But he's asking so much of me. More than just dinner, he's asking for me to let him in. He's asking me to be vulnerable. As if I'm not already so lost. I'm so far down that deep, dark hole, scrambling for purchase, when it's clear I'm already going to fall all the way down. And as all of these thoughts swirl through my mind, they suddenly dissipate because all I can focus on are the sharp lines of his jaw and the warmth from his hands and the way his eyes are staring at me like I'm completely exposed.

"Someone will see us." My voice has transformed into this low whisper because all the air leaves my chest as I gape at him, and he stares back. It only makes everything feel more intimate.

"So?"

"So, what about the cameras?"

"I can fix that." His eyes light with the challenge, but he doesn't pull away from me. "It's going to happen eventually. People are going to catch on whether we hide or not. Say yes."

All I see are green and gold.

And I realize that in my daze, I just nodded my consent.

He drops his hands, and I try to keep from stumbling as I walk to the gate. The line along my jaw where his hands were resting continues to burn.

Kai waits to make sure I get inside the house alright before he drives back to the main road. Once I know he's out of sight, I take a deep breath. I just lost that battle. And the war isn't looking so promising either. Judging by the way my heart is still pounding in my chest, I'm already done for. The worst part is I'm not upset. Not even a little. My self-control was my most-valuable weapon, and now it's crumbled with a simple touch from Kai's hands. My emotions are rushing in, clouding my mind. And I don't even try to hide the smile that curls on my lips as I walk inside.

CHAPTER NINE

I do everything in my power to push away thoughts of Saturday, but my attempts are useless. Especially because I can't keep away the thoughts of our kiss—his hands in my hair, the heat from his body so close to mine, his lips needy but gentle, like he was holding back, like there was so much for him to discover.

I suffer through my tutorials, finish *Wuthering Heights*, master a piece on the piano, work on my French conjugations (not too successfully), and plug in equations for calculus. I dedicate myself to my schoolwork, hoping that it will get me through the week faster, but Kai is never far from my mind.

I've never been on a real dinner date before. The idea of dressing up and going out makes me bite my bottom lip to suppress a preteen squeal that threatens to leap out of my throat.

When Saturday evening finally does arrive, I watch from my balcony, waiting to see his car. My hands run down my thighs, smoothing the lines of my simple black dress. It's cut low in the front, flaunting my curves in just the right ways. When the seamstress finished the garment, my mother forbade me from wearing it. She said it was too revealing for a girl of my stature and age. I secretly kept it in the back of my closet. I never thought I'd have a use for it, but tonight I'm going to dinner wearing it. For the first time in my life, I feel truly beautiful. And it isn't just the dress. Something inside me is changing. There's an awareness that wasn't there before. My reflection doesn't seem so distant anymore.

Impatiently, I stare out at the fence in the distance, and then glance back at the clock.

The clocks, which had seemed to be moving so slowly all week, quickly begin to tick off minutes as the hour of our date approaches. First ten minutes pass, then fifteen … then a half an hour … and an hour.

His car doesn't appear at the gate.

I call his phone, but it goes straight to voicemail.

Kai's never been late before.

I call his phone again but get voicemail just like before.

Maybe there was a miscommunication. Maybe he said Sunday instead of Saturday? Maybe he was waiting for me a little farther down the road, and I just couldn't see his car from my window. Maybe he couldn't get his camera app thing to work and so he had to ditch Plan A, and he's trying to figure out a Plan B to get me out of the house.

I grab for my bag and start to head out, but my mother meets me at the top of the stairs.

"Lilith."

"I'm going out."

"Lilith."

"Mom, stop trying to stop me." I try to skirt around her, but she's in front of the stairs blocking my path like a goalie.

I heave a sigh and drop my arms. "Mom you've got to stop trying to...."

She's holding her phone tightly in one hand. Her eyes narrow sharply, and deep lines embed her forehead, aging her significantly.

"What?" I ask.

"I just got off the phone with your father."

"So? Mom, I'm late to meet Kai." I try to dodge her again, and this time I'm able to get past. I trot down the stairs.

"You aren't meeting Kai, Lily." Her voice is so soft I almost miss the words. She referred to me as Lily. I freeze about halfway down the steps.

I shift back toward my mother. "What?"

"He's been shipped out on a mission."

"What?"

"He's gone."

"What?"

Her voice is stoic. "He left this morning."

"What? No. He wouldn't have left without saying goodbye. He would have told me."

"He didn't know. It was an emergency operation."

"Where is he?" I ask. "Where did he go?"

"Your father wouldn't tell me. He couldn't tell me anything other than that he's gone. Apparently he volunteered for this operation a few months back and assumed he hadn't been chosen. He got a knock on the door this morning telling him to report for duty."

"What?" I don't know why I keep saying that but it's all that's circling around in my head. "He would have told me. He would have called. He wouldn't have just left."

"He wouldn't have had a choice." My mother is trying to be consoling. Instead of the usual clipped tone she uses with me, her voice is low and steady. It's condescending.

"Did Dad have a part in this? Is this your way of making sure I never have a life?" My voice rises steadily. "I finally find something normal, something real, and you take it away. He wouldn't just leave like that. He told me...."

He told me what? That I could trust him?

He never promised I wouldn't be alone or that he would never have to leave. In fact, he said himself that he promised his country another year.

I sink down the stairs and drop my head onto the railing.

"How long will he be gone?" I mumble, already steeling myself for the worst. What if I never see him again? I have less than eight months before I'm a Taken Eighteen. The Revealed probably won't wait that long.

My mother knows what I'm really asking. She comes and sits down next to me, gently putting a hand on my knee, and I know she won't be able to tell me anything.

Kai is gone.

What if I'm taken before he gets back?

Two hundred and thirty-six days until I'm nineteen. That means 236 days of opportunity The Revealed have left to take my life.

"I'm gonna get some air." I stand and my mother's touch drops.

She just nods.

Usually being outside helps clear my thoughts. But today, it doesn't stop them from spinning.

I walk down to the gardens.

The sun is setting around me.

I imagine Kai and myself at dinner, sitting tucked away in a dark corner on an outdoor patio. I don't know where he was planning on taking me, but in my mind it was a place like this. Where we could just be teenagers on a date and no one would know our names.

Then my thoughts drift to the last time I saw him. The way he held my face and stared into my eyes was more intimate than our kiss. I try to remember everything about his face and his expression then. The determination that burned gold beneath the green in his eyes. The way his jaw held firm, not taking no for an answer. And the gentle way his hands held my face, imploring me to just let go and say yes.

If that's the last time I ever see him, will it be enough? When I'm gone, will he tell people that he was grateful for just those few days? Or will he be angry he didn't get any more?

A light breeze kicks up around my face.

I shut my eyes tightly.

The breeze becomes stronger, lifting the ends of my hair. It moves through the garden, and I can hear it swaying in patterns. It twists around the plants, taking on a life of its own. It swells around me as though it's coming from the center of the garden itself.

It flaps loudly against the branches, bending and twisting the vines, making them scream for mercy.

Yet, no dirt or debris hits my face.

Nothing but the gust of wind blows around.

It happens so suddenly, within a matter of seconds.

My eyes snap open.

The wind dies instantly, and the vines drop around me with a sudden plunk as they hit the dirt.

Everything around me is still.

I stand and spin in a circle.

"Hello?"

It feels like someone is watching me.

Am I crazy? Because I could have sworn that the vines from the plants around me were floating, hovering in the air like the wind was manipulating them.

"Hello?"

I didn't realize that twilight had crept into the sky, and it's suddenly hard to see.

I tense but don't wait any longer. I sprint back to the house. A quick glance over my shoulder makes me shudder.

The wind has gone completely, making the silence even more overbearing.

It's too quiet. Unnaturally so.

I run around the corner of the house and collide with an "oomph" into a pillowy, broad chest. It's Darren, Jeremy's overeager second-in-command.

"Ms. Atwood." He braces me with his hands, surprised. Then he looks me over. His eyes widening at the sight of my little black dress. "Where are you off to in such a hurry? Can I help you with something?"

I shake my head, glancing back over my shoulder. "I just thought I saw … or I mean heard …," I can't bring myself to articulate any sort of crazy explanation for what I experienced in the garden. "I'm fine," I sigh, "just being paranoid." I try to laugh it off, but goose bumps are still raised on my arms.

"Makes sense." He grins, revealing his crooked teeth. "Want me to escort you inside?"

I shake my head. "I'm fine."

"Well let me assure you, the premises are clear. No one is getting on this property without us approving it first." He stands a little straighter, as if that helps prove his point.

"Right," I say, and I don't hide the hesitation in the word. I know Darren is just trying to be comforting, but his efforts feel useless in light of the black notes.

I glance back over my shoulder once more and head inside.

CHAPTER TEN

I've been going outside.

My mother's not pleased about it. Neither is my father, but he hasn't been around enough to make an issue of it. And my mother realizes it's a useless battle at this point. Her only other option would be to tie me to a chair. I think she would, except she'd be worried the press would find out, and that wouldn't look too good for the campaign.

My father's been living at his office. He sleeps there most nights. He's hot on the campaign trail—ahead in the polls and determined to stay there. My mother goes and visits him, brings him lunch that Ilan cooks.

The election occupies little thought in my mind.

I think about Kai. I wonder where he is, what he's doing. But more than thinking about Kai, I think about that drive we took before he left. The unspoken words about continuing on the road and never looking back. I wish we had. I play it over in my mind, imagining what it would have been like if we had just continued on the freeway. I imagine we could have reached the West Coast. I would take the wastelands any day over this.

I sit in my room for the rest of the morning, into early afternoon, trying to get homework done. I barely get through two problems. My pencil just hangs there, suspended between my fingers and forgotten amidst the other thoughts flying through my mind.

Finally, I close the book and grab for the car keys.

My mother is just walking in the door as I breeze past her.

"I'm going out!" I call over my shoulder.

"Excuse me?" She turns, dropping the shopping bags in her hands. "Lily," my mother says, walking to the entryway. She stops and puts her hand on her hip. She looks like she is in the mood to fight.

But instead she sighs. "You're going whether I put up a fight or not, aren't you?"

"Yes," I nod. I'm done with staying indoors. "And I'm a legal adult so you can't stop me and if you try to kick me out of the house, it'll only look bad for your campaign."

My mother sighs. "It isn't the campaign I'm worried about, Lily."

"I know you're afraid, Mom." I take a couple steps toward her. "I'm afraid, too. But keeping me here isn't doing anything. Let's be real, they crashed your gala without so much as a hitch. I'm not any safer here. You have to let me go."

"I don't ever want to let you go," she says in a rare moment of affection. It surprises me. Then she purses her lips in an attempt at composure. "Will you at least take Jeremy with you?"

"Deal." I reach for the door and head outside before she can change her mind.

Jeremy is standing on the porch at his post.

"Come on, chief," I say, and nod my head at him. "Mom says if I want to leave, you have to come, so hopefully you don't mind a road trip?"

He clears his throat. "Where to?"

"The gym."

I don't mind that he comes with me, really. Jeremy is pretty cool despite the fact that he's my father's watchdog. But he lets me drive and doesn't try to dictate where I go.

"How's the gala investigation?" I ask.

"Pretty much over," he says dryly. "There isn't any evidence."

"Like always," I sigh. "I'm a sitting duck."

He laughs lightly, which catches me off guard. I glance over at the easy way he smiles.

"It isn't funny," I tell him, though a smile plays at my lips— mostly because I'm not sure I've ever seen him laugh like this. "You have no idea what it's like—feeling like at any moment someone's going to snatch you away. I can't trust anyone."

"You seem to trust Kai Westerfield." Suddenly his tone drops back to … I dunno … it sounds like concern.

"Maybe." I glance out over the road and rest my hand on my forehead. "Not that it matters anymore."

"Two hands on the wheel," Jeremy prompts.

I give him a wry look but clutch the wheel at ten and two, mockingly.

"Actually," he tells me, "you're supposed to hold it at nine and three. Gives you a wider turn radius if you have to swerve, plus if your airbag deploys being positioned at nine and three will protect your hands from damage."

I slip my grip down but feel awkward about it.

"So this is what they teach soldiers, huh?" I drop one hand.

"You have no idea what they teach us." His voice is suddenly cold, and I find myself swallowing limply. Did I offend him? Did I say something wrong?

"I'm sorry," I mumble.

And suddenly his face flattens. He shakes his head. "You have no reason to be."

We drive the rest of the way in silence. It's almost fall now and the leaves are just beginning to brown.

I drive into the small parking lot at the back of the gym.

Working out with Elias has become somewhat of a respite for me. It helps to calm my nerves and get out some of the frustration. It gives me time to think. Mostly about Kai. I haven't seen him in over a month. I imagine what he's doing right then as I'm throwing my fists into the bag. Somehow my mind always drifts to him with a weapon raised high, running through the wasteland. But there aren't any enemies in the wasteland. Both the Midwest and West were entirely deserted after the war. There was too much damage and too few people to occupy the space. Everyone who survived moved to the Eastern Coast, which was relatively undisturbed—as undisturbed as possible in a nuclear war.

It's highly unlikely they shipped Kai west. But where is he then? What use could they possibly have for the military in a time of peace? I know that sounds naive. Of course the North American Sector still needs protection, but it seems we would need the most protection around the land we occupy. It would make the most sense for him to stay here. What could he possibly be doing that it would be too dangerous for him to contact me?

Maybe he's at the borders? The North American Sector does have checkpoints from the Gulf Coast to northern New York, all along the Mississippi and Ohio Rivers, and everywhere in between.

But it wouldn't be a secret if that's all he was doing. I could drive out to the edge of the colonies right now if I chose, and visit those men who control our borders. People do it all the time. And they aren't plucked randomly from their homes. They are given a schedule of their terms of duty well in advance. It's a rotation system. Basically a regular job.

The mission Kai is on is different.

"You're focused today." Elias walks around behind the bag and holds it steady while I drill my fists into it again and again. "Anything you'd like to share?"

I drop my arms and shake out my hands.

"You miss him, don't you?" Elias asks.

That makes me cringe. Elias isn't the only one asking that question. Every newspaper in the sector seems interested in the gossip over my heartbreak with Kai.

"He's not dead," I say stoically. "He'll be back soon."

"Doesn't matter," Elias says, shrugging, "I saw the two of you in here, rompin' around on the ground like a couple of kids. You make each other happy."

"I barely know him," I say.

Elias's eyes narrow. "Right." And just when I think he's going to leave it alone, he adds, "You really believe that?"

"I think I'm going to call it a day."

Elias watches me for a minute with a knowing look. "No, come here." He calls me back and holds the bag. He nods with his head for me to hit. I swing and connect. The bag sways from the force of my blow. I've improved so much in the time I've trained with him.

Again, I drill into the bag. For Rory, who gets to follow her heart while I'm left behind. For my dad, who used to be so much more than my father. He was my friend and mentor but is now almost a stranger. And can I blame him for the distance when he knows his daughter's time is almost up, and he doesn't know how to deal with the fear? For my mother who should have a daughter that prefers high heels and parties to boxing. And, of course, for Kai. But it isn't just for Kai. It's for me. It's for what I could have, maybe, almost had with him. If only we'd just had a little more time. And now it's over. It's over because I'm nearly over. While everyone else gets to build lives, I'm stuck. I got caught in the whirlpool while everyone else continued floating down the river.

"Whoa," Elias steadies me with a hand.

I collapse my face in my hands, feeling frazzled and uncontrolled. I strip the gloves from my hands. "I should go."

"Hey," he squeezes my shoulder then pulls me into a hug. It's startling and all at once comforting. My breathing is shaky. "Take care of yourself, okay? Everything will turn out how it's supposed to. Life has a funny way of working out how it should."

I'm hard-pressed to believe him. But who am I to kill his optimism so I just nod. "I'll be back soon."

I grab my bag and head out.

My father's office is a fifteen-minute drive, straight down Pennsylvania Avenue after the freeway, and I plan on stopping in to see if he wants to grab lunch. Maybe, just maybe, we can talk like we used to.

Jeremy is still waiting at the door when I get outside.

"I'm going to use the restroom before we leave, if you don't mind," he tells me.

"Okay, I'll be in the car."

I walk back out to the parking lot and decide to pull the car around to the front and wait for him.

I get in the car and reach for the seatbelt. It sears my flesh.

"Ow!" I wince and yank my hand from the metal. I bring the burn to my mouth and then pull it away. A red blister swells.

What in the world?

It's almost October and it's chilly outside today. How did my seatbelt get so scorching hot?

I touch it again, quickly to avoid a burn. But the metal is already cool. I touch it once more just to be sure. The heat is gone. The welt on my hand remains. Heat pulses through my finger. The injury is bad enough that I can't pretend the burn is only a product of my overactive imagination. But I can't figure out how the seatbelt got that hot.

Carefully, I start the car. The engine smoothly hums to life. For the second time, I dare to try and fasten my seatbelt. I move to shift into reverse but my hand connects with ice and slips from the gear. There is ice on my steering wheel. And it's growing, spreading across the wheel like it's alive.

I pull my seatbelt off and stare in horror as the ice crystallizes over the wheel.

In a panic, I throw open the door and stumble away from the car.

My eyes scan the surrounding area as I scramble to get away. I trip over my shoes, landing on the concrete a few feet from my car. It's The Revealed. It has to be The Revealed.

I try to regain my footing to run back inside the gym. I don't even have time to stand before I'm blasted by a wave of heat and an explosion so loud it blocks out every other sense in my body. It's like a shockwave rippling through my skin.

Instinctively, I duck down and cover my face with my arms.

Heat rushes over my body, and bits of glass sting my skin.

My ears ring, but the blast subsides. I cautiously lower my arms. The car is still burning, smoke billowing from the windows.

People run outside the building. Elias races to my side and grabs my arms, trying to get me to look at him.

"Lily." He shakes me lightly. "Are you okay?"

I can't tear my eyes away from the car.

The Revealed aren't trying to take me.

They're trying to kill me.

Scratch my countdown. It doesn't matter that I have 212 days until my nineteenth birthday. Those days stretch out as an infinity before me. The Revealed will take care of me long before then.

"Someone call the police!" Elias shouts.

As if on cue, the sound of sirens echoes in the distance.

Jeremy runs outside, sees me and the car, and flips out.

"What happened?" He sprints to my side. "Jesus! Lily, are you hurt?"

"I don't think so," I mumble.

The police pull into the parking lot with the bomb squad.

A paramedic kneels down next to me. "Lily Atwood?"

I nod, confused.

He's wearing gloves and carrying a medical kit.

"I need everyone to back away!" one of the officers is ordering.

"How did you know to be here?" I ask the paramedic as he dabs antiseptic on the cuts from the glass.

"There was an anonymous call. Someone said you were here and that they believed there was a bomb in your car."

The paramedics take me to the hospital just in case, though nothing is broken or seriously injured. Just the burn and a few minor cuts and bruises. Other than that, I'm fine.

Of course, it takes four hours, while I'm lying in a hospital bed, for them to tell me that. Normally it would take longer, but because I'm a "priority patient," they run all of the tests quickly.

Jeremy is right at my side the entire time, apologizing over and over. "I should have never gone inside," he says. "I should have stayed right with you."

"If you'd stayed right with me, we both would have been killed."

"Lily, this is entirely my fault. I should have been watching more closely." His face is full of guilt.

"None of us could have known this was going to happen, Jeremy."

"It's not just that," he says. "I really think of you guys like family. Looking out for your well-being isn't just my job, it's a personal responsibility."

I take Jeremy's hand. "Then trust me," I say. "You couldn't have prevented this, and I'll be the first to tell my father that. It wasn't your fault. Really."

My parents both show up. I would like to say I'm surprised, but their arrival is probably more to do with the press, which has no doubt gotten wind of my ordeal by now. Again, I will be front-page news. It seems to be a trending theme in my life. Every move I make draws some sort of attention from the media.

Everyone seems to want to take the blame for what happened, including my mother.

"I should have never let you go out." She paces as the nurses push me in a wheelchair out to the awaiting limo. Luckily, the press is kept at bay.

"Mom, I'm fine."

My father grips my hand, and that's all I need from him. There's a terror behind his eyes I've never seen in him. He looks visibly shaken, more than I am, and he folds into the chair next to me in the car. He rests his other hand on top of mine.

"If you hadn't gotten out of that car you would have been killed," my mother continues her hysterics.

I look away from my father and back to her, "I wasn't killed, though. I'm okay."

"Yes, well, we're lucky you noticed something was wrong and got out of that car." She waves her hands around wildly.

"Dad," I address him, hoping he can be the rational one here. "I didn't notice something was wrong. I saw ice forming on my steering wheel. That's noticing a lot more than just something wrong," I tell her. "It was The Revealed."

The sound of their name makes her suck in a breath.

"They weren't trying to take me. They were trying to kill me."

CHAPTER ELEVEN

The burns and bruises heal, and life goes back to normal. The country doesn't soon forget my ordeal, but they're swept up by the more important topic of the election. It's only five weeks away.

I stare out my balcony window at the front gate and imagine the Audi that never arrived. There is so much I wish I could say. It's harder and harder to remember him. Sometimes it doesn't feel like he's even real—like the boy I met was a ghost.

And now all that's left is my solitude. Especially following the bombing. All I feel is anticipation, waiting for The Revealed to come and finish the job. I don't feel defeated, just tired. All the time, tired.

One hundred ninety-five days until—

I cut the thought off abruptly. It isn't healthy to dwell on the impossible. Better to accept it and move on.

I turn from the window, calling it an early night again. I crawl into bed and stare at the ceiling until I fall asleep.

When I wake up, the remnants of a dream hang in my memory. A dream that fills me with longing. One with cherry trees and long road trips. Kai is in the car with me, his brown hair tossing in the wind of the convertible we're driving in. He's laughing with me, and the sun is hitting our faces. The warmth of it feels good. I want to curl around it and hold it forever. It's what I want—a life like that. I don't want to be afraid. I don't want to wait in dread and intimidation. That's exactly the reaction The Revealed are hoping for. But I can't live that way—waiting for them to come and finish the job.

I get dressed, fix my hair, and go down the hall to the far wing of the house.

My mother is in her bedroom, working over her desk. Paying bills, by the looks of it.

"I think I'm going to visit Dad," I say.

My mother looks up warily. "No."

"I wasn't asking permission." I decided to tell her this time instead of just plotting an escape because, well, for one I don't have Kai to mess with the cameras anymore. And two, because I'm trying to make my parents understand that I deserve this freedom. It's time for me to make my own choices.

"Why can't you just accept this year as a normal rite of passage?" she sighs.

"Because it isn't a rite of passage in my case. The Revealed aren't sending those letters just for fun. I'm the only eighteen-year-old anyone has heard of that's receiving letters from these people. They're not just going to go away. They're going to come for me. I have the rare opportunity to *know* they're coming. And I don't want to live my last few months or days stuck inside a house."

Her jaw is tight and her shoulders tense. I think she's going to cry—like, actually cry. I've never seen my mother come anywhere close to tears.

"Mom—" I have no idea how to comfort her. My words drop and I stand dumbly in the doorway.

"I was never made to be a mother," she tells me. "Oh I wanted to be, but I don't know how to do this, Lilith."

My chest constricts.

She isn't done. "When the war started, you were so little. You needed so much guidance. Your life was at stake, and I knew how to deal with that. I was ready for the consequences. Your father and I were ready to die for you if we needed to. We were ready to give up our lives. We were ready to hide you from the dangers outside. But now, how do I hide you? How do I keep you from them?" She shakes her head. "Either way, I fail you."

"You don't ...," I try to get the words right, "it isn't your fault."

"But we're your parents. We should be able to protect you. And we can't."

"I don't have to go see Dad," I offer, my voice on the verge of cracking.

"No. Go."

I cross the room and throw my arms around her. We've never been touchy-feely with one another, and she tenses when I wrap my arms around her. I don't care. I hold her close anyway.

Then I'm out the door.

"Take Jeremy with you," she calls, her voice level again.

I nod and wave consent over my shoulder.

Jeremy actually insists I stand fifty feet away from any of the vehicles while he starts the car and drives it to the front of the house.

"No more mistakes," he says as he gets out, offering me the driver's seat.

I stare at the steering wheel. All I see when I look at it are flames licking up the sides and the interior melting away.

"Come on." Jeremy nods his head.

I take a deep breath. I can do this. I have to do this. I won't let my fears keep me inside these gates. I get in the car and shift into drive in one quick motion. The car doesn't explode. Nothing bad happens.

"They have you pretty nervous, huh?" Jeremy asks.

I nod.

"You'd be crazy not to be afraid. But don't worry. I won't let anyone get close to you without going through me first." I see the hint of a proud smile light under his eyes.

"You've saved my life enough times this year. I think you deserve a vacation after all this."

"Oh, I'll get one," he agrees.

Past the gate, I steer onto the freeway, going well under the speed limit the entire drive. I usually never go under the speed limit.

Once I reach Pennsylvania Avenue, I practically crawl across the road. The fifteen-minute drive turns into more like twenty, but Jeremy doesn't say a word. He lets me take my time and overcome the fear on my own. Though we pull into a guarded garage, Jeremy wants to stay in the car, just in case.

I walk up to the second floor where my father has his office.

His secretary, Tracy, is surprised to see me. She fumbles over the phone, knocking her drink over in the process.

I flinch at the noise, suddenly amplified into an explosion in my head.

"Oh, I'm so klutzy," she chortles.

I help her mop up the mess.

"How are you feeling?" Her thick brows pull together, her face animated with worry.

"I'm doing just fine." I don't add that I had the car inspected by security before I got inside.

"I'm just surprised to see you!" she exclaims. "It's been so long. Is your father expecting you? I mean, he didn't tell me to expect...."

What she's really asking is, *Aren't you supposed to be locked up in your house?*

"No," I say to her, "I wanted to surprise him. My mother thought it might be a nice idea, so close to the election," I add.

"Well I'm sure he'll be surprised." She forces a grin. Meaning that my father will be upset. Everyone knows I'm supposed to be at the house.

Tracy picks up the phone. "Mr. Atwood? Lily's here to see you."

Pause.

"I don't know, sir."

Another pause, and then she hangs up the phone.

"He's in a meeting down the hall right now, but he said it shouldn't take long and you're more than welcome to wait in his office."

I walk inside the room, my fingers trace over the books on the desk before I settle on the view from the window. Across the street there used to be a park. I remember running around out there when I was little. It was called The Spirit of Justice Park. It seems a little grandiose for a cozy spot with benches tucked under trees, but it's named for an aluminum statue of a woman who stands tall and proud over the area.

The smoke rising in the distance flattens my nostalgia and makes my gut clench in longing for those days in the sun.

My father strolls into the room looking magnificent, and I turn to greet him. His brown hair perfectly combed back. His black suit pressed and polished with a crimson-red tie. He looks like a president. Somewhere under all of this grandeur is my father.

"Lily! What a surprise," he says.

"I got Mom's permission, if that's what you're worried about."

"A little worried," he admits. "But to what do I owe this visit?"

"Do you want to get something to eat?" I ask hopefully.

My father picks up papers to scan through as he speaks to me. "I wish I could, but we're working on getting a press release out right now about our plans to extend the borders once I'm elected. We can't keep ourselves confined in isolation forever."

"I won't take up much of your time, then. I just haven't seen you in a few weeks and …," my voice trails off as I lose his focus to the computer. "What are you working on?"

"Going over reports from the Department of Defense. They've got some new intel that could be a promising lead to the location of The Revealed." He pauses before adding, "That's between you and me."

"Of course," I say. Who could I possibly tell anyway?

"We previously thought they were coming from west of the wastelands, but now it seems as though we should be looking south."

"Why south?"

"A group surveying the border talked to a gas attendant clerk who said she saw two Range Rovers coming up from Interstate 11. They stopped to fill up their tanks, then headed north. The group was dressed in black. She said she couldn't see any symbols that would have confirmed it was The Revealed. But she snapped a couple of pictures. They definitely weren't civilians."

My father flips the computer around.

The pictures aren't the best quality, but it's easy to see a group of six clustered near the pump. They stand with their heads high, looking around the area. A few hold backpacks and cell phones. The cars are in great shape—that and their cell phones are red flags that these people aren't normal civilians. If they aren't soldiers, they have to be members of The Revealed.

"So we're close then, right?" I ask hopefully. These pictures are solid evidence. They have to provide some leads. This means we could be really close to finding their headquarters.

"Don't get too excited," my father warns. "This is just the first step."

The phone rings. I jerk at the loud thrum on my father's desk. He watches me for a moment, curiosity turning to worry at my skittish behavior.

Bombs will do that.

"Hold on just a second," he tells me and answers. "Jet? I was just looking over the report…. Yes, let's go ahead and release the photos to the press…. I think so, too. Someone has to know these people…."

"Sounds good."

My father hangs up the phone and turns back to me. "Sorry, Lil." This is followed by silence as he assesses me. He folds his hands on the desk. "I have to get back to it," he motions around his desk.

I clear my throat. I have one more questions for him. "Um … is there any information on Kai?"

My father sits back in his chair, annoyed. "That boy is bad news, Lil. I wish you'd forget about him."

I ignore his frustrated tone. He's just tired from all this campaigning. But I have to ask, even if he won't tell me. "You haven't heard anything?"

"Lily," my father says and closes his computer, and now I know the question was a mistake. I've gotten under his skin. "Kai Westerfield arrived back home from his mission two days ago. I've told you from the beginning that boy is trouble. You shouldn't meddle with someone like him. His motivations aren't good. He's a Westerfield. The rest of the world may be charmed by him, but we know better."

I hardly heard anything after the first part.

"He's back?"

"Yes, Lily. He's back," my father sighs. "I don't want to see you get hurt. But you have to know this boy is no good. If the two of you were so close then where is he? Why hasn't he come to see you? Lily, you are too good for him. And I mean it. He isn't someone—"

Turning to leave his office I say, "Sorry, I know you're busy. I'll just see you at home." I don't give my father the chance to say anything else. I sprint out to the car and practically dive into the front seat.

"What's the rush?" Jeremy watches me curiously from the passenger seat.

My mind is going in about fifty different directions at once. "He's back." I wrap my hands around the base of my neck. "He's back."

"You better calm yourself down before you start driving," Jeremy says, watching me closely.

I glance over my outfit. Leggings. Boots. A thick cardigan. I don't even bother asking Jeremy how I look. It's fall. How else can I look but cold?

My stomach flips.

Don't hesitate. Just do this.

I throw the car into reverse, and Jeremy holds on for dear life. "Are you trying to get us both killed?!" he yells as I speed onto the road.

Everything around me is a blur. All I hear on the drive to his house is my heart beating in my ears. Nothing is in focus.

The excitement carries me to his doorstep where a house attendant answers the door.

"Ms. Atwood," the man says in curt recognition.

"He's home," I breathe.

"Ms. Atwood—"

I'm sprinting inside the house.

I run my hands along the iron banister as I make my way to the second floor. All I can focus on is the idea of being close to him. It's almost as if I can feel him, just on the other side of the crisp white walls.

But I've never been inside this house, and I have no idea which room is Kai's. As I reach the second floor I begin opening doors.

Where my house is antebellum, blending in with the Capitol's terrain, the Westerfield mansion is contemporary, full of sleek lines and sharp angles. The exterior is white and so is the interior, with dark gray furniture and stainless steel detailing.

"Kai!" I call. There must be at least two dozen rooms. There is even a third floor above me.

I open a door. Office.

Other doors are already open.

I imagine finding him unpacking and running into his arms. He'll tell me he missed me and apologize for not calling before he left.

Guest bedroom.

We'll leave together right now. And spend the whole night just catching up.

Bathroom.

Finally, I reach the door at the end of the hallway and push it open. Instantly, I know it's his. It smells like him—earthy and clean.

"Kai?" I ask, gently pushing open the door and stepping inside.

The bed is made. There's a chair in the corner with a shirt hanging over the back. An empty duffel bag is on the floor.

"Can I help you?"

I jump out of my skin.

Roderick Westerfield stands behind me. His hands are crossed behind his back. His salt-and-pepper hair is slicked back, and he wears his typical shiny black suit. He matches the contrasts of the house. He holds himself with such pompous arrogance, raising one eyebrow at me in mock curiosity.

"Where is he?" I ask.

"I believe that's none of your business," Westerfield tells me calmly. "If he wanted to see you, he would have called."

"Is he okay?"

"Of course," Kai's father replies. "He's with friends right now."

"Friends?" I haven't met Kai's friends yet. And that thought alone makes me realize how not-close we really are.

"He does have friends, Ms. Atwood," he says, clearly not amused. "Now I would appreciate it if you would allow your driver to escort you to your car. I don't encourage people barging in on me uninvited—especially little girls with misplaced affections."

I look downstairs and see Jeremy standing in the doorway. Suddenly I feel embarrassed. More than embarrassed; I'm humiliated.

My father's words weigh on me. Kai doesn't want to see me.

"Excuse me," I mumble as I pass Westerfield.

As soon as I walk outside, the old house attendant slams the door, and Jeremy takes the cars keys from me. I hardly notice any of it. I stare out ahead at the road as we drive, trying to process what just happened, from my father telling me Kai was back to the fiasco at the Westerfields' to this moment, sitting in the car, heading home.

Kai doesn't want to see me.

Jeremy drives me back to the house.

He's been back for almost two days and hasn't even called.

Why?

It isn't until I reach my room and securely close and lock the door behind me that I slide down the wall and onto the floor. My eyes sting and I swallow, fighting back tears. I won't cry. I won't let myself give in like that.

But I don't understand. How could I have been thinking about him and waiting for him all this time while he was just indifferent? How could these feelings have developed so quickly, only for them to be one-sided?

As if this day couldn't get any worse, I glance up to find a black note on my window.

I don't even think. I charge at it, ripping it from the wall and shredding it until a thousand little black pieces float down around me.

"Come on then!" I scream. "I'm right here! I'm right here! Just do it!"

I repeat those words over and over again until I'm exhausted.

No one answers.

No one even comes to check on me.

And I know I'm alone.

CHAPTER TWELVE

There's a newspaper on the stands today featuring a piece on Kai with a mysterious woman. No doubt his so-called friend. The headline reads,

Kai's Back and Ready to Mingle!

My parents don't understand—not that it's anything new. My father hasn't even been home for the past week. I haven't seen or spoken with him since he broke the news of Kai's return.

I stare up from my computer at my mother, who walks in the door with her arms full of shopping bags. "I have some news," she tells me. "Your father and I have decided to go on a last-minute campaigning spree. We'll be traveling to five cities within the next week. We just decided today. Jet said it could be just the golden ticket we need in this race. We leave early tomorrow morning." She's beaming.

"And you want me to stay here?" I ask hesitantly.

"Well, of course not by yourself." She waves a hand at me. "Jeremy will be here."

"Right." I don't know why her announcement pushes me further into a wallowing pit of loneliness. It's not like she and my father haven't left me behind before. But I don't want to be alone now. Can't she see that? I think about the conversation we had the other day. The progress I thought we made suddenly seems lost.

"Can I go with you?" I dare to ask, though I already know the answer.

"Lilith." She sets her bags down and runs a hand through her hair. "You have responsibilities here. You must keep up with your studies. You know that."

I stare at the picture of Kai and the blonde again. It's only a picture of their backs, but I can tell the girl is beautiful, with her hourglass shape and mermaid hair. Most likely a model.

The doorbell rings.

"That must be your English professor," my mother sighs. "I heard you ditched your classes yesterday, and I don't want that happening again. Do you understand? We pay a lot of money for those people, and you might as well get some use out of them."

I spend the rest of the afternoon blankly staring at *The Merchant of Venice* on the dining room table. It might as well have been in a completely different language. That night, I eat dinner alone. Mostly, I just stare at the food in front of me and push it around the plate. Rory is off today. She will be off a lot in the next few weeks leading up to the election if my parents are out of town. With my parents out of the house, there won't be a reason for Ilan to have extra staff around.

I set down my fork. It clatters against the plate, echoing through the house.

Everything is eerily still, even though I'm never alone at the house. There are always maids and house attendants in and out. Security works around the clock, but it's still unnerving, especially knowing The Revealed can slip past them. This house is too big for just a few people. We can't make up for all the empty, dark space.

One hundred eighty-eight days.

I go to my room and get ready for bed, fumbling as I take off my earrings. I'm about to pull my shirt over my head to change into pajamas when I hear a shifting noise. The self-defense reflexes Elias taught me kick in, and I whirl around to fight. There's a shadow on the opposite side of the room, and I'm still standing with my fists raised. The silhouette is leaning, staring out at the balcony. His back is turned on me, his hands buried in the pockets of his jeans.

I relax. At least, a little. A new tension sets in over my body.

I wait for him to turn, as I know he will.

He stares at me for a long moment, our eyes connecting.

"Sorry, I …," he waves to the pajamas still on my bed in explanation for why he'd turned his back to me.

That's all I get? Embarrassment at almost changing in front of him is the last thing on my mind. We have bigger issues.

Should I be angry? Do I have a right to be angry? Should I run into his arms? Should I run away? Call security? Dumbfounded, I just stand there like a dope, fiddling with the hem of my shirt.

There's something different about him. Something has changed. I can see it in him. He doesn't look at me the same way. The fire in his eyes is gone.

"Are you here to tell me you don't want to see me anymore?" I keep my words stoic, strong. I keep the hurt out of my voice, but it lingers inside me.

He doesn't answer.

"What do you want?" My blood spikes with frustration. He just stands there looking at me. I fill my lungs with air to calm my nerves and shut my eyes tightly. "Can you please just leave?"

His voice is low but clear. "I came here to explain." There's distance between us. Miles of it.

I ball my hands at my side. "Spare me. I get it, Kai. I saw the magazine cover."

"It was a *tabloid*, Lily. You of all people should be smarter than that."

"And the fact that you've been ignoring me until now? Is that somehow the tabloid's fault too?"

His jaw tightens. "No."

"That's all I need to hear."

I'm about to turn my back, but the way his eyes narrow makes me pause. His expression looks pained. He seems hurt. He continues staring at me through the darkness. He's holding himself so stiff and strong, but I almost wonder if he's really about to collapse. He's always seemed so tough to me. Physically, he is. And mentally as well. But now, there's something different.

"What happened to you?" My voice barely breaks the silence.

"I'm sorry, Lily," he says, "I'm so sorry."

Without even thinking, I move to him, wrapping my arms around him. It seems like the natural thing to do. He grips tightly, either pulling me closer or pushing me away. I can't tell.

"I'm sorry," he says again. He rests his head against mine. "You don't know."

"Kai, if something happened. You can tell—"

He presses his finger softly to my lips and pulls my chin back so I'm looking up into his gold-green gaze. Electricity runs through me all the way to my toes, and I hate that I respond to him this way. I hate that my heart is beating like crazy. His thumb traces across my mouth and he replaces his fingers with his lips. His touch is light, but I press against him. He laces his hands through my hair and pulls me closer. His mouth crushes against mine, and it's suddenly so desperate. I wrap my hands around his shirt. His hands bunch into my hair. Our bodies are flush against one another, and his heat keeps away the chill in the room. But just as soon as I think that maybe everything is okay, he pulls away and untangles his hands from me. He walks to the window so we aren't touching at all.

"What happened to you?" I ask again, trying desperately to make sense of this moment. "Did someone hurt you?"

"No." His gaze brushes past me as though that one word is a sufficient explanation.

"I want to understand, Kai." I want to be close with him like before. Those feelings are there. The need to be close to him is there, but it's edged with confusion and pain.

His expression has darkened again. "You can't. I need time."

"Time?"

"Away."

"Kai—"

He brushes me off and moves back toward the balcony, slipping off over the ledge and climbing to the ground before I have a chance to say anything else. I watch his shadow until it disappears into the darkness.

CHAPTER THIRTEEN

My tutor, Mr. Shieh, sits with me in the dining room.

I tap my pen and glance at Jeremy, who stands by the entryway. Ever since the car bombing attempt, he hasn't left my side except to sleep. Now that my parents have left on their final leg of the campaign, I don't even think he sleeps.

Mr. Shieh grabs my pen, halting the drumming rhythm I'd been beating against the table.

I mutter an apology and hunker down for the remainder of the lesson, watching as halfway through, Jeremy slips from the room. This is his usual pattern. My tutoring is the only chance he has for a break. I was counting on the fact that he'd follow this routine.

I close the book and Mr. Shieh sputters to a halt. "I'm sorry." I tell him. "I'm suddenly not feeling well."

Mr. Shieh gives me a knowing look, "You've already played that card this week, Ms. Atwood."

Yeah, well, I need to make it work again.

"Right," I tell him. "But this one is actually kind of an emergency."

He eyes me warily.

"You know," I scramble for an explanation and hit on the only one he can't, or won't, argue with, "girl things...."

Mr. Shieh just raises an eyebrow.

"Time of the month...." I make a face that I hope displays my awkward embarrassment.

Mr. Shieh's eyes light up in the way I knew they would.

"Well then," he closes his book as well. "I suppose it won't do any harm to just pick up tomorrow."

It won't do any harm to never study again. Since life as I know it is nearly up anyways thanks to The Revealed.

I do feel bad for sneaking around like this. Jeremy has been really good to me, but I can't just stand by and study politics while my world crumbles around me.

As soon as Mr. Shieh closes the door behind him, I go for the keys to the car, then sprint off down the walkway toward the garage. I wave to a few of the guards on patrol, who greet me kindly and without suspicion. The patrols haven't been as alert and prying lately since my mother has grown more lax on letting me leave the grounds.

I wish I could take the Aston. It isn't like my father ever drives it. But I only have access to the keys for the SUV Jeremy drives, so that's my only option. Jeremy's car is equipped with an automatic gate key, and the patrols glance just long enough to recognize the license plate as I exit the property.

I open the sunroof to feel the breeze. It's a crisp day outside—almost too chilly for me to have the sunroof open, but the wind makes me feel free.

I pull up to the Capitol Building parking lot and walk up to my father's office without anyone questioning my presence. Most of them recognize me.

Tracy is sitting at her desk reading a tabloid on her computer. Kai, looking windblown and rugged on the street, is in full focus across the screen. I try not to focus on the picture—another one with the blonde. "Oh!" she jumps up when she sees me. "Lily! What are you doing here?"

"I think I forgot one of my school books inside when I saw my dad last week," I say, acting desperate, "and I need to have it read before my class tomorrow. Do you mind if I go in and take a look? It would really help me out. You can call my dad if you need to."

"Oh," Tracy waves me off, "not a problem. It's not like you're a member of The Revealed or something," she chuckles. "Go on in."

"Thanks," I sigh with mock gratefulness, "I'll just be a minute."

I walk inside the office and then peek back around the corner.

Tracy has gone back to her computer. As soon as I'm sure she isn't going to come in after me, I turn to my father's desk and begin rifling through his papers.

I want information on Kai, like where he was stationed for his mission. Something happened while he was gone. There is a reason he's acting so strange. If he isn't going to tell me, I'll figure it out on my own. My father knew that Kai was back home before it was announced publicly, which means he looked into the case. He has to have the records somewhere.

I look under the random folders on his desk. I flip through the stacks of papers in the drawers. No luck. I place my hands on my hips and scan the room, glancing at the door. I'm running out of time. I poke my head around the corner again, just to make sure. Tracy is still sitting at her desk. But it won't be long before she'll get curious and come investigate.

My eyes scan the room again and rest on the computer at my father's desk.

Of course! He probably didn't have a hard-copy document delivered to him. Services like that are expensive and less efficient. He would have simply shot an email to the right department and received word back electronically.

The computer is off. It takes a moment to boot up. I settle into my father's cushy desk chair. Immediately a prompt for the password pops up. A password I don't have a hint about. But I'm his daughter, so I figure I may have a shot at guessing.

I try Mark Atwood.

It doesn't work. Then I try my mother's name, then mine. Each is incorrect. I try all sorts of combinations. All our first names. Just our last name. Capitalized. Not capitalized. Birthdays, my mother's maiden name, phone numbers. Hopefully there isn't an alert set up on this computer if someone tries to log in and fails too many times.

Finally, I try the last thing I can think of: president.

The computer takes me to the main page.

I should have known.

I open his email and find all the messages he received on the day Kai returned home. There isn't anything related to the military in his file. I go back to the date when Kai left.

And there it is.

From a General Colin Solemn. It's a form document, which I open.

"Lily?" Tracy calls from outside.

I jump, and my knee slams into my father's desk.

"Sorry Tracy!" I call, "I can't find it." My eyes prick with tears and I rub my knee. Ouch.

"Well, it's almost six, and I'm usually out of here by five thirty."

The sun is already setting. I check the clock, 5:57 p.m.

"It's no problem," I call back, "I'll just have to do without it."

As I talk, I quickly scan over the form. The date when Kai left home. The date of his expected, now confirmed, return. And then the purpose of the mission.

There's a shuffle outside as papers are folded and drawers are closed. Tracy is pushing away from her desk.

As fast as I can, I click *PRINT* and shut the computer down. The document just finishes sliding out of the printer when Tracy sticks her head inside.

"Ready?" she asks, purse in hand.

"Of course," I say, nodding. "I was just looking around his desk because I thought maybe he found it lying around."

"Oh, I remember those days." Her eyes soften with the memory. "Before the war of course. High school was brilliant."

As I walk around the desk, I slip the paper from the printer and shove it into my bag while Tracy is daydreaming. She shakes her head, clearing the memory. My eyes go wide as I wait for her to speak, terrified she saw me pull the document out of the printer.

"Enjoy your youth while you've got it," she advises. If she did see, it didn't register enough to raise suspicion. Tracy closes the door behind me and locks it securely—too excited the day is done to worry about me.

The roads being what they are these days, traffic getting home is horrible. By the time I get back to my house, it's dark outside. It gets dark so early now that summer is over. It isn't even seven yet. At least I have time to go over the form I printed at my father's office. Just before I reach the phalanx of the security cameras, I pull the car over onto the dirt shoulder. I smooth out the crinkles in the paper on my steering wheel. Using the light of my phone, I scan over the document.

NORTH AMERICAN SECTOR GOVERNMENT MEMORANDUM
FOR OFFICIAL USE ONLY

ANY UNAUTHORIZED REPRODUCTION OR DISTRIBUTION OF ENCLOSED DOCUMENTS IS TREASONOUS AND WILL BE PROSECUTED TO THE HIGHEST DEGREE ALLOWABLE BY LAW.

Mission: OM05386
Location: Wasteland of Texas, 31°59' N, 102°4' W
Purpose: To identify active headquarter location(s) for The Revealed.
Description: Cell traffic and eyewitness sightings of The Revealed suggest they enter through the southernmost area in the North American Sector (NAS) colonies. Analysts believe that their headquarters are located within easy access of the sector, probably established in the once-heavily populated wastelands.

The military has established a series of missions aimed at pinpointing the location of The Revealed. The government is hopeful that these missions will conclude with the successful arrest and capture of the terrorist members of this organization.

Refer to document OM02674 for a detailed list of all intended missions. Status report to follow upon completion.

I read it again. Then again.

The mission Kai was sent on concerned The Revealed. He was trying to find out where their location was in the wastelands of what used to be Texas. But what does that mean? Did he find them? The document doesn't say anything about whether or not the mission was a success.

This document only gives me more questions. These aren't nearly the answers I'd hoped for.

Does that mean Kai will leave again?

I press my forehead into my hands.

My eyes drift to the gate, which I can see only because I left my headlights on.

My heart skips. There is a black note taped to the fence.

I stare out at the darkness around me. The security guard stand at the gate is dark. Where is everyone?

The Revealed could still be here.

It was a stupid move to be out this late. I've made myself an easy target. In the darkness, I'm vulnerable.

Are The Revealed just beyond the road, waiting? There are thick trees on either side of me, chilled with frost from the night air. I imagine dark shadows waiting for their moment to strike as I sit helplessly, just watching through my window.

My doors are locked, but what does that matter against The Revealed? Sitting in my car is the worst thing I can do. I'm easy prey in this small space with a seatbelt latched around my waist.

The SUV has an automatic gate opener, but it's not working. I have to get out of the car to punch in the gate code. Either I sit here and wait for them to attack, or go for the gate and try to get out of here.

I turn the headlights off.

"Just do it then!" I growl at my cowardice.

My eyes adjust to the darkness. Everything around me is shadowed.

"One … two …," I grip the door handle of the car, "… three!"

I throw open the door and jump from the car, sprinting to the keypad, I type in the code … still nothing. Placing my back against the fence so I can watch the forest behind me for movement, I grab at the note beside me, ripping it off the gate and tearing it open. The note contains one word:

Run

Someone reaches through the bars of the gate and grabs my shoulder.

CHAPTER FOURTEEN

I scream, scrambling to pull away with all my might as the hand latches on.

Zero days. Zero days until I'm dead.

Panic claws at me even more painfully that the fingers through the gate.

"Lily, Lily!" Jeremy holds up his hands. "Geez! What do you think you're doing?"

I turn to find him staring at me on the other side of the gate, confused.

My heart pounds. My body shakes from the sudden dose of adrenaline. And then the relief rushes through me so quickly that my head spins.

"You just took off on me like that!" he says. "Do you want to get caught? When will you learn… ?"

All I can do is stare at him. My heart is still pounding so loudly, and I'm gripping the black note like it means life or death—it just might.

"Why don't you come inside?" Jeremy suggests.

I nod, shivering in the cold, and get back in the car. It takes me a moment to recover. I collapse my face against the wheel.

Jeremy manages to open the gate and gets inside the car with me. We drive down the road and around to the garage.

As I turn off the ignition, Jeremy holds out his hand and says, "Keys."

I give them over. "Sorry about lying to you this afternoon and sneaking off."

"We all tell lies now and then."

"Yeah, well, g'night." I head toward the house.

"Why don't you come to my place for a bit?" he offers. "I could make some tea? Maybe put on a movie?"

I look back over my shoulder at the still, vacant mansion behind me. With the fall frost, it seems like something out of a *Dracula* movie.

"Okay," I say, grinning. "That sounds great."

Jeremy's quarters are small compared to the mansion next door, but much homier. I would rather live in a place like this. He has a fire going, and above the mantle, a mirror reflects the warm light of the room. Papers are strewn on the kitchen table—things like bills and other letters.

He puts a tea kettle on the stove and then joins me in the living room, sitting across from me. I hand him the note over the coffee table.

"They're just taunting you," he says, crumpling it up. "No one's on the property that isn't supposed to be. Security would have seen them. It's okay." Jeremy twists to the side and raises his arm slightly, showing me the gun holstered at his side. "Security doesn't just walk around helplessly."

This I know.

It still doesn't comfort me.

I just stare back at him.

"Maybe I should call someone or something," I say, my voice unsteady, "just to be safe."

"Would it make you feel better to talk to your parents?"

"No." They probably won't even answer if I call anyway.

Deep breaths. I focus on my breathing, counting each inhale for five seconds.

Still, I'm shivering, and goose bumps run up and down my body. This feeling has become familiar to me—the fear that jolts through me whenever I see one of their notes. The anxiety stays with me, and I don't remember what it's like to live without it.

"You want to talk about it?" Jeremy asks, snapping me out of my trance.

"Not really," I shake my head.

"You can talk to me, you know." Jeremy leans forward, resting his elbows on his knees.

"There's not much to tell."

"What about that boy you were seeing? Kai? He's back, isn't he?" he asks. "Are you still talking to him?"

"It's complicated."

"Well, I worry about you," he admits. "I don't trust that kid. He was the one that leaked those photos of you to the papers wasn't he?"

My gaze snaps to him. "No," I say. The response comes so instantly, but truthfully, I'm still not sure. Jeremy is right to have his suspicions. It's too easy to trust Kai even though I know there's another side to him—the side he hides from me. I have to try and separate my emotions from the situation. I should be wary.

"Why do you want to know about Kai?" I ask Jeremy.

"Just curious." He relaxes back into his chair. "You've been different since you met him. I think he's manipulating you, Lily. I really do think you should be careful."

A shrill whistle comes from the kitchen, and I jump at the noise.

"Tea's ready," Jeremy grins and goes to fetch it from the kitchen.

I glance at the mirror above the fireplace and try to comb through the tangles in my hair with my fingers, playing with the strands so I don't look so disheveled. My gaze is strained. I look tired—exhausted, even.

I rub my eyelids, and pull open a drawer in the coffee table, searching for some tissues. I push the papers aside until I realize they aren't papers. They're pictures.

I freeze, my fingers just resting on top of one.

There's a realization.

I'm in them.

And confusion.

I shuffle through the snapshots.

One of me driving the silver Aston Martin out of the gates of our house. One of me standing in the fields with Kai. It's an original copy of the picture from the magazine cover. One of me standing in front of Elias's gym. Then one of just my car in Elias's parking lot. Something with wires is strapped on the bottom, next to the left front tire. It's a bomb. This is a picture of the bomb that almost killed me. I throw the image down as though it burns my skin, feeling the need to get far away from all of it.

The pieces fall into place.

It's Jeremy.

Jeremy's a member of The Revealed. And he's trying to kill me.

Worse, I'm alone with him.

I drop the pictures and begin backing toward the door just as Jeremy walks out of the kitchen with two cups of tea in his hands.

I tense.

He looks at me, then the pictures on the floor, then back at me. His eyes narrow with understanding.

Calmly he sets the tea aside. "You just had to go snooping," he says, and sighs. "Well, this isn't exactly how I'd planned for the night to go, but I suppose we'll have to speed things up."

He reaches into his back pocket, and I don't wait to find out why. I unlatch the door and sprint from the house. I'm not a runner, but the adrenaline propels me.

A camera is positioned just before the entrance of the house, and I stop in front of it, waving my arms wildly to try and alert the other security guards on duty.

Jeremy laughs behind me. "Don't bother," he says smoothly. "I gave them the night off. Figured they could use the break."

I look back over my shoulder. He's close. His expression so easy and relaxed that it sends shivers down my spine.

I sprint inside the main house.

Everything is pitch black, and it takes a second for my eyes to adjust as I scramble around in the darkness. I make it to the end of the hallway leading into the kitchen. It's deserted. More than ever, it feels like no one lives here. Abandoned and quiet. Everyone is gone. Jeremy has been planning my murder for months. It's perfectly plotted—just what you'd expect from The Revealed.

My hands fumble around in the darkness, searching for a weapon. What did Elias teach me? Stay low. Get something to defend myself with. Run if I can. If not, fight. Don't be the prey for the predator. Fight back. The house stretches with stillness. And I am the beacon of sound, my shuffling along the floor echoes throughout the empty house. My small frame seems so lumbering and unskilled. Every step is an alert. I have no doubt Jeremy will reach me, and once he does, there are thirty acres of land surrounding me—a long distance for a scream to travel.

The moon doesn't provide more than a soft glow through the windows.

I huddle in the back corner of the kitchen, behind racks stacked with pans.

My hands fumble for the phone in my pocket.

Nothing else moves.

There's only one person I can call.

One other person I know who can afford a phone and is in Capitol City.

The dialing rings sound so loud in my ear as I wait for him to answer.

There is a click.

"K-Kai …," my voice shakes so badly that I can hardly speak.

"Lily!" He hears the terror in my voice. "Lily, where are you!"

"I'm—Jer!"

A shadow appears in front of me and I scream. In my panic, the phone falls from my hands. Before I can move, Jeremy's in front of me, shoving me to the ground. I slide across the floor, scrambling to get away.

"Why are you doing this?" I scream at him as he pins me beneath him.

Jeremy kneels over me, slipping his hands around my throat and squeezing.

He's so calm. "It's too easy, really. I kill you. Westerfield kills your father." He applies more pressure, and I scramble against his hold, hands flailing, trying to push him off. "We blame your death on The Revealed. We blame your father's death on the Eastern

European Sector. The world turns to us as the heroes. Like taking candy from a baby."

I choke and spots begin to dance in my field of vision.

Westerfield? He's working for Westerfield?

Not The Revealed.

"Roderick Westerfield used your family like pawns, and now you're all going to die. I've spent years following your bratty ass around, and finally it's all worth it."

Self-defense.

What did Elias teach me?

Kai.

I remember the first day when we were in class. Don't turn around. Swing forward and kick. The elbow is the strongest. Take the attacker by surprise. For a fraction of a second I allow my body to relax on the floor, giving in to Jeremy's hold. It's enough to make him think he's won.

It's all I need.

I press my chin down, loosening his hold so I can breathe and throw my fist up, connecting with his stomach.

It isn't enough to break his grip, but it's enough to distract him. I latch on to his wrists and press down against the veins, squeezing his pressure points until the pain is too much and he loosens his grip. As soon as he starts to let go, I grab one of his arms with both hands and twist his wrist around until I hear a snap. The sound makes my stomach lurch, but there isn't time to think about it. If I stop now, I'm dead.

Jeremy bellows, swears, and recoils. His wrist lies limply, and he's screaming in agony, cradling the broken joint with his other hand. I scramble from underneath him in a crawl.

But he attacks once more, latching onto my foot with his uninjured hand. I stumble. With his strong grip, he pulls himself toward me, trying to pin me to the ground again. I kick off his hand, push myself up, and manage to run, though he's close behind. A broken wrist doesn't stop him from running. If he has as much adrenaline coursing through him as I do, he won't feel the pain anyway.

I wildly sprint into the foyer toward the front door. I yank on it, but it doesn't budge. Jeremy's footsteps are heavy down the hall. One after the other, getting closer.

My hands are shaking so much that I'm fumbling with the locks. Finally, I give up and run upstairs.

I race down the hallway, pushing myself even though my muscles burn. The house is dark. All I see are shadows dancing on the walls. I grip the door frame of my room and push my way through. I don't know how far away Jeremy is. But I don't hear anything. The house is silent, though it feels deadly instead of peaceful.

I pick up the phone on my desk, but there's no dial tone, of course. My cell phone is somewhere downstairs, abandoned while I was trying to stop Jeremy from strangling me.

I need a weapon. Something to protect myself. I fumble around in the darkness, feeling for anything I can use. My eyes flit between my searching hands and the doorway. I try to stay as quiet as possible, but I'm shaking too much, rattling everything I touch: makeup, cans of hair spray, brushes.

I move to the side of the dresser, feeling my way around until the shadow in the doorway stops me cold.

He moves slowly toward me, still keeping his smug composure despite his broken wrist. The Jeremy I knew is gone, replaced by this monster that was hidden under the surface all along.

I grab for anything on the dresser. Perfume. Lotion. Not very effective weapons, but I try anyway, throwing the bottles at him, hoping I will at least distract him. All the while I'm backing up toward the window.

The balcony doors are unlocked, and I push them open, heading toward the railing.

"You're making this too easy," Jeremy says. Ghostly moonlight hits him as he steps outside after me. "I push you over the edge and you're done." He leans to grab me, and I barely skirt out of the way.

"Jeremy, listen." I try to reason with him, holding up my hands. "You … you don't have to do this. M … my … family will give you whatever you want."

"No!" he yells so loudly his voice echoes. "Your family is worthless. Roderick Westerfield is the one who has what I want, and all I have to do is get rid of you. Enough with the games." Jeremy pulls out his gun—the gun he was given to protect me. "I didn't want to resort to this. But you haven't really left me a choice, have you?" He cocks the gun.

And I stop thinking.

Thoughts take too much time. All I can do now is react.

I reach out for the weapon, grabbing hold of his arm and yanking the gun aside as the shot rings out.

Then I run.

Back down the hallway, down the stairs, to the front door.

I look back over my shoulder.

Jeremy is running at me with such feral anger it pierces the darkness. He raises the gun again.

My fingers shake as I undo the locks.

A bullet zings next to me and hits the door. I yelp—a pathetically helpless noise, and manage to throw open the door and run outside.

I swallow the pain in my throat. I'm wheezing, struggling to breathe.

Jeremy is still behind me, but I don't have time to look. My heart is beating so franticly I can't hear anything.

I glance over my shoulder and stumble. My ankle twists and pain shoots up my leg.

My fingers dig into the soil as I try to pull myself up. My leg is on fire.

Jeremy catches up and steps in front of me, and I hear a gun cock. "Think of it this way, Lily. At least your death will actually do something significant—something you wouldn't know anything about."

My body tenses.

The gun blast echoes.

Tears stream down my cheeks.

There is no pain.

Something hits the dirt next to me.

Hands reach out to me, picking me up and pulling me close.

"It okay." Kai's voice is soft against my ear. "It's okay. You're alright."

I glance up at him and then across the grass where Jeremy's body lies in a motionless heap.

"He's dead," Kai assures me.

A sob escapes my throat, and I bury myself in Kai's chest, shaking, still so afraid.

"Let's get you out of here, okay?"

I nod against his chest and he picks me up, cradling me in his arms and carrying me to his car. He sets me down in the passenger seat and turns the heat on. Still, I am shivering. Tears slide down my cheeks, and I don't have the energy to wipe them away.

"What?" I force a hysterical grin as Kai gets in next to me. "You're not going to let me drive?"

"Not tonight."

We pull back out onto the main road. I assume he's taking me to his house. Instead, he turns in the opposite direction. Probably toward the hospital.

I just want to get away from this nightmare.

I close my eyes and sink into the seat. When I shut my eyes all I see is Jeremy's face and his hands around my neck, intent on wringing the life out of me. I moan and try to steady my breathing.

Gently, Kai cups his hand over mine.

It works to calm some of my nerves, though I'm still rattled, and my ankle is throbbing.

"I'm going to take you somewhere safe, okay?"

I nod.

It's probably best that I'm going to the hospital anyway. My ankle is definitely hurt, maybe broken, and my throat burns from Jeremy's hands.

"What happened?" Kai asks.

"He was making me some tea. I found pictures in a drawer— pictures of everything. He's the one who leaked that story about us to the press. He's the one that put the bomb under my car. Kai," I say, glancing up at him to gauge his reaction, "he's working for your father. Your dad's planning on having my parents assassinated."

Kai's eyes narrow, but he stays very still.

I follow his gaze out along the road.

"How did you get to me so quickly?" I ask.

He lets the question hang in the air.

Suddenly, I realize where we are.

The fields.

"What are we doing here?" I ask. His actions don't make any sense. And he won't talk to me. I just want him to tell me what's going on. Maybe he's lost it? This could be some sort of creepy post-traumatic stress disorder from his mission, and he's lost all rational thinking.

He comes around to my side of the car and picks me up.

"Kai—"

"It's okay." His voice is rough but gentle.

He carries me toward the center clearing.

"Kai?" I expect him to tell me what's going on, but he's silent. He doesn't even look at me. "I think maybe someone should look at my ankle," I say uneasily.

He pushes through the tall blades of grass, making his way to the center. The dusty smell of dried earth fills my nose, and I cough.

"What's going on Kai?" The panic begins to rise again. "Just put me down, okay?"

He doesn't.

And I'm not in a position to put up a fight.

He sets me down when we get to the middle of the circle, but he keeps his arm wrapped around me so that I can stand despite my ankle.

The night air is sharp and cold, and I'm shivering from the chill and leftover adrenaline.

"Kai, you're freaking me out," I say, staring around the clearing. "Will you at least say something?"

He shakes his head. "Lily, nothing's like we thought. All of it's a lie."

"What's a lie?" I ask hesitantly. "I know what your father is planning. I don't blame you, okay? Just take me back. I need a doctor."

This isn't right. My skin is crawling, my legs are twitching with a need to flee.

"I want to go back, Kai."

He stares out at the opposite end of the clearing, and I follow his gaze.

My eyes narrow, and then I hear it.

Something slaps through the stalks.

Swap. Swap.

Like dominoes falling, coming closer and closer.

Finally a wind breaks into the clearing, pushing me, knocking me.

And then I see them.

Shadows come through the stalks one by one in their inky black outfits, in perfect stride.

I stare at Kai, the betrayal sinking in.

"No!" I try to tear myself away from him but he holds me still.

He won't look at me. I want to run, but he holds me tightly against his side. I push against him. "No!"

"Lily, you have to go with them," he tells me.

"Kai, what are you doing?"

"You have to trust me," he says.

A woman walks to the front of the group. She has striking blonde hair, which she keeps in a high ponytail. I remember her from the gala. Her eyes are deep blue. "It's okay, Lily," she tells me, holding out her hands, palms up as though she was in prayer.

"I won't go with you!" I desperately try to pry Kai's hand from my arm.

"This time, it isn't a choice."

I don't have the energy to run anymore. Even if I could break away from Kai's grip, I would only fall to the dirt. My ankle is too weak.

"Please don't do this, Kai," I beg, near hysteria. "Please just take me home. I just want to go home!"

"Hey." Kai cups my face between his hands.

"No." The word is hardly more than a whine and I keep crying, wishing this is all just a bad dream.

I feel someone place a hand on my shoulder, quickly followed by a sharp pinch on my forearm.

The world falls away, until all that's left is green and gold, then blackness.

CHAPTER FIFTEEN

The sound of wind beats in my ears, echoing around me.

The noise grows steadily louder and louder until it's a scream inside my head. It blurs together, screeching around me, and instead of a steady pitch it breaks with an explosion.

I blink my eyes open and white light floods my vision.

The wind stops abruptly.

Everything is silent. Nothing moves around me. My eyelashes brush against one another as my vision adjusts. A soft, steady beep catches my attention, breaking the silence, and I turn my head in the direction of the sound.

I'm losing my hold on the place in my mind where I was before. It's slipping, and I don't want it to leave. I want to go back.

My eyes open. Instantly they are flooded with color. It's too bright. Vivid color reflects off every surface.

"Where am I?" my lips try to form the words, but they end up a jumbled mush, slurred together incoherently.

No one answers. My eyes open more easily the next time. A shadow looms overhead, blocking the light; when it moves, the colors flicker against my pupils. Why isn't the color going away? I don't remember anything looking like this before. It's harsh and bright and overwhelming.

I continue staring at the light, trying to focus on the rainbow in front of my eyes. Eventually, I see it isn't a rainbow, but more a kaleidoscope, the light shattered and reflected as it would be through a lens, the colors bold and clear. So strikingly clear that it hurts to look at, but I still want to reach out and touch the light, feel it between my fingers.

A shadow passes over me, and the light dances.

"Everything looks strange," I whisper.

"Don't worry," a friendly voice says, "everything is fine. Are you feeling any pain?"

I search my body. Arms. Legs. Chest. I try breathing. It comes easily. My eyes flutter once more.

"No." But I still see dancing, vivid shapes around me. "No, I don't feel anything."

I'm in a hospital, but I can't remember hurting myself. What do I remember last?

Nothing.

My mind is blank. White. Too bright.

"I'm going to ask you a few questions. Is that alright?" the female voice says.

I manage to nod, though I'm distracted with my memories—or lack thereof. It isn't that I forget. I just can't seem to pinpoint specific moments. I vaguely recall being in my father's office.

"What is your name?" the woman asks.

"Lily," I say, absently rifling through my thoughts. What's missing? I came home and it was dark out. There was a note taped to the gate.

"Lily what?" she asks gently.

Doesn't she know? She's a nurse after all. She's probably looking at my chart right now.

"Lilith Atwood."

And then there was a hand reaching through the gate.

"Where are you from?"

"Capitol City. I live in Capitol City."

"How old are you?"

Jeremy grabbed me and....

"I'm—"

I'm eighteen.

The memory slams to the front of my mind. I sit up straight.

I'm not at a hospital.

The blonde woman stands in front of me. Her features are so angular and jutting, they cut through the light like a knife.

I take in my surroundings. A white bed. Silver, stainless steel walls. Equipment hanging on clips around the room. It looks like a hospital, but it isn't. It definitely isn't.

I grab the dark shirt I'm wearing and my hand touches something raised on the fabric—the symbol with a lick of flame looped into a circle, crossed with a defiant X. The silver embossing contrasts sharply with the black outfit. I want to rip it—tear the fabric off me. "Get it off!"

"Lily, please just wait while I—"

I swing my legs over the bed and head for the door. My first step on my right ankle is tentative, but it's completely healed. I have no problem running. My heart pounds in my ears, and I have no idea where I'm going. I need to find an exit. The door leads to a maze-like network of hallways, and I blindly begin to sprint down one.

My mind spins as I try to gain some sense of place. There are no windows. All I can see are stainless steel walls. I continue running even when I can no longer breathe. I bump into a few people all clad in black uniforms along the way and shove past them. There are long stretches of hallways that turn in patterns. This place is a maze of white light and stainless steel.

I sprint into some sort of open room, like a banquet hall. The ceiling stretches above me, at least twenty feet high. There are rows and rows of tables, a few people milling around. Four hallways split off in opposite directions around the room. Between the hallway entrances are tall windows.

It's night outside.

I run to the closest window and throw my fists against it.

Instead of glass breaking, something cold seeps through my fingers. At first I think maybe the cold is the first sign of pain, and I've hurt myself. Instead, the cold continues to move through my veins, spilling out onto the glass.

I jerk my hand away and the ice melts instantly, dripping from my fingertips. I bring my hand only inches from my eyes and stare at it—more in horror than wonder.

Ice! Ice just came from my fingertips!

"I wouldn't do that if I were you, babe."

I spin on my heels.

"Rory! What are you doing here? When did they take you?"

She raises an eyebrow and saunters toward me. She's wearing the same black outfit with The Revealed's symbol sealed across her heart.

I notice there are other people in the hall, dozens of them, all dressed like Rory ... and me. They're staring at me with looks of pity. Some are giggling. They recognize me, and my face heats as I realize my current situation, and the display I just put on for them. I must look crazy. But then I correct myself. I'm not the crazy one. These people are The Revealed. *They're* the ones who should be embarrassed.

"Look back at the glass," she tells me instead of answering my questions. "Look up."

I stare back outside and can't see anything. The only thing I'm able to make out is a small streak of light cascading down. The moon? But why does it look so weird and refracted?

A fish dances across the glass.

At that moment, it hits me.

It isn't the moon.

It's the sun.

We are underwater. *I* am underwater.

I turn back to her. "Rory!" Everything sways around me. "Where are we? We have to get out of here!"

"Well, I can tell you're taking this *real* well," she snorts.

"You're—"

"A member of The Revealed?" In answer to her own question, she snaps her fingers, and a flame flickers over her hand. "Never would've guessed it, huh?" She grins excitedly.

I back away, pinning myself against the glass.

She shrugs and puts out the fire. "You'll get used to it." She pauses, looking me over. "Deep breaths."

I realize I'm panting, and my arms are shaking.

Behind Rory, the sharp-featured woman comes sprinting into the room. Her shoulders grow slack with relief when she sees me with Rory. "I'm glad you found her," she says, then turns to me. "Lily, like I said before, just give me a chance to explain. First of all, my name is Julia."

I keep my back pressed firmly against the window.

"No one here will hurt you," she promises, then waves a dismissive hand at everyone watching. "Break it up, people. You were new once too."

The people milling around the hall oblige and begin filtering back to tables to eat and talk, but I still see their quick and curious glances in my direction.

"Who are you?" I ask.

"She's kinda our leader," Rory says. "Everyone here is part of a team. There are no superiors and definitely no inferiors. We work together, but Julia has been here since the beginning. She knows the most about us."

"Us?" I demand, horrified.

"I'm not asking you to accept all of this yet," Julia says, "but I'd like a chance to explain."

"I just want to go home."

"Not exactly possible," Rory replies. "Trust me."

"I don't know who to trust anymore," I snap, shrugging away from her. "You take me here, mess with my head! That ice—" I point at the window, "came out of my fingers!"

Rory shrugs. "Pretty cool if you ask me."

"It's not normal!" I yell. "I want to go back."

A few people in the hall raise their eyebrows at me. Julia lifts her hands in a gesture meant to calm me down.

I put a hand on my head. What have they done to me?

"If you go back," Julia says, "Westerfield will kill you just like he's planning on killing your father."

That snaps some reality into me as I remember what Jeremy said. He was supposed to take me out, and Westerfield would handle my father. My stomach heaves.

"Lily, Westerfield's goal this entire time has been to start another world war," Julia explains. "He wants to take over the rest of the territories around the globe, and he'll get away with it if we don't do something to stop him."

"Westerfield? He's crazy but ... a murderer?"

"Your father's assassination will be set up to look like it's coming from the Eastern European Sector. If he can force them to surrender to the North American Sector, then it's only a matter of time before the others fall as well. He'll control everything."

"I don't believe you," I say firmly and look at Rory. She's supposed to be my best friend. How can she do this to me? She's been lying to me this whole time, working for The Revealed.

"You don't have to yet," Julia says. "Just listen."

"Fine." I cross my arms over my chest, waiting for her to start talking. It's not like I have many choices here. I'm at the bottom of the freaking ocean.

Julia nods. "Good. Follow me."

"I thought you were going to explain."

"And I will," she promises, and then beckons me to follow. I walk warily to her side. Julia places her hands behind her back, walking steadily with me through the stainless steel corridors. "About fifteen years ago, a group of researchers calling their organization The Revealed requested government funding to unlock the potential of the human mind. The lead scientist in the group, Anthony Roben, wanted to better understand why humans didn't utilize all of their brains. At a given time, in a normal person, only about ten percent of our minds are active. His theory was that by upping the percentage active at any moment, he would greatly expand human capabilities. Do you understand?"

I nod tentatively. I've never heard anything about this Anthony Roben or any secret experiments.

She continues, "His research lasted for two years before he discovered a breakthrough procedure he was convinced would change the world. The government refused to fund the program. The surgery was too risky. In order for the procedure to work, the subject had to be young enough that the brain wasn't fully matured, but old enough that the body could handle the surgery. Eighteen was chosen as the prime age, but no parents were just going to hand over their children to the government for testing. It wasn't possible. Dr. Roben knew he couldn't give up on this research, however, and so he went underground, experimenting in hiding. Eventually, he perfected the surgery with the help of volunteer subjects. His child was actually one of the first to undergo the procedure. Then, he was ready to make his results public. That was eight years ago. The war struck before he had a chance to share what he'd learned. Roben was killed during the war, but I was able to protect his records and continue on with his research. After the war, we discovered what Roderick Westerfield was planning and couldn't risk the information falling into the wrong hands. Instead, we continued recruiting new students with the hope that we could stop Westerfield and avoid another world war."

I glance down at my hands again. "But what does the surgery do?"

"The procedure is complicated. But in a nutshell," Julia says, smiling knowingly, "it expands the capacity of the mind, making it possible for humans to manipulate the elements. Fire," she snaps her fingers, sparking a small flame. "Wind," a breeze kicks up, blowing out the flame. "Earth," she grabs something from her pocket; a small seed began to sprout on her open palm. "And water," she places her empty hand on the stainless steel, and ice forms beneath her touch; the sprout in her other hand shrivels and crumbles through her fingers onto the gray counter.

I picture the lights going out suddenly at the gala, the glass shattering throughout the building, the winds that kicked up around my face. All of the rumors are true.

"After a while, and with more procedures, we found a trend. Only certain types of people can survive the surgery."

I cut in without thinking. "People died?"

"Sacrifices must be made. Something no one is proud of, but if it means we can stop Westerfield from forcing what's left of the world under his control, then it's all worth it."

"And that's worth all the kidnappings?"

"We're talking about another world war, Lily," she says, "but in truth, we aren't kidnapping anyone. No one is forced to stay. For that matter, I've never heard a student ask to leave once they understand. It has to be done this way. If we were to take the potential students in front of the whole world, we risk exposure and corruption. We have to keep ourselves hidden from the government, which is why our facility is underwater. If they found us, we'd all be dead."

The weight of her words hangs heavily on me. I'm not sure I believe any of it, but it doesn't seem to matter one way or the other. By now, the government will know I've been taken. The world will know it was The Revealed. Julia is right. I can't go home. Who knows what they'd do to me if they saw me? Whether I like it or not, they performed this procedure on me. I'm one of them now.

I snap my fingers like I saw Rory and Julia do.

No flame.

"It takes practice to control," Julia explains. "Let me show you to your room." She leads me down the west wing. "We have coed living quarters for our students—" Julia motions to the line of stainless steel doors in the hall, "but we expect all of our students will demonstrate the utmost respect for one another."

A spritely boy leaps from one of the rooms into the hallway before us.

"Watch out!" he calls. He throws his hand out, and a spark of fire reflects off the walls. The tiny ball of flames grows larger. Another boy, this one with a large build and curly short hair, follows the smaller boy into the hallway only seconds later.

The sprite throws his ball of fire into the air like it's a baseball.

I gasp.

The blaze explodes, and I duck away from it.

The curly-haired boy doesn't even flinch as he dodges the fire. It explodes and peters out against the wall. Now the stainless steel makes sense. He pulls something from his pocket, and it rapidly begins growing. It's green and twists quickly from his hand. Vines! He now holds a plant that snakes out toward the other boy.

"Romni!" Julia puts her hands on her hips.

The curly-haired boy folds his palm over the vines, and the leaves droop and turn brown.

"Sorry Julia," Romni says, shrugging. "We were just practicing."

"It was just a little fire," the blond boy says mischievously. "It wouldn't hurt anyone."

"Nero," Romni shoots back, "you nearly took off my arm!"

"Yeah right!" Nero rolls his eyes. "That orb was half the size of my usual ones!"

"Boys." Julia holds up her hand. "Classrooms are for dueling," she scolds lightly, "not the hallways. You're scaring our new student."

"Hey!" Nero's eyes light up. "You're Lily Atwood!"

He walks closer and sticks out his hand. "I'm Nero."

I don't take it. What if that spark thing comes out of his fingers again? He could burn off my whole hand!

He raises an eyebrow. "It doesn't work like that."

My shoulders tense.

"The fire," he clarifies. "We can control it."

"How did you …," I trail off, watching him skeptically.

Nero's lips curl into a proud grin.

Romni pushes Nero aside and smirks at me. "Don't mind him. He's a little stupid sometimes."

I look to Julia. She has one eyebrow raised at the boys.

"Alright, that's enough boys," she finally says. "She's overwhelmed as it is."

Nero lifts his hands in surrender and begins walking backward down the hall. "Fine, fine. We're going down to the dining hall to get food anyways."

"Lunch was two hours ago," Julia says.

"Exactly," Nero says, "I'm famished. See you later, Lily!" He grins before turning around.

Romni gives me a wink before running to catch up with Nero.

"Those two." Julia shakes her head.

I just stare at her, disbelief clouding my vision.

Julia takes me to a room at the end of the hall. It looks like the college dorm rooms from old movies, only a stainless steel version. There are two desks, each with a laptop on them. The beds are neatly made with colorful sheets. Drawers are set against the wall. One is cracked open, and I can see the dark pants inside. No doubt the other drawers are filled with folded black T-shirts as well. The Revealed don't seem to wear anything else.

I walk inside the room and move to the empty side, which I assume is mine. The other side is untidy. The bed isn't made and the laptop lies askew on a pillow. A black tank top is strewn across the desk.

"Surprise!" Rory pops her head in the door.

I jump.

"I'm your roommate," she says cheerfully.

"Roommate? I'm not staying here."

"What do you mean? You have to stay."

"No, I have to go warn my father. Roderick Westerfield is planning on having him assassinated, and someone has to get my parents to safety."

I stride to the door, but Julia is standing in the frame. "You need our help, Lily."

"I don't need anything from any of you." I can feel myself losing control of my emotions again. "I've spent the last six months thinking my life was about to end and now it's just, 'Surprise, join the club'? No way."

I push past her.

She follows. "You can't stop Roderick Westerfield on your own. You need help. His operation is much bigger than you think. He has a whole cadre of power-hungry people working on his side— almost as expansive as our organization. Warning your father makes him aware, sure, but it doesn't stop Westerfield. You really think your father is that blind to Westerfield's hidden agendas?"

I think about all the times my father warned me about Kai. He told me the entire family was rotten, not to be trusted.

"So what?" I spin on my heels and face Julia. She's taller than I am, but only by a bit. It's enough that I can hide how intimidated I am by her. "You want me to just stay here and do what exactly?" I manage to ask rather defiantly.

"We want you to train. You have abilities now. It's important you learn how to use them. We brought you here to keep you safe. But now that you are here, we want your help."

"And then? How do you save my father?"

"We stop Westerfield. He's planning his attack on Election Day. He wants to assassinate your father and make it look like the Eastern European Sector is to blame. We've been tapping his phone and his computer, but he's careful to use codes. He's paranoid and smart. We've cracked some of his code though. From what we can tell, he's going to have a sniper in the crowd on Election Day. He's been importing illegal arms—AK-47s, to be exact."

"So why don't we take him out now?"

"It isn't that simple. He knows we're after him. We have to be more clever about our tactics. He was originally going to conduct the assassination at the gala. We got there in time to stop him, but someone had tipped him off about our arrival before we got there. He'd fled the scene. Election Day is a time and a place he can't avoid. He has to be there so when the assassination takes place he won't be considered a suspect. This means he won't be able to flee the scene if we show up. And we'll finally have him."

"Are you going to kill him?"

"No. We'll hold him in custody until we can gather enough evidence to prove, without a doubt, his guilt. Then we'll hand him over to the proper authorities and let due process run its course. My guess is the justice system will be the death of him—either by rotting in a cell or by lethal injection."

"And his followers?"

"We'll take out as many of them as we can. We suspect once Westerfield is in custody, the others will disband on their own. We'll still be here to keep an eye on things though."

"So?" Rory asks hopefully as she comes out of the room. "Will you stay?"

I take a moment to think and realize it isn't enough. "I need time," I say, "to process all of this."

"We'll give you private quarters this evening," Julia offers.

"Thank you."

"No one will disturb you until you're ready to talk more. And I do hope you'll come to me with any questions you have. I suspect you will have quite a few."

CHAPTER SIXTEEN

The next morning, I find Rory in the dining hall. She pats the seat next to her, offering me the empty space, and I take it.

"How are you?" she asks. "Anything you want to talk about?"

I look around at the rest of the table; Nero and Romni sit across from us, as well as another girl with dark ringlet curls and chocolate skin. I'm not sure if I want to discuss my doubts in front of this crowd, all of them strangers, as well as members of The Revealed.

Rory waves it off. "It isn't anything they haven't been through."

"So I'm not the only one who's thought about leaving?"

The girl with the curls laughs. "Everyone thinks about leaving. It's a shock, suddenly being in this new place. You need time to adjust."

"Lily, this is Maya. Maya, Lily," Rory says.

The girl sticks out her hand, and I shake it.

"Nice to meet you," she says, and grins widely.

"You too," I mumble, still afraid one of them is going to zap my hand somehow. Like these niceties are just some kind of joke.

"Listen," Rory says, "you have to understand. None of us came from the background you do. Most of us lost everyone in the war. We were out of school, working in the factories. I was living on the street when The Revealed found me. Both my parents were dead. I didn't have anywhere to go. Everything but the clothes on my back had been destroyed by the war. I hadn't eaten in two days." Rory presses her lips together, the memory hard for her to recall. "I would have done something bad," she admits. "I was desperate." She looks away from me for a moment. "Being taken was the best thing that's happened to me. Yeah, I was scared. I thought they were evil just like everyone else. But Julia gave me a room and food. After time, I also found a family. I learned the mission and gained a purpose. Now I'm working for something good. I am someone good."

I take in everything Rory tells me. And after a long moment of silence, all I can say is, "Rory, I'm sorry. I didn't know."

"I didn't want you to. I don't like pity parties," she waves it off with a few flicks of her wrist.

"So I take it this means The Revealed isn't going to kill me."

Rory snorts and rolls her eyes, "Of course not."

"Well that's a relief, at least."

"Get something to eat," Rory tells me. "I want to show you something."

After shoveling eggs down my throat, I follow Rory into the east wing.

She takes me down an elevator to a basement that houses dozens of computers on desks. Next to them are shelves with rows of books, articles, and boxes, which I assume hold more papers. It reminds me of the libraries I went to with my mother before the war. A lot of books were destroyed in the war. Of course, there are still some bookstores and archives, but most information was placed in an online database that is accessible to everyone. This makes research much easier. Rarely do people—my father being an exception—keep collections like the one I am now looking at. It takes a lot of time and wealth to accumulate artifacts like these.

"Why is all of this here?" I ask, thumbing my hand across some of the loose papers.

"Evidence." Rory strides down one of the aisles, peeking into random boxes as she goes. "The government's tracking abilities are too strong for us to risk compiling our evidence online. Any information we want to store, we print out and organize here. That way, we don't run the risk that someone will discover us online and become suspicious of what we're doing."

Rory pulls out a few more boxes before finding the one she's looking for. She carries it to an empty table and takes off the lid. Inside are more papers.

"Here." Rory lifts a stack of pages and hands them to me. "Be careful to keep them in order though."

I look through them sheet by sheet. Some are emails, others pictures. There are even a few formal contracts, though I'm not sure how The Revealed got their hands on these.

How could Westerfield be doing this? My heartbeat pulses in my ears. I feel so many mixed emotions, but confusion and fear top the list. My whole world has been turned upside down in less than forty-eight hours. And to think, Westerfield is behind it all.

A breeze picks up, tossing my hair.

"Calm down, Lily." Rory places a hand on my shoulder, and after a moment, the wind around me dies. "You need to learn to control your emotions. Your abilities are connected closely with your mind. If you lose your focus, bad things could happen."

I created that wind!

I take a deep breath.

"Where did you get this?" I stare down at a transcript of a phone conversation between Roderick and Kai.

"Kai allowed us to tap his phone," she explains.

"He allowed you to tap his phone? How long has he known about you?"

"Since shortly after he left for his military assignment. They'd sent him to track us and gather information. We found him, showed him what we're showing you. The facts told him everything he needed to know. He agreed to help us."

"Why didn't you do the surgery on him, too?"

"It doesn't work like that," Rory explains. "The surgery isn't compatible with everyone. The mind needs to have susceptibility that's hard to describe unless you understand the procedure. I don't even understand it fully. But not everyone can survive. If performed on the wrong person, bad things can happen. Kai isn't a candidate for the procedure."

"But he's one of the strongest people I know," I say.

Rory smirks. "I'm sure he is, but it isn't about physical strength. It's something genetic, inherent. We can test for it using DNA sequencing. Usually we find a hair sample or a tossed paper cup. We track all of our potential members to ensure compatibility before they're taken."

"And Kai trusted you enough to let you take me?"

"Yes, but he also knew that if we didn't, his father would have you murdered. Jeremy wasn't the only one working for him. Kai did this because it was the only way to protect you."

My hands absently slide to my neck. I picture the gun in Jeremy's hand and shiver.

Rory answers my silent question. "His body was found the next morning. I'm so sorry, Lily. We had no idea Jeremy was working for Westerfield. I never should have left you alone in that house with him. We knew Westerfield was after you, but I never thought Jeremy could have been involved. I thought you were safe with him. We were more worried about Westerfield targeting your father at this point. We didn't know who was sending the notes. We knew they were coming from someone in the Westerfield camp trying to set us up, but I never in a million years would have guessed it was Jeremy. I'm sorry," she reaches out and touches my arm.

"It isn't your fault," I say.

She purses her lips and shakes her head. "Jeremy was trying to make you believe The Revealed were after you instead of Westerfield. That way, when he ... succeeded, The Revealed would be even more reviled. If you suddenly disappeared then it would be easily explained away. No questions. Plus, he controlled your trust. When he taped that note "Run" to the gate, where were you going to go? Of course, you'd turn to the head of security in your panic. He'd lure you in and then take your life, setting it all up to look like The Revealed."

"That's insane."

"Well," Rory continues, "along with your disappearance, the murder has been pegged on The Revealed. Just like Westerfield wanted."

"What? You were blamed for what happened?"

Rory shrugs, "We're used to it."

"How are we going to stop Westerfield?" I ask. "Do you have a plan?"

"Yes," Rory tells me, "and we'd like you to be a part of it now that you're here. We didn't want to take you like this. We wanted to avoid it if we could. But after everything that happened with Jeremy, we decided it was the safest move for you. I'm sorry you're caught in the middle of all this."

"What do you want me to do?" I ask.

"You have to learn to control your abilities. Right now, your mind is sensitive. The abilities are new to your body and unfocused. It could be even more detrimental to your family and the mission if we send you out there without the proper training. We have about two and a half weeks until the election. During that time, you'll train. Every day. If, at the end of it, we think you're ready, you can help us."

"If I'm ready? No." I shake my head. "I have to be there. My parents' lives are in jeopardy. I'm not just going to sit at the bottom of the ocean while you go up there."

"If you aren't ready, being there could cause more harm than good."

"No. No way. If you want me to even consider joining this band of vigilantes, you can't keep me down here on Election Day."

"I can't make that promise." Rory remains firm.

"I thought you said this was my choice." I feel my temper rising again.

"It is. You are welcome to go back to Washington and live in your father's shadow again. But I know that's not what you want. You have an opportunity for something great here. Lily, you'll get to travel the world and help people. Isn't that what you've always wanted?"

I don't answer. Because she's right. It is everything I want. Desperately.

Rory isn't done. "But if you're going to be a part of our mission, you have to be part of the team. Sending you up on land before you're ready doesn't just put your life at risk. You could risk *everything.* The mission could be compromised. Your parents could be hurt. The Revealed could be exposed. Not to mention the countless innocent lives that could be lost. I know you're worried about your parents, which means you can't think rationally about this situation. So I need you to trust me and the rest of The Revealed. We'll make the decision if you're ready."

"I don't know if I trust you," I tell her.

She looks taken aback, swallows, but then nods. "I hope you decide to."

"I'm trying." Ready to change the topic, I ask, "When do we start training?" Just because I haven't decided I completely trust The Revealed, doesn't mean I'm just going to sit here helplessly.

"Now."

We walk back upstairs. My presence draws whispers and stares as we pass people in the halls. Rory glares at them and shakes her head.

I watch them as we walk, unable to hear what they're saying.

Rory shakes her head and sighs, "I told them not to do this." She tries to be as casual and familiar as we once were. "But you're the hot new topic, babe. Everyone's curious about Lily Atwood."

"Great." I roll my eyes. The last thing I want is to attract attention.

"You're part of the family now." She grins. "The attention will die down."

"Do you even like to cook?"

She gives me a sidelong glance. "Sure. I just don't do it very well. Why do you think I was always asking for your help? The only reason I was there was to watch your back." Rory shivers. "The idea of you alone in that house. When we got the call from Kai saying he was going to get you, I was so worried. And out in the field ... you have to know Lily, it was never our intention to scare you. It definitely wasn't Kai's intention. Once he got back from his mission, he went back and forth on his decision. He really didn't know what to do with all this new information. He wanted to tell you, but was worried for your safety like the rest of us. He asked to meet with me several times before actually agreeing to go through with the plan."

"That's why he was acting strangely. And you were the woman he was photographed with in the magazines." It was all falling into place. I should have recognized Rory's blonde hair from those pictures.

So Kai wasn't dating a model. I stare at the ceiling and can't help the laugh escaping my throat. I allow myself to enjoy that one shred of good news.

"Yeah. It was really hard for him. It's hard for anyone to take in all of this information. Plus, no one wants to believe their own father is a murderer."

I think about the turmoil in Kai's eyes when he came to my room. It made sense now. He wanted to tell me everything that night. He wanted to keep me safe. All this time he'd been protecting me.

We walk into a gymnasium. It reminds me of Elias's gym, in a way. There are punching bags hung throughout the room, along with assorted workout equipment. A cool breeze hits my face from the large vents tunneling along the ceiling. It smells like plastic and sweat. But this gym is different. It's meant for people with unique abilities.

There are a few other people already working out. One snaps his fingers and repeatedly lights, then extinguishes the flame of a candle. The flame grows progressively larger and larger until it almost reaches the ceiling. I can feel the heat from where I stand. Others have lined random items against the far wall. They stand a measured length away and throw out their hands, freezing the items, melting them, and then repeating the process again from a greater distance. The last person in the room is standing in front of one of the bags; she doesn't touch it, just stares with intense concentration. I watch her for a moment. Her hands are resting at her sides. She takes a deep breath and throws out her palms. The bag flies back so forcefully that it makes me jump.

My fists ball at my sides in anticipation. My muscles twitch with the desire to move in that way, to control the world around me as they do. I resist the urge to reach out and try right away.

"She's using wind to increase her strength," Rory explains when she sees me staring.

"Ah, Lily." I jump again and turn to see Julia approaching. "Right on time. You're going to train with me today if that's alright?"

Rory takes a seat against the wall to watch. I wish she wouldn't. I'm already nervous enough without her staring.

Julia doesn't look like she's messing around. She holds a glassy ball in her hands. "This is what we call a training orb. It'll help you practice and learn to control your new abilities. Got it?"

"Okay," I say, but I'm not sure I am. What if I can't do this? Sure, I've done a few weird things since I got here, like creating that ice on the glass, but what if the procedure didn't work? What if I can't learn to control my abilities, and I'm some fluke of a failure? How am I going to get out of here to help my parents then?

Julia hands the sphere over to me.

"Now I want you to use wind to make the orb levitate," she instructs.

I stare at her for a moment, then down at the orb in my hand, then back to Julia. My stomach knots. Levitate? Is she crazy? She

192

watches me steadily. She fully intends for me to give this a shot. A helpless sigh escapes my chest.

"Just focus," Rory calls out.

My brow furrows as I stare at the tiny glass ball in my hand. I don't even know where I'm supposed to begin. I look hesitantly up at Julia again, and she nods encouragingly.

"Um," I stare down at the orb. "Float!" I command, and I think maybe it shakes a little.

Rory snorts and my cheeks flush. Julia glares at her.

"I'm sorry," Rory holds up a hand, not looking the least bit sorry with that dopey grin still plastered on her face.

"It doesn't work like that." Even Julia is smiling a little though. "The commands don't come from here," she points to my lips, "they come from here," her finger taps my forehead.

"So I have to think what I want? I *was* thinking about it."

"It's emotional, Lily," Julia lectures. "It's more than just a command. You have to feel it. When you move your arm, you don't say 'move.' It's intuitive. This is the same thing. You must simply feel what you want."

I'm not sure about what she's saying, but I focus again on the orb, wanting it to rise from my hand so badly that I start to feel frustrated. But glass orbs aren't supposed to float. If I snap my fingers, fire isn't supposed to appear. Lifting my hands shouldn't create wind. Having these abilities is counterintuitive. I can't do this. I don't understand. I drop my hand in resignation.

"You're thinking about this too logically," Julia says, her thin arm coming to rest against her hip. "Raise your hand again."

I hesitate as the frustration begins to rise, but do as I'm told.

"Now," she begins, "you aren't trying to make this orb float, alright? What you are doing is connecting with everything around you. Think of yourself as part of everything here." She waves her hand around the room. "This is not negative space. There is substance here whether you can see it or not, and you are going to grab it and use it just like you would move your arm. You know you can."

I take a deep breath and close my eyes.

"The human mind, through evolution, disconnected itself from the particles around it. It separated itself instead of being part of the whole. The surgery brings us partly back in tune with everything around us so we can utilize its potential while retaining our selfness. Does that make sense?"

"Kind of," I tell her.

"Feel it inside, not at your fingertips. Feel the warmth of it."

When I think of warmth, I think of Kai, and my heart aches. All this time, everything he's done has been to help me. When he handed me over to The Revealed, I assumed he was giving me over to the enemy. Instead, he was saving my life, and I can't even say, "Thank you." Rory told me it was too dangerous to communicate with the outside world. The Revealed send people directly if they ever need to communicate. With the surveillance technology available these days, there's no doubt the government would be able to track any calls or emails, and locate The Revealed's headquarters. So while I'm here, I am completely shut out from the outside world.

"Concentrate, Lily." Julia snaps me out of my daze.

My hand wiggles unsteadily and the orb falls from my grasp. It shatters on the ground, spewing glass around my feet.

"I'm so sorry," I blurt out, moving to pick up the pieces.

Julia waves me off. "Don't bother. Do you know how many broken orbs we've had? If you hadn't broken this one today, you would have made history. Why don't we move on to something else and get back to the orb tomorrow?"

We clean up the pieces, and then Julia guides me over to the candle where we practice fire skills until I manage to make the edges of the wax melt on command. I'm not quite at the point where I can create a real flame, but it's a start.

At the end of the lesson I'm exhausted, though Julia tells me I've done well. My body hurts as though I've run a marathon.

"Let's get some food," Rory says, taking my arm and leading me to the cafeteria. "You need to keep your strength up. If your body isn't alert, neither is your mind, and your abilities will suffer."

The dining hall is set up like a high school cafeteria. There are long tables in the center and round tables around the outside. The food line is run by a group of kitchen staff, all preparing fresh dishes. Behind the service counter I can see the kitchen. Chefs in black aprons work on a line that reminds me of my kitchen at home. The grill sizzles with meats and fish. The charred smell hits my nose. The air is circulated quickly in the building though. I've noticed how efficient the vents are, streaming in fresh air so smells are whisked away and replaced by others. Now I can smell potatoes in the fryer. Then the scent of something sweet after that.

Rory leads me past a full salad bar, stocked with four different lettuce options and over a dozen vegetables. My eyes light up with the myriad colors, from purple beets to orange carrots.

At the end of the cafeteria is a sandwich station. The sandwiches are displayed on top of the case, each labeled. Rory grabs a turkey sandwich on wheat bread. It's exactly the sandwich I want. She puts it on my plate knowingly. "It's important you always take care of yourself, otherwise you might get into a position where you temporarily lose your abilities due to lack of energy."

"Good to know." I take a bite of the sandwich.

"The food here isn't super-gourmet—nothing like the creations from Ilan's kitchen—but it's good," Rory continues. "We won't be spending a lot of time here though," she warns. "Most members are in and out. We're always going on missions around the world, helping out where we can. A group just went to the Western European Sector, actually. They're going undercover to help develop clean drinking water supplies. It makes a big difference when you can draw water out of the atmosphere with a flick of your wrist. We have to be discreet about it, though, otherwise people get suspicious. But we do what we can."

She finds a table and sits down. "Eat up," she pushes the tray closer to me until it nearly teeters on the edge of the table.

"We have less than three weeks until the election," Rory says.

And that hits home.

Time is running out.

I take a deep breath to steady my nerves, the weight of my decision bearing down on me. Nineteen days until The Revealed stops Westerfield, or I watch my parents get killed.

CHAPTER SEVENTEEN

The next morning I shower and put on the black pants and tank top, grazing my thumb along the silver symbol over my heart as I do.

Before I begin my training again, I sit in front of the computer, reading up on the election news coverage. By now, I am sure my father and mother have discovered I'm missing. But the media isn't reporting it yet. I picture Jet scrambling to come up with some sort of cover story. This is not the kind of press my parents need just before the election.

I can't help but wonder if they are more concerned about the press or the fact that their daughter has gone missing. Is Dad calling out the troops? Is Mom conspiring with Jet to keep my disappearance under wraps? Will they assume I've been taken by The Revealed? I have little doubt the answers to these questions are "yes."

And then my fingers find their way back to the keyboard, clicking open my email account. My hands hover over the keyboard. Where do I begin?

I'm breaking all the rules Rory laid out for me yesterday. No email. No texting. No phone calls. I must be cut off from the outside world. But surely that doesn't apply if someone on the outside already knows about our existence. Surely, there's an exception if that person on the outside is already helping The Revealed and supplying them with information.

I need news of Kai. I'm already desperate to hear from him. My body aches with the constant realization of his sacrifice for me. He is no doubt struggling to accept that his father is a sociopath. But in the midst of all that, he managed to save my life and ensure my safety. How can I be satisfied to just let that go without a word? I can't. I won't just leave him alone. He didn't leave me when I needed him the most. He has to know I'm here for him. I may be at the bottom of the ocean, but my thoughts and my heart are in his hands.

So I type out the email.

```
Kai,

    Has it really only been a few days? It
feels like only moments have passed and,
at the same time, an eternity if that
makes sense. The Revealed want my trust.
And I think the only thing that is
holding me to them, forcing me to
consider putting my faith in them, is
that I know you did. You threw
everything you knew away in order to
save my life so I can at least give them
```

```
a chance, can't I? Please tell me I'm
making the right decision.
    I know I shouldn't be writing. Rory
told me it's dangerous, but right now,
without you, I'm all alone. I don't know
how to do this on my own. I think about
you every second, and I need to know you
think about me too. I can't stand the
way we left each other.
```

There's noise in the hallways. I'm running late. My hands hover again before I sign off.

```
Always,
Lily
```

I click send before I lose the guts to.

Then I walk into the same gym I used yesterday and meet Julia and Rory, who are waiting for me.

There is a boy with them, and I stop when I see him. He's staring at me with these striking blue eyes, his stare intensified by his jet-black hair. His body is that of a fighter—lean muscles honed by months of training. He's young, maybe only a year or so older than I am, yet I'm intimidated.

He stands on the mats of the gym, stretching his lean muscle, throwing an arm over his head and swinging his shoulders around. I watch the way his limbs move so gracefully, fluid with every motion he makes. He's in touch with his body, every gesture controlled into a dance-like pattern.

His eyes never leave mine, though my line of sight goes from the padded mats, back to this boy, to the padded mats again. I know this setup. I've trained at Elias's gym and know what this means. My eyes search for the boxing gloves but I don't find any against the walls.

Julia is watching me from the sidelines with Rory, and her gaze tells me everything I need to know. She intends for me to spar with this obviously well-trained boy.

Are they crazy?

"Lily, meet Skylar." Julia beckons me forward.

They're crazy.

Then something weird happens. The boy's face suddenly turns a deep shade of red, in striking contrast to his dark hair. He straightens and sticks out his hand. "You have no idea what an honor it is to meet you."

Now it's my turn to blush. I shake his hand.

"Your father is my hero," he continues. "While I was still in the colonies, I planned on joining the military and then working my way up to politics. I've watched everything your family's ever done."

Rory pats Skylar on the shoulder. "Calm down, cowboy."

"Sorry," Skylar shakes his head with a grin. "I promised Julia I wouldn't freak out but meeting you is just ... you have to understand, your family is like, the hope for our future."

"Not my family," I try to shrug off my extreme embarrassment, "just my dad."

"Okay," Julia cuts in, and I'm grateful. "Let's get to it, shall we? Skylar's only been here for about eight months now, but he's already the best we have at hand-to-hand combat. You're going to try and pin him on the mats."

I cringe. I look back and forth from Julia to Rory. Julia's gaze is steadfast, and Rory's seems to say, *No, she's really not kidding.*

Rory backs away from the mat, signaling that my training is to begin.

I suddenly miss that damn orb.

"I'll go easy," Skylar promises.

I step onto the blue cushions that really don't feel like they'd soften a fall all that much. There's no way I'm going to be able to summon my abilities quickly enough to use them defensively. Flipping through my memories, I try to come up with a series of self-defense moves Elias taught me. I have a feeling this isn't going to be gentle.

Rory stands against the wall to observe. Julia puts her hand up between us so she can cue when we should start. Skylar situates himself across from me.

"Don't hold back." Julia eyes me. "Go!" She drops her hand and steps back.

Skylar leaps into action. He grips my shoulders, trying to pull me to the ground. This pairing doesn't exactly seem fair. I guess Julia knows that.

As Skylar jerks my body to the left, I grab his wrists and we topple over one another.

Immediately, he's back on his feet. A mischievous grin spreads across his lips.

He comes at me again.

I catch him just before he strikes me. His hand covers mine and instantly becomes so hot that it burns my flesh, and I yelp. Skylar takes advantage of my surprise and flips me onto the mat, knocking the air out of my lungs.

After heaving for a few seconds, I look over at Julia from the ground. "Can he *do* that?"

"Do what?" she asks innocently.

"Burn me like that!" I hold up my arm and show her the small welts rising across my forearm.

"Of course," Julia shrugs. "You're a member of The Revealed now. Your survival hinges on your ability to use the resources at your disposal."

"But I can't control them like he can yet," I argue.

She smirks. "Why do you think we're doing this? What better way to learn? This will catch you off guard. Haven't you realized that when your emotions—fear, stress, excitement—are built up, your abilities unconsciously emerge. That's what we're trying to replicate today so you can recognize it and control it."

I sigh and splay my arms out across the mat.

"Again," Julia claps me to attention.

Skylar helps me up and mumbles a quick apology before returning to his stance across from me, fists at the ready.

"Go!" Julia shouts.

This time there isn't even a small chance for me to respond. Skylar takes hold of my arm, twists it behind my back, kicks up a wind under my feet, and yanks me to the ground.

I groan. "I didn't even have the time to raise my hand!"

"But you had time to think," Julia points out. "Use your mind. Again."

Skylar helps me up once more, and I shake out my muscles, which are already starting to cramp up. "Get angry," he suggests. "It helps. Know what you want and pin me."

I think of Westerfield. Roderick Westerfield makes me angry. That kind of evil is beyond my understanding. Knowing that someone wants to harm my family pushes me to the edge, and I want him dead. I've never felt that kind of hatred for another human being, but it comes easily when I think of him. I don't want to just stop him from hurting my family, I want to stop him from doing anything ever again. I want to see him rot away in a small cell until that smug grin he wears fades to skin and bone.

"Go!" Julia calls.

I reach out and grab Skylar's arm, trying to copy his technique. My fingertips smoke slightly with my efforts. Still, he doesn't seem affected by my touch at all. Instead, his hand closes over my grip, and ice begins to smother my heat. Then he flips me to the ground, laying a hand on my chest to pin me.

"This is impossible," I yell.

"Again," Julia orders.

And on and on it goes. Each time Skylar pins me, until finally my whole body feels bruised. I don't even want to stand up again. The last few times Skylar spars with me, I'm so exhausted I can barely put up a fight. I just let him barrel over me.

"We'll pick up on this again tomorrow," Julia says finally. "I recommend you get some water and food, Lily."

"Tomorrow?" I whine. I don't move from the mat, where I'm sprawled after the latest tackle. If it weren't for my family, I'd be so over this.

"It was really nice to meet you, Lily." Skylar sprints to my side and looks down at me, offering me his hand for the last time today. "Hopefully I'll see you around."

"And hopefully it won't end with me on the floor again," I say. I take one more long breath before accepting his hand and standing shakily, trying to ignore the bruises.

"Ya never know!" Rory sings, snorting at her own joke as we walk away.

"Please." I roll my eyes.

"Come on!" she teases. "You can't deny that Skylar's hot— *totally* hot!" She glances back over her shoulder as we leave the gym. "And he's already in love with you."

"He seemed more in love with my dad. Plus, I like Kai."

"For now—"

I hold up my hand. "Stop." I don't want to hear it. After everything I've been through with Kai, there is no one else I can even imagine being with. I don't want anyone else.

My mind wanders back to the email I sent this morning. Will he have read it by now and responded? My body almost physically twitches with the desire to get back to the room so I can look, but Rory has other plans.

"Come on," Rory takes my hand, "there's something I want to show you."

The dining hall is at the center of The Revealed's headquarters, the hub to its four corridors, each of which are clearly marked as it's hard to remain oriented underwater. Designated living quarters are in the west wing. Research facilities and surgical centers occupy the east wing, which requires approval to access. In the south are the gyms and classrooms. The north holds the greenhouses and tools used to grow food and sustain plant life.

Rory tells me that The Revealed tries to grow as much of the food as possible at headquarters. This avoids the need to plan dangerous missions to grocery stores in the colonies. Of course, some things can't be produced underwater or are too prohibitively expensive to farm; for example, meat and dairy must be sent for. But with the abilities The Revealed have, growing grains and vegetables aren't difficult.

She leads me down the hall of the south wing, where all of the classrooms and a few more training gyms are housed.

"Please don't make me go to another gym," I plead.

Thankfully, she rounds the corner.

"Stop being such a baby," she laughs. "And, no, I'm not taking you to the gym. There's still something you haven't seen."

At the very end of the hall are two large doors that stretch all the way up to the ceiling. Rory opens them both, swinging out her arms and unveiling what's inside.

My breath catches in my chest.

It's like walking into another world. There are trees stretching to the ceiling, which must be thirty feet tall. Rows and rows of small saplings fill the room. Bushes rise along the walls. Vines twist around the beams that support the middle of the football field-sized room. Flowers of all shapes and colors decorate the landscape. It's a greenhouse, though I've never seen a greenhouse like this. Maybe the biosphere came the closest. But from the pictures I've seen of that experiment, this is the biosphere times a hundred.

The warmth and humidity hits me as we walk inside under a large sunlamp overhead. All of it is simply spectacular.

Rory kicks off her shoes and walks into the dirt, carefully avoiding any plants.

There's the thick, heady smell of soil mingled with the humid warmth of the room. The walls are covered in white, vinyl-looking material, but warm light seeps through. It can't be possible. We are underwater. Yet the rows and rows of plants stretch before me like a field.

I continue to gaze all around and up at the ceiling.

"This is my favorite place," Rory says as she goes to the side of the room and grabs a handful of seeds from a bucket on the shelf. She slips them into her pocket. "You can take as many as you'd like."

"It's amazing." I'm so awed by the room I'm hardly paying attention to her words.

She heads to a small, empty spot on the soil, getting on her hands and knees and pressing a few seeds into the dirt. She waves her hand over the area and soon, small sprouts pop up, uncurling from the surface.

I bend down next to her, watching the small plants reach for the light. Little leaves pop open before Rory drops her hand.

"How is this possible?" I stare in wonder at the plant Rory has just created.

In answer, she pokes a finger to my forehead.

"Can you teach me?" I ask, heading for the seeds on the shelf. I put a handful in my pocket. I pinch a few seeds between my fingers and walk back to the clearing, crouching and pressing them into the dirt. I mimic Rory's style and hover my hand over what I planted, willing them to grow.

Before long, a tiny seedling pokes through the dirt. Elation fills me. I've created something real and tangible just by desiring it. Rory bends next to me and places her palm over mine. With our combined efforts, the small plant springs to life and twists rapidly out around the dirt. It matures so quickly that soon I have to jump out of the way.

Rory stands and proudly observes our work. She drops another seed in my hand, encouraging me to coax it too to life. It's a fun game, and I continue to practice, wanting to be as skilled as Rory.

"Come here," she beckons me over after a few minutes, and I join her in the center. On either side of us are rows and rows of young plants. "Look."

She levels her hands between one of the rows, palms up, and I can see her eyes narrow in focus. She builds the electricity inside herself before unleashing it around the room. The plants shudder in her wake, coming alive as they dance with Rory's abilities. She raises her hands slightly and the plants shoot from the earth, growing taller. Rory's eyes practically glow.

I reach out and grab her wrist.

Her focus is broken. I stare around the greenhouse as the plants crumple and fold back into their original positions.

"How did you learn to do that?" I ask, astonished.

She shrugs. "I've been practicing. In fact, I used to practice in the gardens of your house during my breaks. Impressed?"

"Impressed? Rory, can all members of The Revealed do this?"

She shakes her head, suddenly coy.

"It's amazing, really."

Rory beams at my compliment. "Yeah, well, I may not have been the best at cooking but *this*? This I can do."

That evening, my first move is to open my email, of course. But there are only a few junk messages and news alerts on the election. It was announced that my parents cancelled the rest of the tour and flew home, but no one is talking about my disappearance yet. It won't be much longer now, I know.

Much to my dismay, I haven't received a reply from Kai. He may be somewhat of a techie, but I know he isn't the type of guy to live in front of his computer. I reconcile with the twinge of disappointment. It's only been a few short hours really.

After my sweep of the Internet, I clear the guest suite of my few possessions—basically just the clothes I was wearing the night I was attacked and my ID card—and move in the dorm room with Rory. She's at her computer, facing me, when I walk in the room. I beam at her, dropping my clothes on the floor to prove I'm making myself at home, then collapse face first onto the bed.

My brain hurts from all the training. Plus, I just want to go to bed so that I won't look at my email again. Maybe by the time I wake up, I'll have an email from Kai.

"Welcome home," I say to myself with a smile as I smash my face into the pillow, ready to sleep.

"Lily, someone's here to see—"

I interrupt with a loud yawn. "I don't think I can move, let alone see anyone else today."

Someone clears his voice. Immediately, I sit up. If I weren't so tired, I would have seen him standing in the room the whole time. His crystal-blue eyes shift to my wide-eyed expression.

"You!" I say, scrambling up.

Skylar chuckles, and his cheeks turn red. "Me again. I promise I'm not stalking you for your autograph."

"Yeah," Rory scoffs, "because I made him promise he wouldn't."

Skylar turns a deeper crimson, and it's so funny to me that someone with such a strong constitution can blush so deeply.

His eyes seem to soften around the edges. "I just wanted to drop this off for you." He holds out a book, his eyes still connected with mine. I stare back, startled. "I was going to give it to Rory to give to you, but since you're here now, well, here it is."

He's staring at me the way I *think* he's staring at me, right? I glance at Rory, who wrinkles her nose the way people do when gushing over a cute puppy. I look back at Skylar. He's definitely giving me those eyes, those *I really just couldn't get you off my mind* eyes. He adds, "I thought it might help you with the elements. I've already finished it."

I clear my throat, suddenly anxious, and take the book he offers. "Thank you." I glance at the cover. It's called *The Energy of Us*. Anthony Roben—the man who founded The Revealed—is the author.

"And I also just wanted to say that I'd like to hang out with you sometime, if you want to. You know, get to know each other better," Skylar offers. "I know that back in Washington you were sort of seeing Kai. At least, that's what the paper said. But I mean, everything's changed now hasn't it? Now that we're here?"

"Are you asking me out?" I look between him and Rory, who is staring at me with laughing eyes and pursed lips. She begins biting her bottom lip, trying to hide her grin. I want to chuck the pillow at her.

As if trying to navigate the elements wasn't enough, now I have to navigate boys. I'll take the elements over the opposite sex any day.

"I'm sorry, Skylar," I say, and shake my head. "I was—am—seeing Kai."

He shrugs, and that boyish grin of his returns. "Hey, it was worth a try, right? I'll see you around. Let me know if you change your mind."

"Okay," I breathe, feeling put off by the whole situation. He just had to do this tonight.

But instead of trying to convince me again, he says goodbye to Rory and leaves, closing the door behind him.

Immediately, Rory rounds on me. "I can't believe you just turned him down!"

I brush her off with, "I want to be with Kai, Rory."

"Yeah, but I didn't think you guys were ever like, super-official or anything, right? I mean, he'll understand. It's like Skylar said. Everything's different now. You could at least get to know the guy. It's not like you can go prance back to Capitol City and date Kai. The paparazzi would be on you like a bloodhound and then you'd be arrested by the government or something crazy like that. And Kai can't exactly come here."

She acts like I haven't thought of this already.

In fact, it's been on my mind since Julia mentioned the danger I'd be in if and when I return to the cities.

"I can't do this right now." I pull out a drawer and find some pajamas. "I need to stay focused on training. My parents' lives are at stake here."

"I don't know why you seem so attached to that boy, but you two really are like peas in a pod aren't you? You do realize his father is the one trying to kill you?"

"Kai isn't his father. Kai's the one who brought me here."

I walk to the bathroom and change. But instead of returning to the room, I stare at myself for a long moment in the mirror.

I'm the same girl. Chestnut hair, almond eyes, pale skin. I run a hand through my hair, searching for the scar. It's at the base of my neck, so small and insignificant, it's barely noticeable. I run my fingers over the scab and recognize the pattern. An open circle dancing to form a flame, crossed with an X stitch that separates it into four pieces. I pull my hair up farther to see the mark. It will leave a scar, no doubt, branding the organization on my skin.

I interrupt Rory, who is now on her computer.

"What is this?" I ask, keeping my hair up.

She keeps reading but lifts up her hair. There is the faintest trace of the same brand at her hairline.

"See this?" She traces the X through the circle. "Each of the triangles it creates represents one of the elements—earth, air, water, and fire. After they perform the surgery and stitch the incision, they brand the skin closed with this mark. No one can ever know it's here. The boys are marked here," she says, and points about an inch into my hairline, "so it's covered once the hair grows back. But you can still see it if you pull back the strands."

She turns back to the computer. The headline reads *North American Sector Prepares for Elections*. It's all the world can talk about. Capitol City is being transformed for the announcement, which will take place in front of the Capitol Building.

"Let me see that," I peek over Rory's shoulder at the news.

My parents went home immediately after rumors of my disappearance got out. My father has dropped in the polls; the election is too close to call. He and Westerfield are running neck and neck, according to the most-recent surveys.

People are starting to suspect, though my family has yet to confirm the news. Westerfield is using my disappearance against my father. He said, "If Mark Atwood can't even keep his own daughter safe, how can he protect the country?" The line seems to be working in his favor.

"How are we going to stop him?" I ask her.

"We're going to find the sniper he's planning on planting at the election announcement."

"Easier said than done."

"We've kept detailed records of Westerfield's correspondences. It's just a matter of piecing together the information to discover his plan. Kai is helping as well."

"You're in contact with him?" I respond, too hopefully.

"Julia is."

I'm desperate for any information about him. Kai is staying out of the limelight in recent days. He's only been photographed once, and he pulled up the hood of his jacket to hide his face. I stare blankly at that article.

I know Rory is right. My face is too well-known to risk a return, and Kai can't become a member of The Revealed. The only logical thing to do is move on.

If only it were that easy.

I don't want to move on from Kai. I don't want to stop thinking about him. As soon as we save my parents, I could go back. We could figure out our lives together. We could find a way to make a difference on our own. I don't have to be a member of The Revealed. I have the option of going back, right?

Rory snaps her fingers in front of my face, "Earth to Lily."

"Sorry." I shake my head, clearing the thoughts.

"Yeah," she says, grinning, "you definitely need some sleep."

CHAPTER EIGHTEEN

My body jerks awake.

I look over to the bed across the room. The rhythmic rise and fall of the sheets tells me Rory is still fast asleep.

The room is dark.

I wipe my hand across my brow, trying to dispel the cold chills that spread from my skin to my bones. I shiver and stand, unable to take being in the small, cramped bedroom anymore. I need air.

The dim hallways are a welcome calm in the middle of the night. I twist my hand, and a breeze kicks up around me, cooling my face. I feel like I can breathe again, though the memory of the dream doesn't fade.

It's more a nightmare, actually: standing with my family on a stage before the entire world. Kai is next to me. He is holding my hand. Beside him are Rory and Skylar. Slowly, they all begin to disappear, until I'm standing alone in front of millions of people.

I rub the back of my neck, trying to shake the images from the dream. I walk into the dining hall toward the large windows that cover the far wall. I stretch my hand across the glass, and ice extends from my fingers. Just like I practiced. I stare out at the darkness around me. A single streak of blue overhead is the only thing I can see.

The moon. It's bright tonight.

I withdraw my hand, and the ice retreats from the glass.

I hear the soft steps approaching behind me before he speaks.

"You can't sleep either?"

Lazily, I turn around, leaning my shoulder blades against the glass.

Skylar is standing in front of me with his jet-black hair and blue eyes that seem to pierce the synthetic night lights.

"I thought you said you weren't stalking me?" I ask, raising an eyebrow.

He shrugs. "I'm assuming you aren't sleeping for the same reason I'm not."

I shrug back. I'm not about to tell him my dream. I barely know him. He won't understand, anyway. No one can understand what being in my position is like, except Kai. Not only can he relate to my situation, he knows *me*. I feel comfortable with him in a way I've never felt with anyone in my life, and, if I'm being honest, I'm kind of lonely without him around.

He has yet to respond to my email.

I stare back out at the ocean because the loneliness starts rising in my throat, and I don't want Skylar to see my lips trembling.

He stands next to me, glancing up, seeming perfectly content in the silence. He rests his hands on the glass, staring in wonder. I'm glad the amazement at being at the bottom of the sea doesn't fade.

I rub my eyes, trying to rid myself of the dream and the image of Kai burned on my brain. Right now I need to stay focused. My parents' lives depend on it. I'm not going to lose them. I'm not going to let Westerfield take them.

"We're going to stop him," Skylar says after a moment.

"You don't know that."

"Yes, I do. It's like a good-versus-evil thing. Don't you ever read comics?"

I give him a sideways glance.

"Okay, maybe that's just a 'me thing,'" he chuckles. "But we're like the superheroes. And Westerfield is the bad guy. If my abilities have taught me anything, it's that there's a balance to the universe. People like Westerfield don't succeed. Sure, the world thinks The Revealed are the bad guys and Westerfield may or may not be elected president, but he'll get what's coming to him eventually."

I'm grinning without meaning to. I don't believe all the superhero stuff, and the dream still lingers in my mind, but I can believe everything will be okay. I can let small fragments of Skylar's optimism dig under my skin.

"So you wanna go hit the bags or something?" Skylar asks.

"Sure."

I take the lead and we walk to south hall, where the classrooms and gyms are located. We choose one and go inside. I throw my hand in the air, and a small ball of light illuminates the room. It's just bright enough that we can see our movements, but dim enough that it won't alert anybody if they walk by. The last thing I need is an audience.

"You're improving," Skylar says, looking at the light that dances like glitter in the middle of the room. When I glance over at him, I see he's carefully watching me. Was the doubt that apparent on my face?

I shrug, "It's an easy trick."

He concedes, "One of the easier ones," and I punch his arm.

"Whoa," he rubs the spot. "Put your gloves on before you start swinging, princess."

"I am *not* a princess," I gripe, but grab my gloves nonetheless.

"Whatever you say," he teases, walking around to hold the bag for me.

I watch him with a wry expression as I slam my fist into the hard cushion in front of me.

"That's it," Skylar encourages, holding the punching bag steady as I pound it again and again. "Gotcha angry, didn't I?"

I sigh, a little out of breath, and hit again, "Not angry enough. How long until I'm at your level?" I swing again.

"It's different for everyone. You'll get there," he promises.

I know my body is transforming, adapting to strains it never had to worry about before. I can already feel it even though I've only been here for a handful of days. It makes me realize how capable The Revealed really are. There is a good chance they could actually stop this assassination. They're an organization built on teamwork and careful honing of their abilities. If anyone has a chance to save my parents' lives, it's them.

All I can do is focus on training to keep from panicking about what Westerfield's planning. Every time I get tired or out of breath, I think of my parents. They need me now, and they need The Revealed, even though they don't know it yet.

"Alright," I say and straighten. "Let's go again."

I hit the bag.

"Try throwing your palm out after you punch," Skylar suggests. "You can create ice or fire. It's a good technique that will give you the edge in hand-to-hand situations."

I punch again but this time, do as he suggests. My ice doesn't work very well. It melts as soon as it touches the bag.

"Like this," he pulls away from the bag and shows me the step. His hand slices through the air, knuckles perfectly aligned. He makes a slight "umph" sound when his hand hits. Just as he pulls away, he throws out his hand, and ice spreads across the curved surface of the bag, crackling along its path.

"I'm doomed," I sigh. "If someone attacks me during Election Day I'll just have to accept death."

He shakes his head with a grin and faces me. "You were able to get away from that guy at your house."

The reminder brings back images of Jeremy's wild eyes and his hands choking my neck. I fidget uncomfortably. I was somehow able to get away from him. I will never forget the sound his bones made as I twisted his wrist. The memory of the way it cracked still makes my stomach squeeze.

"Let's try something different." Skylar lifts his hands into a boxer's stance.

"What are you doing?" I ask hesitantly, but I raise my fists in protection.

"Let's go for a round of the mats," he lifts his chin, egging me on.

"No way!"

"Come on. This is the only way you'll really learn."

"We already tried this, remember? It ended with me in pain on the ground."

"Come on!"

I take a deep breath and swing.

He catches my fist in his hand and holds it, using the leverage to spin me around in his grasp. He clasps me around the waist, immobilizing me.

"The way you're hitting right now is too slow. Use your mind like it's a part of your body. Don't think, just do." His breath is warm against my ear as he holds me tightly, our bodies aligned. For a moment, I lose what he's saying and imagine his body is Kai's. Like the time we were at Elias's gym together. It's just a moment. Then it's gone. And I realize the awkward way my shoulders are bunched around his arm. I'm sweating and uncomfortable. I stiffen in Skylar's grip. "Sorry." He drops his hand and I stagger back. His cheeks turn pink. "I didn't mean to make you uncomfortable."

"It's okay," I say quickly, "you didn't. I just—"

"Like Kai," he finishes for me. "I don't get what girls see in that guy."

I open my mouth to say I'm not like those girls but what's the use? I don't want to add salt to his wound. He swallows his pride and shakes his head. Then there's a grin on his face, one that seems genuine. He beckons me forward. "Let's go," he says.

I hesitate.

"Come on, soldier, I don't have all night. I'll have to get my beauty sleep eventually. Let's go."

So I punch, trying to create ice, and he smacks my hand away, sending me stumbling. I regroup and go toward him again. This time I'm able to make contact, but he uses my surprise against me and retaliates, pinning both my arms. I squirm out of his grip and spin around in an attempt to recover.

Quickly, Skylar's back on the offensive. His hand shoots out toward mine, and it barely misses my stomach as I slide out of the way. My back is to him, and I jab with my elbow. He dodges and moves around in front of me. I duck as he swings his fist. Then he tries to kick my legs out from under me, but I jump and jab out at him. He narrowly avoids my swing, stumbling back a few steps. He is quick to recover, moving toward me again, and I reach for his arm, my hands already burning with my abilities. I connect with his flesh, but he's already guessed my move. His arm is icy cold. He uses my momentum against me and flips me over onto the mat.

"Ugh!" I groan. I stay on the ground, staring up at the reflective metal ceiling.

After a long silence as I recover my breath, Skylar offers me his hand. "That was much better."

I allow him to pull me up. "Do you ever think about your home?" I ask him.

"The past is the past," he says, brushing my question away.

"Right." A lot of the people here want to forget. Their pasts are full of poverty and death. They want to look forward. There is an underlying hope here that one day soon, The Revealed will be vindicated and accepted into society. Then the members will be able to return to their families without risk.

He clasps his hands on my head, shaking me playfully. "Focus," he says into my eyes with a laugh. "You can't let that mind of yours get away from you."

"I know." I swallow against the fear for my parents that creeps over my spine like vines The Revealed control. It makes me want to swat at the invisible threads over my skin.

"Let's call it a night," Skylar says, realizing I may be too distracted to continue.

"I'll see you tomorrow," I tell him as we reach the hallway.

"Get some sleep."

But I don't sleep. I'm too nervous. Every thought I have makes my head spin more and more. My room slowly becomes bright, as the sun begins to rise and the light creeps over my bed. Finally, Rory's alarm clock begins to buzz with the morning.

But I'm still exhausted. The reminder of the bad dream lingers, flashing white through my mind. My parents are dead on the ground. Red oozing from their sides. And me, standing in the background, helpless and alone.

Kai tries to run to me, but suddenly, I'm at the end of a long hallway and even though he's running in my direction, he never gets any closer. When I look down I realize my side is sticky. Red seeps through my shirt. I grip the wound, trying to make the red stop, but it pools at my feet. And Jeremy is holding the gun and laughing.

I'm on a stage in the middle of Capitol City. There's so much blood.

Jeremy continues laughing loudly, but suddenly I realize he isn't the only one laughing. The entire crowd has joined in, laughing while I lose too much blood to stay standing. I fall to my knees. My surroundings begin to blur. All I hear is dark laughter. And when I close my eyes, Westerfield is there with a glass of thick, gold liquid and a smug grin.

CHAPTER NINETEEN

"Lissa wants to work on my technique this afternoon," Maya groans at lunch the next day. "She says if I don't maintain my conditioning it only takes like two weeks or something to lose the form."

"Practice, practice, practice," Skylar waves his fork like it's a magic wand.

"Nerd," Maya slinks into him with her arm, her curls bouncing with her effort.

He shrugs and takes another bite. "I like hand to hand."

"I'm a lover, not a fighter," Maya counters.

"So am I," Skylar says. "But if it's kill or be killed, you better believe I'm not going to hold back."

That's a mantra I can relate to.

"Well, I hear Julia wants to put together a group to attempt a wasteland colonization effort. Apparently, we're getting too many members. We'll have to expand soon."

"It's true," Rory nods. "The problem is going to be security. This facility is practically a fortress. The only way in is via submarine and ours is the only surviving vehicle I know about. On land, it's a whole other story."

"Either way, sign me up for *that* mission," Maya says.

"No way," Romni shakes his meaty head. "I'm taking down the bad guys, starting with Westerfield. There is no chance I'm missing out on that action."

It isn't until Rory grabs my wrist that I realize I've been swirling my food around my plate. It's my "tell" when I'm anxious. One she knows well by now.

I grimace.

She shrugs, "It's not like you're ruining my plate decor anymore." Her grin is reassuring, but it falls flat. My mood is hopelessly somber. She takes a breath and tries again to muster some energy. "You did really well today."

"Yeah, until that wind she created whipped her hair all over her face and blinded her," Nero says, laughing with a big dollop of potato salad rolling around on his tongue.

Nero and Romni decided to watch the spectacle of my training today as well. Even Maya and a few of her friends stopped by before lunch.

Rory flicks her finger out and a quarter-size ball of ice hits Nero on the side of his head with a thud.

"Hmm," she says at the noise, "I guess that means there is something in there after all. Doesn't sound very big though."

Nero rubs the side of his head, glaring at her with spritely emerald eyes.

Rory raises an eyebrow, pointing her fork at him as both a dare and a warning. He wisely realizes Rory's abilities greatly outweigh his and shuts his mouth, sulking and massaging his head.

"It really is impressive," Maya assured me. "You've only had a little over a week. I didn't get sent on a mission for months after I arrived at The Revealed. You should be really proud."

I don't feel proud. I feel pressure, overwhelming pressure to be better and stronger.

Rory turns back to me. "We'll practice again this afternoon and maybe spend time in the greenhouse?" her voice ticks up to ask the question.

I run a finger across my tense brow. "Okay." I shove another bite of sandwich in my mouth and push the plate away. "Ready. I'll meet you in the greenhouse in a few minutes," I tell Rory and rush out of the room before she can ask where I'm headed.

A few people smile at me as I make my way down the hall. Faces are starting to look more familiar, and the black outfits no longer make me uncomfortable. I run my hand along the symbol embroidered over my heart. It's becoming a habit. I used to hate and fear this symbol, now I have put my faith in it.

Without looking at the pattern I can trace its curve. Whether I decide to stay with The Revealed permanently or not, they have left their mark on me—both beneath my hairline and in a deeper way. My soul is slowing becoming entwined with the mission here. I'm aware that if I allow it to continue, it will become too tangled to unravel without pulling myself apart in the process. The Revealed have changed me for the better.

That doesn't mean I'm ready to leave Capitol City behind.

When I get to my dorm room, I quickly flip open my computer and log in to my email. No new messages.

It's been long enough that I can't pretend like he just hasn't checked his email. It sends my guts twisting. I'm not ready to leave my past behind, but what if Kai is? It's a constant fear within me. The insecurity that suddenly, he'll decide I'm disposable makes me feel weak and incapable. It makes me want to go hiding under the bleachers again and never come out to face the world.

"What are you doing?"

I whirl to face Rory. She's peering over my shoulder looking at my email.

"Just wanted to check the news," I sputter quickly.

She moves around me and clicks on the "SENT" folder before I can stop her. My message to Kai pops up at the top of the feed.

"I knew it," she shakes her head.

"Rory, I had to talk with him," I exclaim. "I couldn't leave things ... like that."

"You have no idea what you've done. This isn't a game! The government can track this, Lily. This could lead the North American Sector right to our front door. You have to leave your other life behind. A message like this could compromise everything, including your parents' lives. You know that. Your life. His life. The life of this country, they all depend on your ability to move on and accept this new path. Isn't this what you want?'

My mouth opens, then shuts, then opens again wordlessly. A life with purpose and making a difference for people is what I've always wanted. If The Revealed is everything they say they are, I will have more than ample opportunity to explore the world like I've always wanted and see new things. But how am I supposed to do all of that and forget about what could have been with Kai? I don't want to wake up and realize that I let him get away. I don't want to see him on the news, accomplishing things and building a life without me. Before The Revealed, there was Kai. Kai was the first person who didn't want to hold me back. It's because of him that I'm with The Revealed.

Rory grabs my shoulders, "Get with the program!" She shakes me slightly.

"I'm trying."

"We're running out of time for trying. You have to make decisions and make them quickly. If you keep stewing over this instead of acting, you're mind will be all over the place and you won't be ready for this mission."

"I'm trying," I repeat, throwing her arms off me. I don't need another mother. I need a best friend. I need her to understand what I'm dealing with. "I just need some time." I push around her, heading out of the room, the pressure threatening to crush me under its weight. It's hard to breathe past the anxiety.

I go to the citrus grove greenhouse, which is dedicated to oranges, limes, and lemons, spaced in neat rows. The fresh, floral smells roll over me the instant I walk in the room: a relaxing aromatherapy. The warmth clouds around me like fog. I roll up the ends of my black pants and take off my shoes, feeling the dirt between my toes.

I run my fingers over the leaf of a lemon tree, and rub the wax between my fingers as though it were perfume.

My pulse finally feels like it's returning to normal, and the relief that washes over me is enough to make the tears form at the corner of my eyes. Now is not the time for tears. Rory is right. Now is the time to make decisions.

I sit at the base of a tree and stretch my back against it. The greenhouse lights almost make me feel like I'm sitting in the shade on a sunny summer day.

When I close my eyes, I am there: it's before the war, and I'm six years old. I'm rushing through the desert outside our adobe house. There's the soft scurry of a rabbit running with me. My house is an oasis amongst the cacti and gravel.

My father used to love citrus. He planted fruit trees in our backyard—one orange, one lemon, and one grapefruit. When they bloomed, the smell from those trees wafted through the whole cul-de-sac.

I would turn the hose on and spray the grass and dirt of my backyard to watch the butterflies collect at the puddles. My father would sit outside with me, and we would bask in the sun in afternoons with nothing to do but be together.

Absentmindedly, I reach my hand up and twirl the end of a lemon branch around my fingers. The smooth bark glides beneath my touch.

What I wouldn't give for those days again. Things were simple. I didn't know anything about good or evil, other than what I saw in Disney films where the bad guy always lost.

Now everything seems to be shaded in the gray of uncertainty. My choices, my responses, mean life or death. When did that happen? Rory is right. That email was a mistake.

I'm a part of a team now, and my actions don't just affect me. The Revealed are affecting change that I could be a part of if I let myself, instead of sabotaging everything because of my petty feelings. There's a big world out there, one I've just started to see the edges of.

I would rather live in the gray of uncertainty if it meant I got to experience life, wouldn't I?

That six-year-old I was hadn't really understood or appreciated the beauty. She hadn't been able to see a bigger picture, because all she'd had was sunshine.

Maybe that's okay for a while. It's good for a kid.

But I'm not a kid anymore. It isn't enough.

And I know in myself that even if Westerfield wasn't coming after my parents or The Revealed hadn't taken me, I still would have sought out more in life. I want a life beyond the small one I've been living, a bigger adventure to explore. I'll take the messy, uncertain gray that comes with taking such a risk, if it also means I get to experience life and can make a difference.

Something shifts in front of me.

I jerk at the sound.

Rory. "How long have you been there?"

She's leaning against the trunk of an orange tree. Her blonde hair falls loosely over one shoulder. Her arms are crossed over her chest.

"Long enough to see you've been holding out." She tips her chin at the lemon I've just created on the tree. It's plump and ripe, perfect for picking.

"I'm not holding out," I say in a clipped tone.

"You need to let yourself go. Let yourself experience whatever it is you're bottling up inside of you."

"I'm not—" But I can hear it, even in my voice. It sounds harsher, stressed. And I think back to the dream and rub my forehead.

"Let it out." Rory, my eternal counselor, grips my shoulders.

I try to shake her off.

She holds fast.

And when she won't let go, I shove my hands against her shoulders.

She continues holding so I push again. And the wind that bursts from me is so strong that she falls back.

"I don't think I can save them," I say, tears springing to my eyes.

But she's smiling. "You will if you use your abilities like that."

CHAPTER TWENTY

I find Julia in her office.

It's stainless steel just like the rest of the facility, with a white couch to the left of the room. It looks unnaturally clean and sleek, almost like Julia herself. Everything is modern and sharp. A white orchid sits on top of the black desk Julia is behind. She must keep the delicate flower alive herself, since the lights are all artificial here.

Julia is working at a computer. When she sees me, she takes off her square-rimmed glasses and closes the laptop.

"Have a seat," she gestures to one of the plush, black chairs in front of her desk.

I settle in.

"What can I do for you, Lily?"

I realize I'm biting my bottom lip and stop, before looking at her squarely. "I just wanted to let you know I'm ready." It's been two weeks since I've been with The Revealed and the election is only a week away.

She smiles and clasps her hands on the desk.

"You have to let me do this mission."

"The only one that will stop you is yourself."

"Then I choose to go," I tell her.

Julia hands me one of the glass orbs, and I will it to hover above my open palm. As it floats above my hand, I stare back at her. She can't fault me for my skill. I've been working night and day to find some semblance of control over my abilities. I'm no Rory or Skylar, but I've certainly got a rudimentary control of my new capabilities.

"You have improved," she concedes. "Maybe the fastest I've ever seen anyone advance. Then again, I don't think anyone has had quite the motivation you have."

I continue to toy with the orb, letting it dance across my fingers.

"The mission doesn't just stop once we save your father. You realize that, don't you?"

"Of course."

"There are hundreds of Westerfields out there and millions of people who could benefit from our abilities. We have a responsibility not to turn our backs on them. But we also have a right to choose our own paths in life." She snatches the orb from me with just a flick of her finger. She wants my undivided attention apparently. My eyes meet her crystal gaze. It's like staring into a different sort of orb, equally as hypnotizing. "Whatever you choose, there is no going back."

"I don't want to go back," I say automatically, and then an image of Kai filters through my mind. I don't want to go back to the way things were with my parents, inside that shell of a house, but I'm not ready to leave Kai behind. So maybe I don't want to go back, but can I move forward? I'm not sure. It's a white lie I allow to hang between Julia and me.

She buys it. Sort of. "I don't think you do. But I don't think you're ready to make the decision about where you belong yet, either. And because you aren't invested in this organization, I'm not sure I can trust you in the field."

"I won't stay here and watch my parents get murdered on national television," I stand suddenly from my chair. "I won't let you keep me here while—"

Julia stands up too and puts a hand back up to silence me. "Sit back down, Lily," she says steadily. "I would never propose to take you away from your family like that when they are in danger."

The relieved breath that escapes me is so sudden, I choke on it and find myself coughing slightly as I breathe.

"But," Julia holds up a finger. "You must swear to me you'll listen to everything Rory and your team members tell you."

"I promise."

"And you will remember that there are thousands of lives at risk. Your parents are our priorities, but there is also the greater good to consider."

"Yes."

"And you will think long and hard about what you want after this mission. I've said it before, and I'll say it again. I would hate to see you leave. The potential for you here is extraordinary. Don't waste the opportunity to do something important with your life."

"Okay." I begin to imagine what it would be like to be one of them, but concern for my parents and those sneaky thoughts of Kai dominate my thoughts.

Julia seems to be reading my mind.

"Lastly," she says, "you will follow protocol and stay away from Kai Westerfield. Eyes will be on him during Election Day, and I can't risk exposure if you're spotted."

My cheeks flush a little with her being so public about my relationship with Kai. She discusses it like a business deal.

"No calling. No emails. No eye contact. I need your word on this one. No more sneaking correspondences. At least until the election is over, though I think we would all feel more at ease if you two decided to part ways. It isn't just about you anymore. You hold the potential to destroy The Revealed."

Well, when she put it like that she made my email sound treasonous.

I bite my lip, take a deep breath, and agree. "I promise."

"Good." There's something like pride in her eyes.

From there, Julia spends an hour briefing me on the mission. She goes over everything including the satellite phone I'll be provided for communication as well as the highway routes we'll take to get to the capitol. She already knows the size of the stage that will be set up for the announcement and the number of people expected to attend. The polls will close at 5:00 p.m. with the announcement scheduled at 8:00 p.m. to allow for proper vote tallying. Depending on traffic, we are scheduled to arrive at the Capitol Building between 3:00 and 4:00 p.m. This will allow for a solid window of time during the afternoon to locate the sniper and subdue the threat before my father ever steps on stage.

After the plan has been drilled into my mind, Julia finally dismisses me.

"Oh Lily," she calls me back with one final thought before I can open the door, "the submarine leaves at 7:00 a.m. sharp. It's the only one we have, so don't be late."

I nearly stumble from Julia's office I'm so filled with relief at being allowed to help with the mission. And then I realize that just because I've gotten what I want doesn't mean The Revealed is any closer to saving my parents' lives.

But I'm closer to figuring out mine, and that has to count for something, right?

Until this point, my life has been about being contained and composed. Now, for the first time, I'm becoming something wild and unexpected. There's no straight line toward anything for me. It's both exhilarating and terrifying, but I know I'm alive.

There's nothing that can kill that electric shock of life faster than a research project, but that's where Skylar, Rory, and Maya are spending their afternoon, and I promised earlier in the day I would help.

They're gathering information to take with us on our trip to land. Anything that could be useful to stop Westerfield is being compiled.

We'll take a handful of the most-incriminating evidence to turn over to the authorities once Westerfield is apprehended.

With any luck, by the end of Election Day, Westerfield will be in jail and people will know the truth about The Revealed. Then we don't have to hide anymore. We can integrate into society, and I'll have the chance to make things work for real with Kai.

There are quite a few people milling about the research room, toiling over folders of papers. Just like a library, the light shuffling of pages is the only noise aside from the backdrop hum of air ducts imbedded in the walls of the facility.

I walk down the aisles of shelves filled with organized boxes and files. It looks like how I imagine a police evidence room must be. Everything is a mess, but somehow also in its rightful place.

Rory has a box at her feet and a manila envelope in her hands. She's sifting through papers and unceremoniously tossing the useless ones on the ground.

Maya scrambles behind her picking up the dropped files and reorganizing them back into the box.

I throw out my arms in a victorious gesture. Rory barely looks up. She grabs another handful of papers in one hand and tosses them aside. In the other, she splays two between her fingers and her eyes flit over them quickly.

"I'm in!" I tell her and that gets her to drop the documents she's reading.

"Julia gave you the all clear?" she asks hopefully.

"Yes! I'm going with you and we didn't even have to plot another elaborate escape attempt."

She hugs me, "That's fantastic news, babe."

"Knew it," Skylar says, rounding the corner with a box in his hands.

"Another one?" Rory sighs. Her fingers spasm. She was definitely not made for a desk job.

"Shh!" A girl with a high ponytail hisses as us. Then she meets my gaze and her expression pales before she quickly buries her nose back in the books.

I give Skylar a sidelong, apologetic glance.

Rory snorts, "Prude," before going for the second box.

Skylar snatches the box from her before she can undo the tape securing the top. "I think it's time for a break," he tells her.

"I'll take over," I offer.

"Do you even know what to look for?" Maya calls me out.

I grimace, "Not exactly."

"I'll be in the greenhouse," Rory says, backing away quickly before I can change my mind and beg her to stay.

"I'll show you," Skylar says, picking up one of the folders and propping it open on his arm. "Right now we have the email records from Westerfield over the past few weeks. Now, he knows The Revealed can track his communications so he's most likely only corresponding face-to-face or via some sort of code. We're not the first to go through these files, but a new set of eyes can't hurt. Look for any sentences that seem out of place or any correspondences that don't match up."

"So you're telling me, we're looking for some sort of hidden message that may or may not be in any of these emails, that we may or may not be able to decipher."

"Well, when you put it like that—"

"It's not unlikely," Maya pipes up.

The girl with the high ponytail gives us another pleading glance to be quiet.

Maya shrinks and lowers her voice, "He's done it before. It was an email that first led us to believe he was attempting to assassinate your parents. The letter was coded so that the first letter of every other word, was a letter in the real message. It ended up spelling, 'Atwood attempt. Gala invite,' or something like that."

I think back to the gala, flecked over in my memory with gold glitter thanks to my dress and the little shards of glass that reflected off the fabric as they rained down.

That moment seems like a lifetime ago. It was a lifetime ago. I am no longer the girl that fears The Revealed as some sort of terminal cancer I can't avoid. Or the girl that cowers in the wake of some glass shards.

I'm also not the type of girl who runs away from a challenge. I'll find the needle in the haystack. We have to find it....

With a huff of breath, I take the papers from Skylar and begin sifting through them.

I have to force myself to read through the conversations, knowing that most of the chatter is useless. In fact, the only thing Westerfield seems concerned with these last few weeks is planning campaign stops in the North American colonies. No wonder my parents felt such a need to make some last-minute stops.

It doesn't take long before I'm throwing the papers on the ground just like Rory. The threads of doubt weave their way through my veins.

And then I stumble on an email correspondence that catches my eye.

```
TO: m.lancing@n.america.gov
FROM: rwesterfield@n.america.gov

Marg,

I have a keen interest in Pennsylvenia.
Please consider an endorsement that
would allow our mission to reach through
the people and into our future
endeavors.

All the best,
Roderick Westerfield
```

```
TO: rwesterfield@n.america.gov
FROM: m.lancing@n.america.gov

Dear Roderick,

I'm not sure our visions align on the
matter of controlling the Capital.
```

Please be advised that when it comes to reaching the spiret of justice for the people, I believe we can best accomplish this through what lies with the compromise of independance.

TO: m.lancing@n.america.gov
FROM: rwesterfield@n.america.gov

Thank you, Marg. Perhaps my campaigning efforts would be better focused on Marylend then.

TO: m.lancing@n.america.gov
FROM: rwesterfield@n.america.gov

Yes. I believe that is your best course of action, sir, but remember, campaigning in one state will not win you the election.

Something strikes me about this particular email string.

"Have you read this?" I ask Skylar.

His eyes are glassy when he looks up and shrugs. "Probably. I feel like I've read through these boxes a hundred times."

"It doesn't make any sense." He takes the paper and looks over it. "Sounds like good old Marg is going with her gut and not trusting the creepy bastard."

"That's the thing," I say, "Marg endorsed Roderick Westerfield after the gala at my house. My mother was pretty put out about it. This email was written only a couple weeks ago."

He laughs, "Good for her for having a change of heart, then."

But something doesn't sit right with me about the correspondence. "This isn't right." I tell Skylar.

"Keep it then. We're looking for anything out of the ordinary so go with your gut."

I set it aside and continue shuffling through the stack in my hand.

It isn't until Rory returns to collect us for dinner that I realize we've spent the entire afternoon holed up in this small section between shelves.

Skylar grins at me when he sees my exhausted expression. I do feel dazed and try to rub away my blurring vision.

"Come on," Rory grabs my hand. "It's time to let the next round of troops take the lead. We have a big day to prepare for."

CHAPTER TWENTY-ONE

Waking and realizing that it's already Sunday morning isn't a pleasant feeling. It's overwhelming. This is it. Today I will return to Capitol City.

It's only been two and a half weeks, but I feel the change in my bones. I'm stronger. I lie in bed and snap my fingers. A flame sparks over my thumb. I stare at it for a moment before shaking it out.

Rory is already up, and she throws open the bathroom door. She has a towel wrapped around her head and another cinched at her chest. "Good morning," she calls. "Rise and shine! We've got to get this show on the road."

"How can you be so chipper?" I ask, feeling terrified for a whole host of reasons. I'm not sure I'm ready for this. Will we be able to stop the assassination attempt on my parents?

But I can't allow myself to think like that. I have to pull it together. There isn't another choice. I force myself out of bed.

Julia has given us street clothes—simple dark jeans and a tank top—so we won't stick out on land. I slip the outfit on and walk into the hallway. It's abuzz with life despite the early hour. People mill around in the halls, whispering to one another. A freckled boy with white-blond hair meets my eye. He smiles at me, but then turns and begins talking under his breath to the girl next to him. It's Maya. I wave hesitantly, and she returns the gesture. She mouths, *Good luck*. She won't be going on the mission with us.

I meet the others down in the east wing where we will depart an hour from now. Outside the glass-enclosed control room is the launch waiting area.

There are six of us surfacing, and we're meeting two more members on shore.

"How are you feeling?" Julia rests her hands on my shoulders. "You look pale."

"I feel a little sick," I admit.

"Good," she says and nods. "If you weren't nervous I'd say there was something wrong with you."

I bob my head up and down, taking deep breaths.

"I'm glad you've come to us, Lily," Julia adds. "You have the potential to accomplish great things. Don't miss it by focusing on your worries."

Rory comes up behind me and touches my shoulder. She smiles and says, "It's time. They've opened the doors to load the submarine."

I give Julia one last hopeful nod before I turn and follow Rory aboard.

None of the members on the submarine have any weapons. We don't need any. We have our minds. The only thing each of us carries is a backpack of supplies—a cell phone, some food—in case we get separated from the group. Most importantly, we each carry a folder packed with copies of the incriminating documents. If one of us gets caught, at lease the others have a chance at completing the mission. Hopefully it's enough to convince my father of Westerfield's intentions.

One of the members of the crew takes my bag. He's a few years older than I am, with a shaved head that doesn't do a good job of hiding the mark on his neck.

He sees me staring at it. "My job doesn't require me to wander the streets on missions, just power this beauty here," he gives the submarine a love tap.

"Oh," I can't muster anything else.

"First mission?" he grins with crooked teeth.

"Yes."

"I'm Kellen," he offers me his hand in a firm shake. "Welcome aboard," he gestures for me to come inside like an emcee introducing a show.

The submarine is lined with blue-tinted windows rimmed in silver chrome. Beyond the windows, I can see the bottom of the ocean. We descend a ladder from the top hatch into the vessel, which is separated into three main compartments. The captain—a boy who doesn't look much older than I am and is probably skinnier—sits in the middle compartment. The two compartments on either side are stocked with snacks and lined with plush couches. I sink into one of the cushions on the left.

I sit next to Rory, who sits next to Skylar. Nero and Romni grab a couch across from us. "I just can't wait to see the look on Westerfield's face when he realizes we're there!" Romni smirks.

"It's a little early to be cocky," Rory warns.

"Confident," Romni corrects.

"Agreed." Nero stretches back across the seat, resting his hands behind his head. "Ten bucks says Westerfield goes running for the hills as soon as he finds out The Revealed's there."

"I'll take that bet." Rory raises an eyebrow. "You've never met the guy before. He's creepy, and...."

My mind begins to focus on the upcoming mission. All I have to do is find my father. My goal is to talk to him, convince him to stay out of the spotlight. If you asked me ten years ago if talking to my father was difficult for me, I would have laughed. Talking to my mother, yes. But my father and I understand each other. He values my opinion, seeks it out. Well, at least, he used to. Things changed when he declared his run for office. Now, I don't know what he'll think.

"Earth to Lily." Romni waves a hand in front of my face.

My attention snaps back to the present. "Sorry. What?"

"Westerfield," Rory says, "creepy?"

"Yeah," I say, trying to recover. "Yeah, he's ... bad."

Everyone stares at me for a moment longer before diving into the next topic of conversation. Skylar gets up and sits down next to me. "Hi."

"Hello." I smile back.

"Listen, the other night when we were talking—"

"Oh, you mean between the times when you were knocking me to the ground ... yeah."

"Yeah, that," he laughs.

"I expect a rematch in a few months."

"Deal. So that means you're staying then?"

I open my mouth to reply, but the response falls short. I don't know what to say. Am I staying with The Revealed? At first, I wanted to go back to Capitol City. I convinced myself that's exactly what I was going to do. Now, it seems like I'd always been waiting for The Revealed to take me. Almost as if it was my destiny.

Luckily, I'm saved from answering when the submarine suddenly shudders. We're slowing down, nearing the shore. The hatch eventually pops open topside.

Nero and Romni are the first ones out, practically sprinting up the ladder, followed by the rest of us.

The sun hits my eyes, and I blink against the rays, shielding my face with one hand. I look past the blinding light to the blue all around me. The sky looms overhead.

The sky.

I blink again just to make sure I'm really seeing blue above me instead of shiny steel. There are soft wisps of clouds floating above.

"Come on." Skylar offers his hand to me, and I slide off the submarine into the water.

The ocean laps at my skin, beckoning me back into its depths. I look over my shoulder. There are only waves behind me. No hint of an entire facility hidden below the surface.

I wade to shore after the others. Rory immediately goes to the trees just beyond the sand, running her hands through the leaves. The branches come alive beneath her touch, dancing and sprouting small buds. Rory is a tough girl, that's for sure, but as she walks through the trees she looks graceful. She's in her element.

Romni sprints down the beach, spreading his arms and catching the wind on his fingertips. "Freedom!" He acts like we've been in some sort of underwater prison. The way he runs about reminds me of a five-year-old in the midst of a sugar rush.

"Some of us don't handle being cooped up at the facility very well."

Skylar eyes Romni as he sprints around shooting up the water with his abilities and yelling, "Wa-hoo!"

I look back at the water and swallow hard. Somehow being on land makes me feel exposed and vulnerable.

The submarine crew unloads our packs. Kellen hands me mine with one last wink. "Make it happen, Lily."

I muster up a confident, "I will." And take the backpack.

These simple black bags will be our lifelines for the next several days. Trucks are parked ahead, waiting for us just beyond the trees. They will take us to Capitol City, a two-day journey because we've docked on the shores of the Texas wastelands in the Gulf of Mexico.

Skylar volunteers to take the first driving shift. I sit up front while Romni and Nero occupy the back. Rory jumps in a different truck.

To occupy myself on the road, I draw out a document from my bag. It's the email correspondence between Marg and Westerfield.

I study the words:

```
Please be advised that when it comes to
reaching the spiret of justice for the
people, I believe we can best accomplish
this through what lies with the
compromise of independance.
```

What is she talking about? Spiret of justice. Independance.

I rub my head. There are pieces here I'm just not seeing.

"What are you staring at?" Skylar asks.

"That email I showed you," I mutter.

"Still? I really doubt Marg Lansing is buddy buddy with Westerfield in his assassination plans."

I sigh, unable to completely disagree. But, if these past few weeks have taught me anything it's, "You can never know who to trust."

"You can trust me. The Revealed, that is."

I look at him, unsure how to respond. Our eyes meet for a moment, and I notice just how handsome Skylar is.

"Get a room!" Nero pipes up.

Romni snorts.

I completely forgot they were in the backseat.

I look away. I like Skylar but don't want him to get the wrong idea. We're just friends. He's been so helpful while I've transitioned to being with The Revealed, but my heart is still back in Capitol City with Kai.

Skylar turns around in his seat and glares.

"What?" Nero shrugs innocently.

We continue driving, following Rory until it gets dark. We have enough gas stockpiled in the back of the truck to get us to the North American Sector. There aren't exactly gas stations in the wastelands, only long stretches of destruction. Crumbling buildings, where people once lived and worked, are now surrounded by miles of barren land. Sometimes the roads are blocked and we have to find a way around, but for the most part, the drive is flat and easy. Everything around us is completely deserted—nothing but ruins and dirt.

There isn't anything exciting about the wastelands. I used to think they were full of mystery. They aren't. The only words to describe these empty areas are sad, lost, and silent. Everything is still except the rumble of the truck's engine. Even animals have abandoned these places. Once in a while, I spot a bird flying between buildings. That's the only movement. Otherwise, it's dead.

We pull over so Romni can drive for a bit, and I get into the backseat, leaning my head against the window and letting my eyes drift shut as I try to imagine what these places must have looked like twenty years ago—sprawling and magnificent, bustling with people and production. Each city with its own personality as though it was a living, breathing organism. I imagine a shopping center here, an apartment complex there, vivid colors instead of the dismal gray monotone that now stretches out as far as the eye can see.

I sleep for a decent amount of time because when I wake up, we are in a city. It's still dark outside, but it's apparent we've made it to the colonies. I check the clock. We've been traveling for over seventeen hours. My legs are stiff and my back has cramped from sitting so long.

The truck is silent. Nero sleeps next to me; it's strange to see him without his mouth moving. Romni and Skylar are both up front.

"Where are we?" I stifle a yawn.

"Almost into Tennessee," Skylar says.

I groan. "I have to get out of this car."

"There should be a gas station somewhere up ahead." Romni stares out at the street. "I'll stop at the next one I see. We need to get gas anyway."

Romni calls Rory, who's driving the truck in front of us, and tells her the plan. After a few more blocks, Rory finds a station and pulls into the parking lot. I immediately hop out of the truck and stretch my legs. The night is quiet. The town is sleepy and small. Not many people are traveling at this hour. Luckily the gas station is open twenty-four hours, because I need the restroom. I grab a hat from my bag and tuck my hair underneath it. It's the best disguise I can muster right now.

"I'll be right back," I tell the group.

"By yourself?" Rory stops me. "I should go, too."

I wave her off. "I don't need an escort." I jog inside. The cashier watches me and grins pleasantly when I look her way. She seems friendly enough. Must be bored out of her mind working this late. She taps on the touch-screen tablet in front of her with languid fingers, browsing the Internet.

Magazines are displayed in a rack beneath the counter. Most feature Westerfield and my father with stern, debate-like game faces. I notice one features me front and center on the cover, proclaiming my missing-person status. I pull my hat down farther and head to the back of the store.

I bend over the drinking fountain and take a long gulp. My throat is so raw. It makes my skin crawl being stuck in such a small place for so long. I lean over, stretching my back again. Then I take another long drink of water and hear the chime of the bells as someone enters.

Boots clatter on the tile floor.

I peek around the corner and then slam my back against the wall.

Soldiers. The gray uniforms give them away as border patrolmen. I don't miss seeing the pistols at their hips, either.

I tip my head around the corner again. The soldiers have both of our trucks blocked in.

"We just wanted to make sure there wasn't anything suspicious going on here, ma'am," one soldier with a red face says to the cashier, leaning against the counter. My heart jumps into my throat. "It isn't often that a bunch of young kids are traveling near the wastelands this late at night, wouldn't you agree?"

"I wouldn't know, sir," the cashier shrugs.

"Do you mind if we take a look around?" the other, taller soldier asks.

I press my back more firmly against the wall.

"Of course not," she replies.

"Is anyone else in the store?" The tall officer scans the room, and I pray I'm hidden well enough that they won't see me.

"There's a young girl here," the cashier tells him. "I think she just went into the restroom. If you officers want to wait I'm sure she'll be right along."

"Thank you," the red-faced officer says and rolls back casually on the heels of his boots, looping his thumbs through his belt loops and facing the short hallway leading to the bathrooms. The hall where I now crouch, barely out of sight.

"Is everything alright?" the cashier asks.

"Everything's fine," the tall officer says, leaning comfortably against the counter.

I slip inside the bathroom. My abilities aren't developed enough yet to get me out of this one. I'll have to figure out a Plan B. There is a small window above the last stall. I bolt the main door and slide into the stall, locking that door behind me as well. Carefully balancing, I stand on the lid of the toilet and hoist myself up high enough to peer through the window.

It's small. Even if I could break it, would I fit through it? If I could, I'd probably fall and break something on the other side.

There's a pounding on the door. It's the cashier. "Miss," she asks, "are you alright?"

I curse under my breath before yelling, "Just a minute!"

I drop back down to the floor and wait, listening for movement. I picture the cashier standing outside with the two soldiers.

After a few more beats of silence, the cashier calls again, "Miss, I'm afraid you're going to have to open the door."

The time for games is over. I take a deep breath and ready my body, focusing my mind.

"I'm coming!" I frantically search for another way out.

There isn't one.

If these soldiers recognize me, our whole mission will be compromised. It isn't like the world has forgotten about my existence. I've seen the online headlines while I've been with The Revealed, and I'm all over them. By now, everyone knows I've been taken by The Revealed. If these men read any sort of news, there's a good chance I'm not going to make it out of here.

I open the bathroom door. "Is there a problem?" I ask innocently, staring between the two soldiers, praying my hat is shielding enough of my face.

The tall one narrows his eyes and put his hands on his hips. "Are you with that group outside?"

"Yes, sir." I nod.

"And just where are you all headed?"

Crap.

No doubt they've already asked the others, and I have no idea what kind of answer they gave.

"Up the coast." I shrug, trying to give as generic an answer as possible. "It's the election, so…."

"The other girl outside said you were heading to the city to start a catering company?" the officer on the left volunteers.

Rory would say that.

"Well, we are," I say, shrugging. "See … we figured that with the election, it would be a good time to start a company … since the country is starting fresh and everything…." What am I saying?

I wait for a moment longer as both soldiers scrutinize me.

"Anything else?" I finally ask.

Neither answers.

"Well, I should probably get back to my friends then…."

"Actually," the soldier on my right cuts in, "if we could just see your identification, you can then be on our way."

ID?

I fumble around in my pockets, though I know it isn't there. Nervously, I laugh. "I must have left it in the car." I point outside and begin walking toward the exit.

"Miss, you know it is sector policy that you carry your identification card with you at all times."

"Of course," I say and nod, "like I said, it's right out in the car."

In reality, it's back in my room at The Revealed's headquarters. It wouldn't do me any good to carry around an ID that reads "Lilith Atwood," better to be caught with no ID.

"We'll just follow you out," the officer says.

"Great," I say. "No problem." They follow me out. As we get closer to the truck, I widen my eyes at Rory. This is bad. This is really, really bad.

"Hey Skylar," I call, "will you get my purse for me? My ID's in there, and these soldiers would like to see it." I emphasize my words, hoping one of them will get the hint.

Instead, Skylar moves to the side door.

I hold my breath.

I hear movement behind me. A struggle, only it isn't much of a fight because it ends quickly.

I turn to find both soldiers on the ground, vines twisting around their waists. They aren't moving.

"They're not …," I can't bring myself to finish my sentence.

"Of course not," Skylar says. "We don't kill unless we absolutely can't avoid it."

I nod distantly. Good to know.

Nero and Romni stand over the soldiers, dusting off their hands and wearing smug grins.

"Come on!" Skylar barks. "We have to get out of here! Now!"

As I run to the black truck, I glance back at the store window. The cashier is already on the phone, clearly having seen the melee in the parking lot. The military will probably be here in less than an hour.

I jump in next to Rory, and we speed down the highway. As soon as we're out of sight I can't help but curse. "That was bad." I shake my head.

"We've been through worse," Rory says. "We'll have to see about getting you a fake ID once we get back though."

"Now the entire military will be on us," I sigh.

Rory snorts. "Please," she scoffs, "they already are. We deal with this sort of thing every time we step on dry land. It isn't new. They won't get anywhere."

By now the sun is rising. I glance out at the world around me. Green grass, clear water, beautiful houses. Six years ago no one thought this was possible. But we've come so far, accomplished so much, and now?

Today is Election Day.

CHAPTER TWENTY-TWO

Some other members of The Revealed are at a small coffee shop on the outskirts of town, waiting for us. They're more experienced members and have made their home in Capitol City, integrating themselves into the government.

We pull into a side yard at the coffee shop that can barely be called a parking lot. It's just red dirt. Tire tracks form worn patterns that could almost be mistaken for parking space lines, if you looked quickly.

By the time we arrive, the sun is high in the sky. People will have been awake for hours. The few with computers will have opened their electronic ballots to vote. Everybody else will go to schools, fire stations, whatever government buildings are left in their communities to cast their ballots in person.

The frosty air hits me as I step from the car, and I zip up my jacket. My nose is surely a nice shade of pink from the cold. Winter has never been my best look.

At this point, we're tired. My rear end is sore from the long trip. I shuffle with the rest of the group into the coffee shop, and the delicious smell of the fresh brew hits us. It calls to me. My body craves the caffeine. My mission isn't to sip hot espresso though.

A bell tinkles lightly as we step inside onto the hardwood floors. It's quiet here. Only a few patrons huddle in corners with their coffees. The rest of the shop is dotted with fresh plants, some off to the side, others hanging from the ceiling. The large windows in the back showcase an empty outdoor patio.

"Right on time." Zared, a veteran member of The Revealed, steps up to greet us. He has a history of successful missions, and I feel better that he's on this trip. Skylar told me on the way that last he heard, Zared was in the Japanese Sector, scouting for new members. It's comforting to know The Revealed take this mission seriously enough that they called one of their best to help. Hell, it's comforting just looking at Zared. He's all muscle, and even his boulder of a shaved head looks like it could take a person out. The thing about The Revealed is that most members are deceptively fragile-looking, myself included. We're barely adults, and most of the group was malnourished until they became one of the Taken Eighteen. Sure, they've been training their bodies and have grown strong, but they still don't look like fighting machines. Zared looks like a threat.

"Shall we?" Zared extends his hand toward the door, allowing us to lead the way. "Cara's already outside prepping."

"Of course she is," Nero scowls. He clearly wants the caffeine as well. For once, I appreciate his frustrated quips.

I stare longingly back at the coffee machine and try to get one more whiff of the freshly roasted beans before sauntering back into the crisp air. I wrap my arms protectively around my chest.

Zared leads us out to his SUV where his partner, Cara, is moving a stack of gear from the front seat to the trunk. She's dressed in leathery black, a sleeker uniform than I'm used to seeing, but the stamp of The Revealed over the heart distinguishes the garment. She pulls on a vest that covers the symbol and flicks her long red locks over her shoulder.

Sometime today, Westerfield will try to have my dad and mom shot. My stomach heaves. Suddenly, I'm glad I didn't have the coffee. With all these nerves, the last thing I need is an added jolt of caffeine right now.

Zared takes off his gloves and throws them in the passenger seat of his car. "Let's get started then," he says to our group.

Nero raises an eyebrow. "Let's."

Zared ignores him. "Who's heading your group?"

Eyes shift toward Rory.

Zared looks her over. "I should have known."

She shrugs. "We didn't really appoint anyone." And the way her cheeks light up, I can tell she definitely doesn't see Zared as a threat.

"Don't disregard your talent," Zared says in a way that only makes her blush deepen. They've obviously met before.

Rory catches me watching their beguiling exchange. I raise an eyebrow, *Another boy, Rory? Really?*

She rushes to explain. "Zared was my mentor when I first arrived at the facilities."

Mentor. Right.

"Whoa, whoa, whoa," Nero holds up his hands, never missing an opportunity to speak his mind. "Mentor?"

"Zared's the one who took me," Rory explains, her cheeks still red. Rory never blushes. Ever. She's always the collected, confident one around boys.

"That's right." Zared puts a hand on Rory's shoulder. I catch the tenderness there too. "And who are you?"

"Nero." He sticks out his meaty hand.

Zared envelops it in his own, brusquely.

"And who are these other crew members?" Zared looks over our group. We seem so motley compared to Zared and Cara, who embody composure and professionalism.

"This is Skylar, Nero, Romni, and—" Rory motions toward me, "our newest addition, Lily."

"Lily Atwood," Zared says, nodding. "I heard you were a candidate. I expect you'll do great things with The Revealed. Pleasure. Now," Zared walks around to the driver's side of his large black SUV, "let's get to work. We've only got about seven hours before the election announcement and Westerfield's sniper is dispatched. We'll head into the city. There's already a crowd gathering in front of the White House. We're about an hour from the Capitol."

Zared doesn't mess around.

"You all know Cara?" Zared rests a hand on her shoulder. "She's been undercover in the capitol now for two years working as an aide in the Westerfield camp. She's an invaluable asset, as she's had the opportunity to work directly with him. She knows how he thinks and operates. Hopefully, it'll give us the edge in hunting down this sniper. We believe he'll be located in one of the warehouses east of the Capitol Building. That gives him the most access to the stage without having to worry about the density of the crowd. We'll check that location while Lily gets to her father. Understood? Between our two groups, we should be able to stop this attack."

Zared walks around to the driver's side and continues talking. "We'll head directly into the city by car as far as possible. Stay close." He jumps into the vehicle.

"Who does this guy think he is?" Nero rolls his eyes, climbing into the backseat of our truck.

Rory glares back at him as she gets in. "*That's* the man who's going to save your life," she snaps.

"Swoon much?" Nero mumbles.

Rory lets it go with one quick huff. No point in arguing with someone who always has to make a point.

We pull back onto the highway and head into the heart of the city.

In my mind, I replay the last time I saw my parents. It's hard to remember the specifics, to be honest. It feels like I haven't really seen either of them in months. But I was just starting to make headway with my mother. We were just beginning to understand each other. Now, I'm back to the beginning. She has to understand me as this whole new person, someone who has seen the world in a different way. My parents don't like change unless it involves an uptick in the social hierarchy. They suffered enough change during the war to last a lifetime. The disappearance of their only child, no doubt, has left them reeling. Now, just before the election, I'm going to show up and rearrange everything they thought they knew. Again.

I'm apprehensive. There's a good chance they'll reject me now. The change will be too much for them, so they'll shut it out completely.

We reach the city, and Zared wasn't kidding. It's a madhouse.

Election Day seems to have brought everyone to the city. People have traveled from the farthest corners of the North American Sector to be at the announcement event. It's like Times Square used to be on New Year's Eve. A mecca for dreams and hopes. There are even a few wealthy enough to have flown here from other countries. It's a historic moment, after all. A day people have been talking about for six years following the collapse of the previous government.

There are people crowding the streets, forcing us to drive slowly, inching our way along. But the closer we get, the more congested it is. We don't have time for this. My frustration rises each time more people step in front of our car. Again, I'm grateful I didn't indulge in coffee. Caffeine jitters combined with my anxiety might just cause a heart attack. In fact, I probably don't even need the caffeine to have one. All I have to do is picture Westerfield's face, and my heart begins to pound erratically.

The sun follows us like sand in an hourglass trickling down as our time dwindles. At least I'm not the only nervous one. Skylar twiddles his fingers atop the steering wheel. We aren't getting anywhere, and we don't have time to waste.

"Maybe we should turn around?" I offer.

"Maybe," he agrees.

We stay sitting in the middle of the street. Zared will be the one to make the call, and he's in the car in front of us.

People weave around our car, all converging on the same place. Skylar moves the car an inch and then stomps the brake to avoid hitting a stout man, who shimmies past the bumper. I press my fingers over my eyes.

There isn't time.

Skylar goes back to twiddling his fingers. Dun, dun, dun, dun....

"Will you cut that out?" Nero's voice breaks the silence.

Skylar freezes. "Sorry." I tense next to him. He drops his hand from the wheel. No point being at nine and three if we're in park.

Zared makes a sharp right into a parking garage.

Finally!

There are only a few spaces left on the top floor. We take them and get out of our vehicles.

"We'll walk from here," Zared says.

I know this area. Capitol Building is about a mile from here.

We have five hours until the announcement at 8:00 p.m.

Everywhere I look, I see crimson red and sapphire blue—my father's and Westerfield's campaign colors. People hold signs, wear T-shirts; some even paint their faces as if this were the largest sporting event in the world.

I stay close to Skylar's shoulder, worried I'll be lost in the crowd.

"Lily," Cara says, coming up beside me. "Your father is in the south wing of the Capitol Building in his office on the second floor. He has three levels of security, but you should be able to get past them as soon as they see your face. Do you think you can convince him? We're counting on you to warn him."

I nod, knowing this was the plan all along. We all have a part to play.

"Good girl." Cara gives me a firm clap on the back. I reflexively grip Skylar's wrist to balance myself. He chuckles and holds me steady. The easy smile on his face makes me recoil. This isn't time for games.

The entrance gates to the Capitol Building are open, but there isn't room for everyone to get through, so the crowd has spilled out onto the streets. People are jumping up and down trying to get a better view of the stage.

I pan the crowd. There are buildings around us, and so many people. It will be impossible to find a sniper in such a large group. The killer could be hiding anywhere. The Revealed have their guesses, but no guarantees.

I scan the windows of the buildings, then back over my other shoulder, looking into the crowd. Such an eclectic group of people. They may *all* be snipers, for all I can tell.

Suddenly, I realize there is no one familiar around me. I got distracted and lost my group in the sea of red and blue. The outfits we'd been given at the facilities matched the theme so we would blend in. My T-shirt is a fitting blue, my father's colors. I glance through the crowd, trying to find the others.

And then I see Kai.

He's standing near the stage in his military uniform, next to security. There are cameras around him, all pointed in his direction from behind the press line. People in the crowd are huddling around him, trying to get a better look, though security manages to keep them at bay. He holds himself high, like usual, but seems distracted today. He ignores anyone calling his name. He doesn't even fake a smile. His lips are drawn in a thin line, and his green-gold eyes are narrowed.

My heart stops.

I have to go to him.

"Excuse me," I say, pushing through the crowd. I squeeze myself between people, forgetting everything around me but him. "Please, I need to get through."

He is so close.

"Lily!"

A hand reaches out and grips my shoulder.

I glance back to see who it is. "Rory."

Then I turn toward Kai again. He's so close all I want is to run into his arms. My body aches to bridge the gap. But I remember the deal I made with Julia.

Rory follows my gaze. "This isn't the time to get distracted." She directs me away from Kai. "Focus." It takes me a few minutes to regain my sense of direction. Luckily, Rory keeps hold of my wrist, weaving me through the crowd.

"Get a little lost?" Nero smirks as I rejoin the group.

I nod, wistfully looking over my shoulder again. All I see now are clumps of people behind me.

I hear a reporter going live on camera off to my right: "Some people have been waiting outside the Capitol Building for days. One man in the crowd said he'd brought his tablet with him so he could vote at midnight. Electronic voting closes at five p.m. The committee on voter authentication has been preparing for this day for years, and their job is coming to a close as the afternoon wanes. We have just been told following the polls closing, the committee will complete some last-minute verifications before the results of the election are announced at eight p.m. sharp. As you can see, there is a crowd of tens of thousands lined up behind me. All of them anxiously waiting to see who the first president of the North American Sector will be."

"Is everything okay?" Skylar asks.

"Mm-hmm."

"Good." Zared steps forward. "Because we don't have time to waste. Lily, you should head around the side of the building. Get past security and find your parents. Skylar will go with you and wait outside."

"Got it," I say, nodding.

"The rest of us will patrol around the crowd and try our best to locate the sniper. We'll split up into groups of two and canvas the area. We'll meet back here in two hours when the polls close to report, got it? That's five p.m. people. Be here."

"Right."

Skylar and I begin sprinting toward the building, dodging people as best we can. "Excuse me," I shout, moving around people. "Can I please get through?" My voice falls on deaf ears.

"Bring them home! Bring them home!" Demonstrators march around us in a cluster. They wave signs pleading for the return of the Taken Eighteen.

My gaze meets Skylar's, and I finally give up trying to be polite. I push through the crowd and don't look back. I plow through clumps of people with my face down, hidden by my hair. The last thing I need is someone to recognize me. Especially because I'm supposed to be one of the Taken Eighteen—I *am* a Taken Eighteen. Anyone who recognizes me would probably freak out.

People glare as I shove past them. "Hey!" a few say, but most are in an accommodating mood, relieved and excited this day has finally come. Eventually, Skylar and I make it around to the side entrance.

Security forms a wall before the doors, blocking people from getting within twenty feet of the entrance. They're all armed. I'm also very aware that there will be Secret Service stationed inside the adjacent buildings as well, with weapons trained toward the crowd as an added precaution. Westerfield will have his own protection, though his snipers won't be for his own physical safety.

"Hang back," I tell Skylar, stopping and extending my hand. "If they realize I'm with The Revealed, they'll either have you arrested or they'll shoot you."

Skylar backs up a few steps. "I'll definitely stay here then."

"Be back soon."

I scan down the security line, not quite sure how to approach. But the decision is made for me. "Ms. Atwood?" Evan steps forward, his brows pulled together. "Ms. Atwood?" he asks again, more certain this time.

There isn't time for me to feel afraid. "I need to see my father," I tell him directly.

"But you—"

"This is an emergency!" I say again, glancing over my shoulder at the crowds.

Evan fumbles to pull his headpiece mic to his mouth. "Lily Atwood is outside."

"Stop playing around, Evan," a voice on the other end shoots back.

"Sir, Ms. Atwood is here to see her parents."

"Excuse me?"

"She's at the entrance."

"You're seeing things, Evan," the voice on the other end repeats. "Lily Atwood is part of the Taken Eighteen now. She wouldn't be—"

I grab the mic from the security guard and hold it to my lips. "Darren?" I ask. Darren was Jeremy's second-in-command, which means he's probably in charge now, and probably the voice I'm hearing.

"Who is this?" the man asks.

"Darren, this is Lily Atwood. Either you authorize my entrance or my parents find out about your negligence. Your call. All I have to do is find a phone, and I can make the call directly to my father."

If Darren has just been promoted, he won't take even the slightest chance at risking his new, coveted authority. There is a pause. Then Darren answers, "I'll be right down."

Smugly, I hand the microphone back to Evan. His expression is a nervous grimace. He's resisting the urge to slink away from me, unsure how to take my sudden emergence.

A burly man in a black suit bursts through the door only a minute later. It's Darren. He takes one look at me and his mouth falls open. He scrubs a hand down his face. But I don't have time for their gawking. "This is an emergency, so if you don't mind." I push around Darren and the others before they can object, and run inside.

"Wait! Ms. Atwood!" I can hear Darren running behind me, but I don't stop. I know exactly where my father will be. I could find his office with my eyes closed.

I sprint down the hallway and throw open the door. Security immediately turns on me, ready to deal with a threat, but pauses.

My father is hunched over a desk with a few other people, making last-minute adjustments to the speeches. He has two speeches—one, a concession speech, the other, the first speech he'll give as president of the North American Sector.

He stops and glances up from his work at the commotion. His expression drops, then pulls together in confusion. "Lily?"

My mother moves around security at the sound of my name. "Oh my God!" She races toward me and throws her arms around me, pinning me into a hug that has no intention of ever ending. "Oh my God." She runs her hands over my hair. Moisture smears my neck. She's crying.

"Leave," my father says, motioning around the room. Despite their curiosity, people begin filing out. Security takes their position right outside the door.

My father is by my side in seconds and reaches out to hold my face in his strong yet gentle hands. "Are you hurt?" he asks. "How did you escape?"

"I didn't." I shake my head, shrugging out of his grip.

My mother pulls back and looks at me. Being her usual self, she starts tucking stray strands of my hair back behind my ears. "It's a miracle," she says.

My father reaches out to me too, "We thought—"

"You thought right." I snap my fingers and a flame appears.

My mother covers her mouth with her hand, horrified. The tears are already drying in streaks across her face.

"What did they do to you?" my father asks.

"It's a surgery, Dad. It improves your mind."

"What?" My mother touches my hand as though she expects it to be hot. It isn't. Nero wasn't joking when he said everyone thinks that at first.

My father is furious. "Where are they?"

"I don't have a lot of time," I say. "This isn't about me right now, okay? I'm fine. They didn't hurt me. None of it is what you thought, Dad. I'm here to help you. Westerfield's planning on having you assassinated if you go up on that stage. Just before a winner is announced. He wants to blame it on the Eastern European Sector so he has an excuse to start another war and take over their territory." I hand him the folder with some of the evidence The Revealed have collected. He takes it and scans through the pile of papers.

"Where did you get this?" He stares down at the files.

"The Revealed have been collecting it for the past few months."

My father sets the folder down on the table.

"Dad, don't go on that stage. I know you think I'm a still child, but you have to listen to me. The Revealed aren't who we thought they were. They've been helping us this whole time. Westerfield has a sniper positioned somewhere out there. There's a slim chance we can find him. Even if we take one out, there will probably be another there to take his place. You have to leave."

"No, I have to go on that stage." My father's resolve is firm. "The winner of the first North American Sector presidential race is about to be announced. This is not the time for the country to question the courage of its leadership."

"The Revealed can't protect you up there!" I argue.

"The Revealed have never done me any favors before. I'm prepared to take all risks for the sake of this new nation."

"You aren't listening to me!" In my passion, a wind picks up around me. I need to focus like Julia taught me. I take a deep breath.

All my mother can do is stare, her jaw slack in mute horror. Somehow her shock still manages to look graceful, and for the first time, she doesn't add her two cents.

"You can't go up there. He's planning on putting a bullet in your head! Both of you! You can't risk this, Dad. For our family and for this nation. We need you."

"Yes. They need me. I have to go out there." My father lays a hand on my shoulder, "They need me now to step up as a leader, not run and hide in the shadows. I understand what you're saying Lily, and you probably mean what you're saying. But the country needs me to stand tall right now. They could have chosen to elect me as their president. Now is not the time to run and hide. I have to go out there."

My voice breaks. "Dad…."

I look back and forth at my parents.

Jet knocks on the door, then opens it. "The reporters are just about ready for you. Again, if you can stress to people to get out and vote if they haven't already, there's still an hour and a half left." He doesn't even notice me. Typical Jet.

"I'm coming," my father says, nodding. He straightens out his jacket. "And please tell security to double their efforts in the crowds and surrounding buildings."

At least he's sort of listening to what I said.

"Will do, sir." Jet steps back, and I can hear him mumbling the order into his headpiece.

I sigh and turn to look out the window at the crowds below, running my hand through my hair.

Then I freeze.

"Darren," my father calls to Darren, who's waiting just outside the door, "please confiscate Lily's belongings. Have them delivered directly to the Department of Security for review. This may be our key to bringing down The Revealed."

"Wait!" I turn on him. I grab for the papers on the desk. Luckily, the one I need is right on top of the pile. I read Marg's words again for the hundredth time in the last day.

```
Please be advised that when it comes to
reaching the spiret of justice for the
people, I believe we can best accomplish
this through what lies with the
compromise of independance.
```

I pull the email correspondence in front of my face. *Spiret of liberty. Independance.* The misspelled words begin to piece together in my mind.

I whirl around again and look out the window.

Spirit of Justice Park!

The realization knocks the wind out of me.

She's talking about Spirit of Justice Park! Independence is the road right in front of the park. It's Independence Avenue, which is why it's misspelled. These are instructions!

I stare back down at the email, my eyes flicking over the information.

"Dad!" I say hurriedly.

He ignores me. "And see that Lily arrives home safely to her room and stays there until after the election announcement."

"Dad, I'm not going with them."

My father turns from me.

"Dad!" He has to pay attention. "Dad!"

"This is for your own good, Lily. They've messed with your mind."

"Dad! I just need to make a call. Just one call!" I scream.

Security moves around me.

"You don't get it!" I say in a panic. "The Revealed are helping you! Look at this email!" The paper is ripped from my hand. "They're at the park. There's someone at the park! Dad!"

"I'll see you at home," my father says. "We'll discuss everything after the announcement this evening. We'll figure all of this out, get you the help you need, and find the people that did this to you. The important thing is that you're home now."

They're forcing me from the room.

"No!" I'm hysterical. "Mom!" She won't look at me anymore; she's crying again. "Mom, Marg Lancing is in on it!"

Hands clasp my shoulders. I shove the paper into my pocket and grab for whatever I can reach, catching a wrist and making my touch burn.

"Listen to me!" I bite my lip and the taste of blood shoots through my mouth. "Stop!"

Evan pulls away cursing, but bringing down one guard isn't enough. There are more where he came from. Security grabs my wrists this time, making sure I can't touch anybody, and escorts me outside.

"This is a mistake!" I yell at my father as I'm dragged into the hallway.

A wind kicks up, lifting my hair and blowing papers to the floor. But it doesn't have enough power to make them let go of my shoulders. I'm not strong enough yet.

I walk with them down to the first floor. No one says a word. Just before they put me in the car I try to break free, yanking my arms toward the center of my body to get them to drop their grip. Their hands release my wrists, and I turn on my heels, sprinting back toward the front of the building.

My eyes connect with Skylar's through the crowd. He's waiting at the back door of the Capitol Building.

"The park!" I scream.

His brows furrow because he can't hear me.

"They're at the park!" I gesture wildly. His eyes go wide as hands clamp around me and pull me back to the awaiting vehicle.

"They're at the park!" I scream one last, hopeless time.

I can hear the cheers of the crowd and the chants of protesters just on the other side of these walls. The noise blurs into a steady hum of energy radiating from the people. *Hurry Skylar. You're my only hope.*

Evan secures plastic cuffs over my hands, binding my palms so they press against each other. Darren puts his hand on my head and eases me into the backseat. There's no reasoning with security. They're under strict orders, and they're trained to follow those orders at all costs.

I'm not giving up. I can't afford to give up. If I don't find a way out of this it won't just mean my parents' deaths. It will mean Westerfield will take over as leader of the North American Sector, make it his mission to hunt and kill The Revealed, and throw the world back into war. He'll become a dictator who will concentrate power in even fewer hands, mainly his own.

Darren rolls the window down as we approach the house and punches in the gate code.

"You have to listen to me." I lean forward. "You can't keep me here."

"Your father's orders." He shrugs indifferently, pulling the car around to the front of the house.

"No," I try again, "you don't understand. If you keep me in this house my father will be dead before they announce the winner. Roderick Westerfield has no intention of letting my father win, don't you see? He wants power any way he can get it, at any cost."

"Miss, your father has plenty of security making sure he's safe," Evan pipes up from the front passenger seat.

"It isn't enough." I try to pull myself closer to him, but hands hold me back. They're smart, because I'm seriously considering my options. "There's a sniper, Evan. Come on, you're not stupid. *Think* about this!"

He gives me a hard look for a moment, and I have him. But then he looks away.

I kick the seat in front of me.

The car stops at the front of the house, and I'm escorted inside to my room. They lock the door behind me. No one bothers to untie my hands.

Now this house really is a prison.

Immediately, I go to the balcony only to find five security members patrolling the grounds below. My father doesn't mess around when he gives orders.

"This is kidnapping!" I yell down.

"It's for your own good," one of the security guards responds. He is a large man, more pudgy than muscular, but I don't doubt he would take me down in a heartbeat if I jumped over the ledge. "If we don't protect you, The Revealed will take you again."

My fists clench and I mumble, "I'm part of The Revealed, you moron." I grind my teeth as I turn back toward the window.

Although, being a member of The Revealed doesn't seem to be doing me much good right now. My mind isn't strong enough yet to use the elements like Zared or Rory. I can't throw out my hand and make the glass explode. I can't move the trees to attack like the others.

For now, I wait. I can only hope Skylar got to the others in time. I'll stay in this prison if it means The Revealed can save my parents and stop Westerfield.

I check the clock. We are supposed to be regrouping with Zared right now.

The polls have just closed.

I use my front teeth to switch on the television and the news comes on. Every media outlet is covering the presidential election announcement. Not just the announcement itself, but all-day footage of the rally. People holding their signs, commenting on the important issues and on The Revealed, especially.

The crowd is going crazy. The vote has ended. The nation has a new leader.

An anchorman's voice rises over the din of spectators, "… only two weeks after their daughter was reported missing. Lily Atwood is the latest eighteen-year-old suspected of being abducted by rebel organization The Revealed. Her bodyguard was found dead on the house grounds with no evidence of Ms. Atwood to be found. Her parents have not heard from her since. Despite everything, Mark Atwood has continued his campaign with valor and strength in these difficult times. He cancelled his campaign plans in the north, returning to Capitol City early to be at home with his grieving family."

Helplessness begins to consume me. I try not to dwell on my small part in this big picture of the catastrophe that's about to unfold. Instead, I need to focus on getting out of here. There has to be a way to escape. Feeling defeated won't get me anywhere.

The news station keeps a digital countdown in the corner. It ticks down the minutes until eight o'clock. Two hours and fifty-seven minutes left.

I slide my wrists together. They move only slightly and the cords burn my skin. The bands don't loosen, but I'm able to twist my hands just slightly so my fingers aren't touching. After repeating this action a few times, I can run my index finger and thumb of each hand against one another. It's enough to give me some range of motion. I hold my wrists away from my body. One of my shoulders pops with the stretch. The position isn't comfortable. But I can snap my fingers and the flame spreads over my fingertips, just not enough to melt the plastic.

I move to the balcony and look over the edge. The men are still there. I jiggle the door handle, and it doesn't budge. There aren't any phones in my room, and I lost my cell when my bag was confiscated.

There isn't anything useful that would aid in an escape. No tools to pick a lock.

The noise of the television in the background does nothing to disarm my anxiety, but I can't bear to turn it off. I can see Independence Avenue in the background of the footage and the park just beyond that.

I have to get out of here.

I pace back and forth, snapping my fingers and then letting the fire burn out.

If only I were stronger. Maybe Julia shouldn't have let me come. I should have trained harder. If my mind were like Rory's or Skylar's I would be out of here by now.

I push my hip against the door and try to swivel my hands around the doorknob.

The door is locked.

Am I desperate enough to burn it down?

If I touch the door I can light a fire. That could keep security occupied long enough for me to get out. Or the fire would spread, and I might be trapped in the blaze. I might burn down the entire house, but then I never liked this place anyway.

I move toward the door.

Just as I am about to set it on fire, it flies open.

I spring back, tumbling over myself as I try to avoid being hit.

Rory stands in the doorway.

Evan is at her side, along with a few other security officers, though they aren't moving to fight her. What's going on? Why aren't they trying to get rid of her?

"Rory?" I ask hesitantly.

"I came just as soon as I heard you were back." She wraps me in a tight hug and then whispers into my ear, "Just play along." She pulls back and stares at me with this worried look on her face. "I was catering your father's after-party event at the Capitol Building. I ran into security at the rally, and was told you'd turned up alive in your father's office. I came as soon as I heard." She wraps me in another forceful embrace. "Did they hurt you? Are you hurt?"

"No?" I say, trying to play along despite my confusion.

"Where are they, Lily?" she demands. "Where are The Revealed?"

"The Revealed?"

I realize suddenly what she's doing. The outside world doesn't know Rory is a member. Only I do. Evan was always infatuated with her, always looking for a way to impress her. She probably fooled him into allowing her into the house. Stupid boy, I'm sure he was hoping to win her affection.

"She isn't talking," Evan explains, putting on this air of superiority. "She says The Revealed were *helping* her."

"Helping?" Rory puts a hand to her mouth. It's all an act. "Lily what have they done to you?"

"I'm fine, really," I say, still unsure which words are the right ones. What I really want to tell her is that there's a sniper at the park across Independence Avenue. I bite my already sore lip. Now is not the time. Now the information would just alert them that we're on the same team.

"She's clearly been brainwashed." Rory shakes her head, gripping the sides of my face with concern. "She should be at a hospital. She needs to be looked at."

"I'm sure her father will make arrangements soon," Evan agrees.

"I'd like a moment, if you don't mind? Alone with her?" Rory's eyes fill with concern. "Maybe I can talk some sense into her?"

Evan immediately objects. "That isn't a good idea. She's stronger than she looks."

"I'll take care of her," Rory promises.

"No, miss," Evan insists, "you don't understand. She can do these weird things with her hands. She isn't safe."

"She won't hurt me," Rory says assuredly. "Please, I really feel like if I had a chance to talk to her I could make her see reason."

Rory saunters up to Evan, and I can see her eyelashes batting even from here. She pouts to emphasize her plea, but I'm done hanging around here. I can feel the guard moving behind me; as soon as he's close enough, I throw out my elbow, slamming into his gut.

The guard doubles over, and I swing him the rest of the way to the ground.

"Lily!" Rory glances back at me. She rolls her eyes. "This was so *not* part of the plan."

I shrug and then point behind Rory where Evan is staring in shock and confusion.

Rory turns back to him reluctantly. "Sorry," she sighs, and then grabs for the gun at his hip, yanking it from the holster. "Down!" Rory orders. "Everyone back or I'll shoot."

I know Rory wouldn't really hurt anyone, but security doesn't. And Evan is too stunned to do anything but fall to his knees and put his hands behind his head. The others clumsily pull out their weapons and raise them.

Rory shakes her head and sighs before she shoves her hand forward and a wind whips toward the raised weapons. It hits the guards and knocks the guns from their hands.

One-handed, Rory quickly melts off my handcuffs. The gun is still raised in her other hand, steadily pointed at the guards as if she's done this before. Maybe she has.

"Run!" Rory pulls me into the hallway.

She doesn't have to tell me twice.

She sprints with me down the main stairs, through the foyer, and out the front door until we are out on the concrete patio, following the path around the house.

As we round a corner of the house, we run into another wave of security. They take one look at Rory and me barreling toward them and freeze, unsure how to react. They don't exactly want to draw their weapons on the potential president's daughter.

"Stop!" they order, trying to tackle Rory instead.

She handles them all like it's a choreographed dance. Her fighting skills are like something out of a movie. I reach for the closest one and use what I've learned in self-defense class to flip him on his back. With only a few quick movements and twists from Rory's wrists, we are past security, leaving them behind us on the grass.

"How much time do we have left?" I ask as we sprint toward the garage.

"About two and a half hours." Rory keeps her eyes forward.

It isn't enough time. "Have Zared and the others found anything yet?"

"Nothing. They're even searching each room in the surrounding buildings."

I didn't expect better news.

"You know your cover is completely blown. Everyone will know you're a member of The Revealed."

"It's about time," she chuckles. "I'm sick of pretending I can cook."

We head for the garage, and I see the guards talking frantically into their headpieces. No doubt they know we've escaped and are waiting for us.

"Ready?" Rory asks under her breath.

"Definitely," I say, feeling my muscles twitch with electric adrenaline.

"Go."

I sprint toward the side of the garage, punching in the security access code as quickly as I can.

The guards raise their weapons on Rory. She bends low to the ground, throwing out her hands.

"Put your hands up!" security yells.

"I don't think you want me to do that." Rory smirks but does as they ask. I see her eyes narrow in focus. I try to pay attention to my actions instead of staring at Rory, but it's hard not to get distracted by her skill. Rory, of all people. My boy-crazy, free-spirited, best-friend-turned-action hero. Who would have thought?

"What is it with these people and guns?" Rory says, annoyed, not showing an ounce of fear. "They just don't learn."

Security shouts into their headpiece mics, "They're around front!"

For a moment, nothing happens.

Then security begins to curse, dropping their weapons. The metal becomes hot under Rory's control, and the pistols burn their hands. Rory twists her wrists and pulls her hands back to her sides. The guns clatter to the ground.

Still, security advances. Darren is at the front acting as leader. His eyes say he has no intention of backing down. He reaches Rory, gripping her around the neck, yanking her to the ground. The garage door opens.

I turn back to help Rory. Maybe my mind isn't as strong as the rest of The Revealed yet, but that doesn't mean I'm powerless.

I run toward Darren, arms extended and mind focused, ramming my hands into his side and using wind to increase the force of my push. Darren topples to the ground, releasing Rory from his hold.

"Sorry," I say, cringing and looking down at Darren. "But I tried to tell you."

I help Rory stand. There are at least a dozen guards closing in around us, and more are sprinting from the fences. Rory doesn't even flinch, swooping her hands around, the branches on the trees near the driveway mimic her motions. She beckons the branches toward us, and they wrap around the legs of security, pulling four of them to the ground. It gives us the space we need to run to the car. I use DNA recognition to get inside, and the engine roars to life. Rory slides into the passenger seat with barely enough time to close the door when I stomp my foot on the gas.

More guns are drawn, and security shoots at our tires, trying to stop our getaway. One of the tires blows and for a moment, the car swivels around the road. I yank the wheel, trying to straighten out. Thanks to the damage-correcting technology of the car, we don't have to wait long. The tire repairs itself, and the car returns to a smooth and straight trajectory. I really do love this Aston. Luckily, with the car's automatic remote control for the fence, we don't have to try barreling through it. I'm not quite sure how that would turn out.

Rory looks through the back window as I focus on the road, speeding to the highway.

"I can't believe we just did that." I shake my head. Word was probably just reaching my father about my escape.

"Believe it," Rory says. "You're free."

"Free." I lean comfortably against my seat, keeping my hands on the wheel. I never have to go back to that house again.

Rory pulls out her phone and dials a number. I hear Skylar pick up on the other end. And I remember the park.

"Got her," Rory says and smiles.

"Good," he says relieved. "Now get back here. We've still got an assassination to stop."

"On our way."

"Wait," I grab the phone before she can hang up.

The battle isn't over yet.

"Skylar?" I turn the phone on speaker. Rory studies me quizzically with quick looks between me and the road. "It's the park."

"What's the park?" He doesn't get it.

"The email correspondence with Marg. It's coded. They're talking about directions to the park. There's a sniper in the Spirit of Justice Park. Can you guys get there?"

He curses into the phone. "We're there."

Relief, so palpable I shudder, fills me to the core.

The drive back to the announcement area is interminably slow. As we near the Capitol Building, it's clear we aren't going to make it any farther by car. Rory finds a parking lot, and we literally sprint into the city. Finally, we reach the center of the crowd.

I call Skylar again, "Did you get him?"

"Cara and I are here now," Skylar says. "There are tourists everywhere. We checked the roof. We've checked all the rooms. Every nook. There isn't a sniper, Lily."

People are milling all around us, pushing and jostling. I can barely see past the herds of people in front of me. I stare at the other roads around me.

Only an hour and a half left until the announcement.

"Keep looking," I tell Skylar.

I follow Rory to find the others, the phone still pushed against my ear waiting for good news.

Nero tussles my hair. "I can tell you're going to be a troublemaker."

Like he's one to talk.

"My dad's going on that stage," I tell them, resigned.

"We figured that much," Nero says. "In the meantime, there's at least one person floating around this crowd waiting to blow his head off."

"Hey," Zared snaps, "that's enough."

"Yeah, well I say that if he doesn't want our help, we let him face the consequences."

"That's my father!" I advance on Nero.

Rory grips my arm, holding me back. "I'd let you go, babe, but it's not quite Nero's turn to get what he deserves today. Westerfield is up first."

I fling back around with a huff.

"If you don't shut up," I say to Nero, "you can leave." A wind whips around my face, revealing the rage I'm feeling.

"I was just saying." Nero throws up his hands as though he's innocent.

I want to smack him, but there's a sudden commotion on the other end of the phone. I hear Cara scream, "Hey!" in the background.

"Skylar?" I ask, pulling the receiver to my mouth.

There's more commotion.

Then the phone clicks off.

I turn to Rory, "What just happened?"

She takes the phone and calls him back.

No answer.

Voicemail picks up.

Rory calls again.

Then again.

Even Nero is like a statue staring stoically at the phone now.

"What just happened?" I ask again.

Rory doesn't have an answer.

She calls again.

This time, the phone clicks on.

There's silence.

"Skylar?" I ask, my voice quaking.

"We got him," Skylar answers between gritted teeth. "Cara disarmed him."

"What?" my voice rises with hope.

"We found him," Skylar tells me again. "We've got the sniper. Cara has him tied to the ground over here."

In my excitement, I drop the phone.

Rory picks it up from the grass as I collapse, my face in my hands with relief.

Skylar's on speaker saying over and over again, "We got him. We got him."

Rory laughs and hugs me. "We did it. We did it!"

But I don't return the gesture. I freeze.

Staring at the streets around me I remember a part of Marg's email I forgot until this point. Her conclusion to the email correspondence.

```
But remember, campaigning in one state
will not win you the election.
```

I grab the phone. "Skylar, melt the gun, see if you can get any information out of the sniper, then get back here."

"Lily?" Rory looks at me warily, her hands still half up in a cheer but they now turn limp.

I pull the crumpled email printout from my pocket and read out loud, "But remember, campaigning in one state will not win you the election." I look up at the group. "There isn't just one sniper. My guess is, they're everywhere."

My mind is turning.

"What are we going to do now?" Nero snaps.

"The only thing we can do. We'll give the world what they're waiting for. If they expect The Revealed to show up, then we'll show up." My mind begins spinning. "I have an idea."

CHAPTER TWENTY-THREE

It's hard to see over the crowd as I push my way toward the stage. The others follow in my wake.

Suddenly cheers erupt. Everywhere people begin to scream.

My father and Westerfield walk out on the stage, each entering from opposite ends. They shake hands and then take their places behind their respective podiums.

"Good evening," the host says into a booming microphone. "In just a few moments, our country will change."

More screams and frenzied cheers.

"Follow my lead!" I yell, pushing through the front line of the crowd. There's a railing blocking people from getting too close to the stage. Rory and Skylar jump over it after me as we race toward the candidates.

Zared and the others stay back along the gates, creating a blockade against security, which is already heading toward us. No doubt they've been waiting for us to make an appearance since my father discovered I'd escaped from the house. If it weren't for my need to focus, I may have laughed at Zared's perfectly feigned composure. We have one chance to get this right.

"Spread out!" I tell my companions.

"Lily, this better not involve us getting arrested!" Rory yells, eyeballing the security closing in on us.

"Welcome to this historic night," the host begins. His name is Riley Fisher, and he's the most-popular news anchor in the North American Sector. He's like a reflector on stage. His gold hair is slicked back, so shiny it catches the stage lights and gleams like a beacon. His tanned skin is in such contrast to the pale, dirt-stained complexion of the average citizen. The combined glint of his eyes, hair, and teeth is blinding. He stands up on stage with the microphone in his hand and a dazzling smile on his face, waving between my father and Roderick Westerfield.

"The results have been tallied," the announcer continues, "and our country finally has a leader!"

My father holds himself proudly, giving the audience that killer look of his, as though he's taking a second to personally connect with each and every one of them. In reality, he can't see past the footlights on the stage. I know from experience that those lights are so bright it's hard to see anything but their rays.

Westerfield stands directly across the stage from him. He's grinning smugly from ear to ear. It comes across as confidence, but I know what his expression hides. He's staring above the crowds. If the lights weren't shining in his face he would be looking to the surrounding buildings, most likely at the exact place where the snipers are waiting.

I try to follow his gaze, but it's impossible to pinpoint the locations. There isn't time to investigate. The announcement is only moments away.

I grip the stage. Ice spreads from my fingertips like I practiced at the facility. Rory and Skylar copy my gesture, but at opposite ends. Their ice moves faster over the stage than mine. Still, it snakes up the side and across the floor to where the announcer stands.

If my father won't get off the stage himself, The Revealed will make him.

The crowd is so loud now, trumped only by Riley Fisher's voice through the booming speakers. People cheer and chant, lifting their handmade signs and pushing in as close to the stage as they can get. No one notices the ice yet, which is creeping like a shadow out onto the stage.

Riley Fisher continues, "After years of reconstruction and months of campaigning, this night finally signals the beginning of a new chapter in the North American Sector's life. We are a new nation, full of promise and possibility. We have taken pieces of our history and carried them with us, never forgetting the war but instead, learning from it to transform this new nation into what it is today. All it needs is the guidance of strong leadership, which is what brings us to this moment."

The crowd erupts, cheering loudly and drowning out all other sound. Riley Fisher waits until the noise dies down and then he waits even longer. All while the ice from The Revealed is wrapping and crackling its way closer and closer to him.

People begin to notice. There is nervous shuffling from the people at the front of the line—VIPs in a cordoned-off section to the left of the stage spot the ice first.

"What's that?" someone asks, pointing.

Riley Fisher finally opens the envelope he's holding, not realizing that the attention has shifted away from him. "And the first president of the North American Sector, with fifty-four percent of the votes is—"

Riley Fisher's breath catches as the ice wraps around his shoe in thick sheets. He tries to shake his shoe off, but instead, his foot pops out and he scrambles backward, tripping over himself to escape the ice.

The audience's silence is broken by a scream.

"It's The Revealed!" someone cries.

Security reaches Romni first and tackles him to the ground. He's still able to push out his hands, causing a wind to strike the guards with such force that it knocks them backward. Romni breaks free and again grips the stage.

Zared and the others throw out their hands, and the guns security hold grow hot. The guards drop their weapons.

"It's not enough!" I yell.

Rory reads my mind. "Go," she says. I jump onto the stage without hesitation.

"It's Lily Atwood!" I hear the crowd murmur.

Cameras flash.

"Lily Atwood!"

"You have to get out of here!" I tell Riley Fisher, who is trembling where he stands. "You have to tell them to clear this place."

"She's a member of The Revealed!" someone yells. "The Revealed are here!"

"No!" I turn back to the crowd, but there are too many of them. "You don't understand. You have to get out of here." But my voice is lost among the sudden frantic chatter that fills the air. "There's someone out there with a gun and—"

"It's okay. Lily—" My father reaches out to stop me, but something cracks through the air. He drops to the ground.

There's blood everywhere, splattered across the stage and my mother's dress.

"Dad!" I scream, falling to the ground beside him.

I can't tell where he's been hit. "Go," he tells me, his voice stifled with pain. "Go with security."

"Dad!" I bend down over him. "Someone get help!" I cry. I pull the buttons of his jacket open and then his shirt, trying to see past the blood. He needs pressure on the wound. But if it wasn't a clean shot, I know pressure will just drive the bullet deeper.

No one seems to hear anything, let alone my pathetic cries for help. Now the crowd is running, everyone is fleeing from the scene. They all think The Revealed are to blame. It's panic. A stampede of citizens—a mob—floods the streets.

People are pushing over one another in their scramble to get away. The hum of terror in the air is thick and constant like a shrill scream that never grows out of breath.

There's blood on my hands.

My mother rushes to my side. She doesn't even look at me, but her presence reminds me of the bigger picture. "Get off the stage!" I tell her. Security runs to my father, and I scramble aside so they can take over.

I stumble into something; hands reach out for me, but I break free of them. Cold eyes stare at me through the haze of chaos.

"You!" I turn on Westerfield.

He's watching the scene with smug satisfaction carved in his otherwise rigid features. He enjoys the destruction. It feels like I'm looking at him for the first time. I can see the hunger in him— hunger for power no one man should possess. The cunning behind his features, the snake-like deception. He masks it all with a cool calm, but his icy gaze freezes my bones.

"How could you do this!" I demand, raising my hands, unsure what I'm going to do but certain I need to act. I'm going to wipe that expression from his face. My fists clench. A wind whips around me.

Westerfield points a finger at me. "She's a member of The Revealed now!"

Security pour onto the stage. They are mostly concerned with creating a human shield around my father and mother and Westerfield. They pick up my dad, his body looking suddenly fragile, and carry him from the stage. I can't see my mother between the bulky bodies of security. Just the wispy ends of her blue dress.

Someone grabs my shoulders again. "You have to get out of here."

It's Kai.

"You have to get out of here." He begins to push me away. "He'll be okay. I'll stay with them." He means my parents.

I stare for a moment at Westerfield, and consider attacking him. He's challenging me to make a move. Wind whips around my face. Deep breaths.

"This isn't the end."

Skylar comes up beside me. "Come on," he says, pulling my arm.

"I can't leave." I look to Kai and then in the direction my parents were led.

"We don't have a choice." Rory grabs my other arm.

"No!" I start to pull away, but my eyes stay on Kai's.

"Go," Kai tells me.

Rory turns me around, her hand firmly wrapped around my arm.

I run.

The crowds are dispersing, charging to get out of the gates, spilling onto the streets. Only a few bold reporters stand their ground, filming the pandemonium.

Paramedics are pushing their way through the crowd to reach my father.

Rory, Skylar, and I break out onto the streets, getting lost in the panicked masses.

Rory keeps hold of my arm, ensuring that we stay together. I scramble after her to the parking lot where we left the car.

"We're never going to get out of here!" I look around at the blockade of cars also trying to get out, horns blaring, engines revving. The streets are full of people.

I glance around at the group. Rory, Skylar, Zared, Nero, and Cara. My heart stops, "Where's Romni?"

Cara flinches. "There's nothing we could have done to stop them," she says.

"Stop who?" I demand.

"Security got him," Zared explains. "There were too many of them. We couldn't hold them all off."

I rake a hand through my hair. This is my fault.

"We should go back," Nero says.

"I can talk to them," I offer. "Most of them know me and—"

"And they also know you're a member of The Revealed," Cara cuts in. "You saw them tonight. Romni knew the risks—we all know the risks—of being members. We chose to fight for the greater good despite that. Your father wasn't killed. He's going to be okay. Romni would say it was worth the sacrifice."

I almost laugh at that, doubtful that's what Romni would say.

"But who knows what they'll do to him!" Nero objects. "No way in hell we're just walking away from here without him."

Zared is firm. "We can't go back."

"I'm not going without him." Nero slings his bag over his shoulder and takes a step into the crowd before Zared yanks him back.

Zared points a meaty finger in his face. "Listen here. I respect every member like family. I don't intend on just letting the government keep your friend. We'll get him back, but now is not the time. Understand?"

Nero yanks his arm away from Zared but doesn't try to run into the crowd again. He crossed his arms over his chest and glares. Romni is his best friend. I don't blame him for being worried, but I also have enough emotional detachment to see Zared is right. We can't go back.

Rory pulls out her phone. "We'll call Julia and have one of The Revealed stationed at the local drop house come pick us up. We'll have to stay with the crowd and follow them far enough out to a road cars can access."

Skylar nods. "Let's go."

We gather around the television at the safe house we fled to, watching Riley Fisher on the news.

"This show serves as a continuation for the election's announcement following the terrorist attack by The Revealed earlier this evening, which left Representative Atwood severely injured."

"You know," Nero pipes up, "anyone with half a brain would realize that The Revealed have never used guns." He scoffs, "Morons."

"They don't want to see the truth," Rory replies curtly, crossing her arms over her chest. "The world wants to make us the enemy and so we are."

"We would like to take this moment now, to inform you of the results of today's election. With a record eighty-five percent voter participation throughout the country, partly thanks to the new electronic ballot system, the results are in. With fifty-four percent of the votes, Mark Atwood is the new president of the North American Sector."

Just like that.

I forget how to breathe.

My father is president.

My father is president.

"Well, congrats," Nero offers.

"Shut up," Rory barks, understanding the look on my face.

I feel conflicted.

I definitely don't want Roderick Westerfield to be president, but my father.... I'm not ready for this. After years of knowing everything he did was building toward this moment, it wasn't real until those words came from Riley Fisher.

"We are told Represen—excuse me, President Atwood will soon be undergoing surgery following the gunshot wound to his shoulder this evening. However, his camp has released a statement saying, 'The nation should expect positive change in the next four years, further reconstruction efforts in the wastelands, improved defense measures to keep the nation safe but, above all, an end to the destruction caused by The Revealed. We pledge to stop them—stop them from taking our children and stop them from attempting to ruin the nation we've all worked so hard to rebuild.' No doubt the Atwood administration is thinking particularly of Lily Atwood tonight as they make this statement."

The camera switches from Riley Fisher to a replay of the events in front of the White House, beginning with a shot of me leaping recklessly onto the stage.

"Ms. Lily Atwood was part of the team that was responsible for shooting her father tonight and destroying the ceremony, in one of the largest terrorist attacks we've seen since the war," Riley Fisher says in a voiceover as the video footage continues to play. "A statement from President Atwood himself regarding his election and the nation's current situation is expected as soon as he has recovered."

Oh God I hope my father is okay.

I need some air. I stand up from the couch and walk outside, letting the breeze waft against my face. It's a crisp, chilly night, and the longer I stay outside the more the frost begins to bite at my face.

The apartment we're staying in is on the tenth floor of a building, and the city stretches out beneath me. I stare out at all of the familiar shapes in the distance. It's quiet tonight. The streets are now lifeless. People are afraid of another attack.

It's funny how in the span of only a few weeks, I feel so disconnected from the place that should be home. despite having lived in Capitol City longer than anywhere else, I always knew this wasn't where I belonged. But now that I've found my place, it feels entirely different being here. I'm the outsider.

I rub my hands together to warm them and cover my ears against the frosty breeze.

I want to say I feel shocked and hurt that my father didn't believe me about The Revealed, but I don't. I expected it. Rory was right. The world wants to make The Revealed the villain, and so everything that goes wrong is blamed on us whether it's logical or not. My father follows the same thought pattern as the rest. I thought the same way only three weeks ago. It's hard to change someone's mindset when they are so adamant in their beliefs. It took brain surgery and an assassination attempt on my parents to get me there. No, I definitely don't blame my parents, but I feel detached from them now. I'm no longer a part of their world. My father is president, and it will probably affect me very little at this point. I will be with The Revealed, not at the White House.

Maybe someday, in the far-off future, the world will be able to understand the truth of The Revealed, and I will be able to reconnect with my family. Someday I might be able to be in their lives again, but right now it's impossible. We're on separate paths.

It's the natural progression of children, I think. We all have to grow up at some point, and distance ourselves from our parents to become our own individuals. It doesn't stop me from missing them, but I know this is the way things have to be.

I'm happy for my father, though. He's worked so hard to become president. People believe in him—even The Revealed. They're right to put faith in him, too. He really wants to do the best job for the new nation. It just turns out that he thinks the most-important part of being president is to obliterate the organization in which I now have my faith.

Rory walks outside with two mugs in hand. The warm aroma of spices is picked up by the wind.

"Brought you some tea." She offers me a steaming mug. "How are you holding up?"

"It's a little surreal," I respond blankly. "My father is president. And then Romni…. We have to get him back. I have to find him. This whole thing is my fault."

"Come on, Lily," Rory scoffs, "you didn't do anything but save your father's life."

"He still got shot. Westerfield got away and now the world hates The Revealed even more. If anything, we just made everything worse."

"The world wants to see The Revealed as evil," she says. "We live with it because we can be proud of the work we accomplish. Eventually, maybe the world will accept we're working for the greater good and then we can collaborate with the government. Until that day, focus on the good. Your father isn't dead, Lily. He's president. If you hadn't jumped up on that stage, it might not have turned out that way, and a lot of people could have died in an unnecessary war that Westerfield wants to create. You did well. The system can't be perfect. Sacrifices have to be made for the greater good."

I nod, but I don't think I believe her. I sip my tea to avoid Rory's inquisitive stare. I know she sees the truth in my features. I cup my hands around the tea and keep the drink warm with my abilities.

"I wish I could be with my father right now, just to make sure he's okay."

Rory raises an eyebrow as an idea sparkles behind her gaze. "Lily, we're The Revealed. If you want to go into that hospital, we can get you in there."

"What?"

She shakes her head with a small laugh. "You're still missing how vast our influence is. Our members rarely stay at the facilities. We're out in the world, climbing the ranks and integrating ourselves into the system. There are members all over the colonies that have made lives for themselves on land."

"They have families?" I ask.

Rory understands what I'm asking. "Don't get your hopes up," she says, her smile deflating. "It doesn't work like that. We still have to be safe. Keeping who we are secret is one of the most-important weapons we have. Unfortunately, you don't have that luxury. I'm going to be blunt with you, Lil, your face is too recognizable to make it possible for you to settle down in the colonies, and especially not with Roderick Westerfield's son. It would never work. Not now."

"I wasn't talking about Kai," I immediately deny, "I was just asking."

She doesn't buy it for a second. "You're better off moving on."

"Rory, really," I scoff. "I've moved on. I barely know Kai. It isn't a big deal."

I nearly gag on the words, the falsehood in them. Kai's never far from my mind. Some part of him has buried itself deep within my heart, and I don't think I'll ever be the same. Forget the surgery and the election. Kai brought change into my life in a way that made me act on what I want. He gave me the fight to make something of myself. I'm better when he's in my life.

Rory lets it go. "Well, see you in the morning, and we'll see about getting you into the hospital."

I'm grateful for the change of subject. It hurts too much to think about Kai. He's the one thing from my old life I don't want to give up. He's the sacrifice I'll be making to be part of The Revealed. I can't be with him.

"Yes," I tell Rory, grateful I may have a chance to say goodbye to my parents.

Rory leads me down the hospital wing. "You've only got about ten minutes," she warns.

"I won't be long," I promise.

It turns out Rory has connections with a nurse, a member of The Revealed who works at the hospital and cleared the wing for us. All it took was one call, and we were good to go. It helps that this wing was vacated of all other patients because of my father's high-profile status.

My footsteps echo as I walk down the hallway and into my father's room. He's sleeping. The nurse confirmed what the media reported last night. The bullet didn't puncture anything vital. He's lucky; he'll be fine. It will take a few more weeks of recovery before he'll be ready to leave though.

I stand next to his bed.

The others are waiting outside for me, guarding the door.

My father's eyes blink open. "Lily?"

"Hi, Dad."

Panic fills his eyes and he pushes the call button near his hospital bed.

"It won't work," I tell him, a little hurt by his reaction. "We've had the floor cleared so I could speak with you."

His body tenses. "Are you here to finish the job?"

"What?" I can't believe he just said that. "Dad, of course not." How can he even think that? "I wanted to make sure you were okay."

"How could you let them do that, Lily?"

"It was Westerfield. It wasn't The Revealed, Dad. We were trying to stop it."

"Or so they told you," he snaps. "I know what I saw."

"I know what you think you saw. You're wrong. It wasn't The Revealed. It was Roderick Westerfield."

He still doesn't believe it. It's like talking to a wall. "Roderick Westerfield bowed out gracefully after the announcement. He's going on vacation. I'm told he left town today."

"He's not gone for good," I warn. "But I'm not here to talk about Roderick Westerfield, and I'm not here to argue with you about The Revealed. How's Romni?"

"Who?"

"The member of The Revealed that you arrested." I grind my teeth together, trying to contain my frustration. The last thing I need is a windstorm to freak my dad out even more.

"I don't know what you're talking about."

I close my eyes and rub my eyelids. "We're going to get him back, you know," I say somberly. "We'll get him back."

"Tell them that would be a *very* bad idea," my father says darkly.

I shake my head. "I'm not here to play the messenger. I'm here to say goodbye."

My father's eyes narrow, but he doesn't respond.

"The Revealed have given me a purpose. I can do something good with them. I know you don't understand, and I'm not asking you to yet, but please just know I have to do this. I'll be okay. They need me and the people here need you. I never belonged in your world, and now I've found a place where I do. Someday maybe you'll understand."

"They've brainwashed you," he says.

"You have a country to look after now, and I can look after myself. You have bigger problems than your teenage daughter."

"Don't go with them," he says. If the comment weren't so stern it would almost sound as if he were begging.

"I'll make you see," I promise. "They're the good guys."

"Lily, I can help you."

"I love you, Dad." I turn and walk out.

"Lily!" my father calls after me, but I keep walking. I don't even hesitate. My life is waiting for me. My life with The Revealed. There is no more time for hesitation.

CHAPTER TWENTY-FOUR

I drive from the hospital with Rory. We aren't heading back to the apartment, though. As soon as I left, there's no doubt my father called for a team to hunt us down. It's time to get out of the city. From here we'll head back into the wastelands and on to the coast where the submarine will be waiting to take us back to headquarters.

Cara and Skylar are in the car up ahead with Nero and Zared. We'll touch base at the rest stop just before the border. We pull out onto the highway and a familiar stretch of land unrolls in front of me. It's a straight shot to the border from here, and then down until we hit the ocean.

I lean my head against the seat and shut my eyes.

For the next few weeks I will continue training at The Revealed's headquarters underwater. Once I've gained more control over my abilities, I'll head out with the others on missions. There's a mission going to China next month. They'll help plant crops. I plan on volunteering. It's a perfect opportunity for me to start exploring the world.

I feel Rory veer off the road and my eyes open in surprise. She's taken one of the exits off the highway.

"Is something wrong?" I ask, staring around the car, wondering what I'm missing. The others didn't pull off with us. It's just Rory and me.

"We need to make a stop," she tells me.

"Do you want me to call the others and let them know?"

She shakes her head. "They'll figure it out once they realize we aren't behind them anymore, babe."

The gas tank is still about three-quarters full, and the car seems to be running fine.

"I didn't believe you last night on the balcony," Rory says.

"Huh? What are you talking about?"

And then I realize where she's taking me. She pulls onto a small road. It's deserted, for the most part. All of the crops were harvested in the last few weeks, and soon the fields will be burned so the colonies can start fresh in spring. Acres upon acres of empty fields stretch out before me, all of them brown and withered.

Rory continues driving deep into the fields almost until the road ends, before she pulls off to the side, driving up a hill. It isn't until we're over the hill that I see his car.

The sun is sinking in the sky, touching the treetops, and sending orange rays splashing along the golden-brown fields. His silhouette is outlined against one of the trees, and he has his back to us.

I glance at Rory to say something, but words don't come.

Rory stays in the car, giving me some time. "Just don't be long," she warns. "The others will start to worry."

I sprint from the car toward him. He hears the car door close and turns. I run into his arms, and he buries his hands in my hair.

"I forgot how good it feels to have you in my arms," he says, pressing his lips to my neck. "I'm so sorry," he says against my ear.

"Why are you apologizing?"

"I should have told you about The Revealed before I let them take you, but I didn't know what to say."

"I'm the one who should be apologizing. All of this time, all you've ever done is look out for me, and I acted suspicious and horrible. I'm an idiot. I shouldn't have ever put you in danger the way I did by sending you that email. I wasn't thinking. I just missed you."

"It killed me not to write you back. I care about you, Lily," he says. "More than I've ever cared about anyone. Don't ever forget that."

He doesn't let go of me, and I realize why.

This is goodbye.

"What about your father?" I ask. "Where did he go?"

"I don't know." I can see the shame and disgust in the way Kai holds his shoulders and stiffens against me. "I got home last night and he was packing. He even let go of the staff. He isn't planning on coming back anytime soon."

"Good," I say without thinking. "Are you okay? He says nothing, just holds me tighter. I sigh, shutting my eyes and taking one more moment to enjoy the feel of being with him. "I have to go back."

"I know."

"When will I see you again?"

"I don't know. For now you need to stay with them. People know you're a member of The Revealed. It's not safe for you here right now."

"Come with us," I beg, taking his hand.

"It doesn't work like that. You know that. I have to stay here. My mind isn't like yours," he runs a light finger over my forehead. "It's your world. Mine is here."

"I don't have to go with them. I can stay."

"No." His voice is certain, almost harsh.

Rory honks the horn lightly. Time is up.

I look over my shoulder then back at Kai. "I don't know if I can do this without you."

"You have to. This is your chance to prove to everyone that you're more than just your father's daughter. You were meant for this." He pulls me close to his chest again and whispers in my ear, "Someday we'll take that drive together."

I nod against his chest.

He takes my hand and we walk back to the car together.

I turn to him, not sure what to say. He stares into my eyes, the green and gold reflecting my own gaze. He cups the sides of my face with his hands and kisses me. One kiss. Our lips touch, gentle at first. He runs a hand through my hair and pulls me closer still. I crush myself against him, lacing my hand around his neck. I don't want to leave. I don't want to say goodbye.

And then the kiss is over. The feel of it still lingers on my lips. I know it will fade. I don't want him to fade from me.

He gives me one more intense look, holding my face with his palms, as he memorizes everything about me as though I'm the most-precious thing in the world. No one has ever made me feel as significant and worthy as I am in his eyes. I will fight to be the person he's seeing in that gaze of his. Then, he lets me go.

"Wait…." My resolve starts to crumble.

He shakes his head. "I won't let you change your mind."

"It's my choice too." I look back at the car and Rory, and realize, I can't have both.

"And your choice is to go with The Revealed."

He's right.

My tongue is thick in my mouth so I just throw my arms around his neck and pull him to me one more time. I bury my face in his neck, my lips brushing against his skin, and I feel his pulse in time with mine.

Eventually, he forces our bodies apart, and I can see the strain on his face reflecting my own. If I wait any longer it will only become more difficult.

"Goodbye," I whisper and walk quickly back to the car.

I slam the door shut and take a deep breath. When I look back up, Kai is already driving away from the fields. I watch his car until it's out of sight.

Rory nudges me with her arm, guiding me back to reality. "You ready for this?" She smiles, snapping her fingers. "The others are waiting. I just got a call from Skylar. They're going to meet us at the rest stop." A flame cracks over her hand. She plays with it between her fingers, letting it dance across her fingertips. "Just because your father's president now doesn't mean the problems are over. We've still got the rest of the world to deal with."

I allow myself to grin. This is the first day of a new era. My father is president and the world is a changing place, full of potential and hope.

I hold my palm out, covering my icy hand over Rory's flame to extinguish it. "I'm in. Only—" I hold out my hand, "I want to drive."

She grins, handing over the keys. We switch places and head back out onto the highway. I grip the wheel, my speed climbing, letting the world and all its possibilities stretch out before me.

301

ACKNOWLEDGMENTS

It's only as I write these thank yous that publishing *The Revealed* actually feels real. It has been quite the whirlwind adventure! And I have an amazing team to thank for every moment along the way. We've come so far together, and the future only looks brighter.

First and foremost, I have to thank my publisher SparkPress, the BookSparks imprint, and founder Crystal Patriarche, who has been so much more than a publisher. She's been there since before the beginning of this novel and mentored me all the way through. Every success with *The Revealed* is because you believed in it and me, Crystal. This novel wouldn't have happened without you. I can't wait to see where the series takes us!

Thank you to my dad for telling me, "Just publish the dang thing." And my mother for always believing in me. It's because of the two of you that I have the strength to never give up on my dreams.

Thank you to the rest of the SparkPress/BookSparksPR team: Heidi Hurst, Wayne Parrish, and Erin Holtgreve, and to their web designer Betsy Cohen for my fabulous author website. The dedication and time you put into this project mean so much to me. Thank you to Maya Rock for giving me the feedback I needed to make the novel stronger. To Jess Riley for making the book sparkle. To Chase Oliver for making the symbol come to life. To Julie Metz for a cover that makes me hope people will judge the book by it.

Finally, to Mr. Don Scott for giving me the creative writing assignment in fifth grade that started this whole crazy passion of mine. You are not just an amazing teacher but an amazing man, who has continued to inspire me to this day. Thank you. Thank you. Thank you.

COMING SOON
THE ENRAGED

Find out what's next for Lily in *The Enraged*,
book two of *The Revealed*.
Coming soon from SparkPress.

JessicaHickam.com
Twitter.com/jhickam
Facebook.com/AuthorJessicaHickam

ABOUT THE AUTHOR

After graduating from Arizona State University in 2011, Jessica relocated to Los Angeles where she now works in the entertainment industry. From acting to working on the Paramount feature *Star Trek Into Darkness*, her experiences have only reinforced her love for living in other worlds—whether they be from her own imagination or someone else's. *The Revealed* is her first novel.

Connect with Jessica at:
JessicaHickam.com
Twitter.com/jhickam
Facebook.com/AuthorJessicaHickam

About SparkPress

SparkPress is an independent boutique publisher delivering high-quality, entertaining, and engaging content that enhances readers' lives. We are proud of our catalog of both fiction and non-fiction titles, featuring authors who represent a wide array of genres, as well as our established, industry-wide reputation for innovative, creative, results-driven success in working with authors. SparkPress, a BookSparks imprint, is a division of SparkPoint Studio, LLC.

To learn more, visit us at www.sparkpointstudio.com.

www.ingramcontent.com/pod-product-compliance
Lightning Source LLC
Chambersburg PA
CBHW020943260626
47169CB00006B/1793